THE SHOTGUN LAWYER

ALSO BY VICTOR METHOS

A Gambler's Jury
An Invisible Client

Neon Lawyer Series

The Neon Lawyer
Mercy

THE SHOTGUN LAWYER

VICTOR METHOS

THOMAS & MERCER

This is a work of fiction. Names, characters, organizations, places, events, and incidents are either products of the author's imagination or are used fictitiously. Any resemblance to actual persons, living or dead, or actual events is purely coincidental.

Published by Thomas & Mercer, Seattle

www.apub.com

ISBN-13: 9781503902275 (hardcover)
ISBN-10: 1503902277 (hardcover)
ISBN-13: 9781503902299 (paperback)
ISBN-10: 1503902293 (paperback)

Cover design by Jae Song

Printed in the United States of America

First edition

To all those who have lost a loved one to gun violence.
May you find peace among the chaos.

The price of apathy is to be ruled by evil men.

—*Plato*

1

This was it. The big show. The final curtain. The last bite of the enchilada.

The defense's main witness was on the stand. My client, Hazel Willmore, a retiree of eighty-six, had gotten both legs broken in a car accident, and I was wondering why the witness was grinning. What sadistic pleasure was he taking in destroying this little old woman's case? Maybe a little old woman had run him off the road once or taken the last doughnut at the grocery store or something.

"And you're positive of that?" I said. "That you saw her run the red light?"

"Positive," the witness said.

"This woman right here, Hazel Willmore? You saw her run that red light and slam into Ms. Gunderson's car?"

He nodded. "Absolutely. You don't forget something like that. The noise and all that." He looked to the plaintiff's table. "That was her, sitting right there. I saw her run the red light and hit the other car."

The jury watched him. Without this witness, Affiliated Mutual Insurance had nothing. Just their client saying Hazel was at fault, and Hazel saying the light was green and it was Ms. Gunderson's fault. This witness was the only thing stopping us from getting a fat paycheck.

I stepped forward. "You're positive *that* woman ran the red light. No doubt in your mind."

"None."

I pointed to the five people sitting in the audience. "Will the actual Hazel Willmore please stand up?"

An older woman rose with the help of her niece. The casts were off, but she had to lean on a walker, and both legs were secured with braces. A few of the jurors gasped and started whispering.

The attorney for the insurance company shot to his feet. "Your Honor! This is enormously unethical! Mr. Game just lied to the jury and to this court! He had another person sitting there who gave *testimony* about—"

The judge, an older African American man named Gilmore Mendelson, who I had known since law school—he was one of my professors—rubbed his face and held up his hand. "Mr. Taylor, please stop shouting."

"Yeah, Clarence, stop shouting," I said.

"Up yours, Pete! I can't believe you'd pull this—"

"Gentlemen," the judge said. "I need you to—"

"You're just jealous," I said to Clarence, "because I got that up-and-comer mention in the Bar journal and you didn't."

"Your aunt was on the supreme court! Of course you're gonna get it."

"No, I got it because I don't sleep with my divorce clients."

"You son of a bitch!"

He made a move toward me and the judge screamed, "Enough!"

The courtroom went silent. I couldn't help but grin. An outburst of this caliber meant an almost automatic mistrial. A mistrial on a personal injury case was the kiss of death for the defense. Insurance companies played the numbers, and preparing and conducting two trials wasn't worth it. They'd settle rather than do it again. I looked back at Hazel, the real Hazel, and winked.

"Hey," the woman at the plaintiff's table said, "can I get my fifty bucks?"

The judge bellowed, "In my chambers, both of you. Now."

We went back to Mendelson's chambers and he took off his robe and hung it on a coatrack. Clarence was so furious he couldn't sit, so he paced behind me as I sat down and put one leg over the other and folded my hands in my lap. The good little choirboy.

"What was that, Pete?" Mendelson said.

"What? Just a little bit of theatrics to show the jury that the defense is playing games with them."

"Theatrics!" Clarence said. "He had a stranger get sworn in, *sworn in*, Judge, and give testimony acting like someone else. He needs to be reported to the Bar. And you damn well better believe I'm gonna do it, Pete."

I ignored him. "That witness was lying. It would've been a miscarriage of justice to allow his testimony to stand. I was just making sure the truth came out, that's all. I mean, that's what the whole system is set up for. Truth. Am I right?"

"I demand immediate sanctions," Clarence said, taking a step forward and pointing at the floor for some reason. "I want Rule Eleven sanctions, I want ethical sanctions, I want it on the record that he committed a crime by allowing a witness—no, forcing a witness—to commit fraud on this court."

"And I'd like it on the record that Clarence slept with his cousin, who was a client of his."

"For the tenth time, she wasn't my cousin!"

"Both of you," the judge said, glancing from one of us to the other, "stop. Just . . . stop it. Clarence, we both know the company's going to settle. They're not going to pay you another twenty thousand dollars to try this case again. And, by the way, maybe vet your witness a little better next time. Make sure he actually knows what the hell he's talking about before you put him on the stand in my court."

"Amen, Judge," I said.

"And you. He's right, I should report you to the Bar."

"You could do that, Judge. But we all know how busy you are, and I would hate to add to that stress. Look, I'll write a letter of apology to you and the jury. Hell, we can even file it and have it officially on the record. I'll go out there and apologize to everyone in the courtroom, and we'll call this little incident a learning experience and move on. No harm, no foul."

"No harm!" Clarence bellowed. I was getting worried now. He looked like he was about to have an aneurism. "No harm! You just lied to a jury and a judge, and if you think you're going to get away with it—"

"Enough," Mendelson said. "I'm declaring a mistrial. You two can work out the details later. I haven't decided whether to file a Bar complaint or not. That'll be all, gentlemen."

Clarence scoffed, uttered an F-bomb, and stormed out. I rose and the judge said, "Sit down, Peter."

I sat back down.

"What're you doing?"

"What do you mean?"

"When you were in my class, I recognized your talent. I knew you would go far. I had high hopes for you. Why did you turn down that clerkship? A Utah Supreme Court clerkship is a ticket to any law firm you want to work at, and instead you're chasing ambulances and pulling this crap."

"Hey, gotta earn a living."

He sighed. "If I flip a coin and it's heads nine times, when I flip it that tenth time, what are the odds that it's heads again?"

I shrugged. "A hundred percent."

"Why?"

"Because nine times in a row is impossible. It means the game is rigged."

He held up a finger. "You see that? One in a million people would say that. Almost everybody else says the odds are fifty-fifty, just like with every other flip. You don't think like every other lawyer that comes through here. You got that street smarts or whatever they call it now. You have serious potential. You could become a justice like your aunt if you really—"

"All due respect, Judge, being an umpire doesn't appeal to me—excuse the pun. I want to be at the plate trying to hit home runs. I want the Ferrari and the penthouse and the trophy wife at my side. I think I've earned that. Or at least I'm going to."

He watched me a second. "One day, Peter, I think you'll find that there's more to life than hitting home runs."

I nodded. "Can I go now? I got a paycheck to negotiate for my client, and I'd like to do it while Clarence is still upset. He won't be thinking clearly."

"Consider what I said."

I rose to leave, and when I was at the door he said, "And, Peter?"

"Yeah."

"You pull that crap in my courtroom again and I'll have you held in contempt."

I grinned. "No shenanigans in your court. Got it."

2

Out in the hallway I expected a good minute of cursing and yelling from Clarence. He got about a minute and a half in and then had to take a breath before he ran for another minute. I glanced at my watch and said, "Clarence, can you just call and leave the rest on my voice mail? I got a client consult later this afternoon."

"You're a shark. You give lawyers a bad name."

"Yup. No argument there. But now I want eighty instead of seventy grand."

"You rat bastard! I'm not giving you a dime."

I rolled my eyes. "Eighty. Have the check ready by Friday. My client has bills to pay."

I turned and left, leaving him fuming in the hallway. Hazel and her niece were standing in front of the courthouse, and I stopped and said, "Well that couldn't have gone better."

"Everyone seemed upset," Hazel said.

"Nah, they're just used to getting what they want. Rich people are like that. And when they don't get it they throw a fit. Speaking of rich, you just netted a cool fifty-five thousand dollars, Hazel. Spend it wisely." I winked. "No gambling or male escorts, young lady."

She chuckled. "Such things you say."

Clarence came out and brushed past me, mumbling, "Prick," as he did so.

"I gotta run, Hazel, but call me if you have any questions. I should have your money ready for you on Friday."

I crossed the parking lot and stood next to a silver Porsche until I saw Hazel and her niece drive off. Then I circled around to my car, an old Honda with a cracked windshield, and got in. On my phone, I checked emails and then voice mails—nothing important.

As I drove away from the courthouse, I played an oldies rock station and tapped my fingers against the steering wheel to "Have You Ever Seen the Rain?" and thought about the client I had coming in. Then I remembered I hadn't paid the woman I'd hired. I turned around and found her waiting in front of the courthouse. I took out fifty bucks and gave it to her. She stood quietly a second, staring at me.

"What?" I said.

"It's just . . . I have rent due. That's why I did this. And I'm still short."

"How much?"

"Another hundred and fifty."

I watched her a second. "Is your rent really due or are you just scamming me?"

"No, it's really due. I promise."

I sighed and took out another hundred and fifty. "*Vaya con Dios*," I said as I drove off.

I passed a bus stop on Third South and saw my face on a small billboard above it with the words **Peter Game, Injury Lawyer: The Best Game in Town** in bold lettering across the top. It was out of the way from my office but I liked seeing it at least once a day.

My office was in a flat, square building that housed mostly graphic designers and therapists starting their practices. The rent was cheap and the landlord left you alone. I was two months behind on the rent, but with the twenty-five grand I netted from this case, I could catch up and pay the rest of the year in advance, and maybe do a little advertising.

Five big personal injury firms got 90 percent of the cases in Utah, and the numbers weren't much different in other states. They spent millions a year on television, radio, phone books, billboards, and sponsored sports events, placing their names on everything from Salt Lake Comic Convention posters to buses, even paying people a few hundred dollars a month to wrap their cars in the firms' logos.

The small guys, like me, had to fight for the remaining 10 percent of cases, usually the crap ones that the big lawyers didn't want. The big boys didn't want to fight in court; in fact most of their senior partners, who had been doing this twenty or thirty years, had never done a single trial. They wanted cases they could flip as quickly as possible for the paycheck. It worked out well because if there was even a hint of a fight, they passed on the case and left it for us scrappers to duke it out over. So the best advertising was getting to know people at the big firms, making sure they always had tickets to basketball games and plenty of drinks over lunch. I had ingratiated myself with two of the firms, and they supplied probably 60 percent of my business through referrals. And we couldn't be picky: we had to take everything that came through the door. They called lawyers like me "shotgun lawyers" because, like the spread of buckshot, we took everything, hoping at least one hit its target and made us some big money.

I parked and got out. Inside, the air-conditioning wasn't on and the place was hot and muggy. I reached my office on the second floor and sat down at my desk. The receptionist I shared with three other businesses wasn't in.

I opened my email—nothing in the inbox. I checked my voice mail again, which was empty, and then leaned back and put my feet on the desk. Dust swirled in beams of light coming through the blinds. I turned back to my computer and went to Facebook. A few people had liked my son's picture of his school lunch, which looked like something between vomit and dog food. The news feed was taken up by another school shooting, this one only thirty miles from Salt Lake in a town called Holladay. I purposely skipped over it. I didn't want to know the details. Life was horrific enough without putting that stuff in your head every day.

After another ten minutes of Facebook, I decided it was time to call it a day. I left the building and walked down to a burrito stand.

"Jorge, how's the rat meat today?"

He chuckled. "You know, you joke about that enough and someone might believe you. You trying to put me out of business?"

"Never, my man. Never. Far as I'm concerned, these are the best burritos north of the border."

He began preparing my usual sweet pork burrito with green salsa and said, "So how's your day going?"

"Oh, not bad. Had a fat case settle. Been kinda slow lately, so it's nice. How's business for you?"

He shrugged. "It's fine. You know the restaurants, they trying to push me out."

"No shit?"

"Yeah, they said that we're not sanitary, which is bullshit 'cause I've worked in them restaurants and they're dirty as hell. But they went up there and got politicians to listen to them. So they're saying I may have to get the same licensing as them, but I don't have the money for all that."

I shook my head. "They're always out to screw the little man, aren't they?"

He nodded as he handed me my plate. "They sure is."

I left some cash for him along with a tip. I was halfway to my car when I remembered I had that client consult in an hour. I sat on the bumper and ate the burrito, watching some of the graphic designers, all of whom were younger than me, come back from lunch. One of them waved to me and I waved back. I put my burrito down on the hood of my car and texted Michael.

Wanna go do something?

Hanging out with some friends after school

I couldn't help but grimace though I didn't mean to. I couldn't remember the last time the two of us had hung out. Another year and he'd be gone to college, then off to who knows where, maybe trying to strike out as far from his father's legacy as possible, the way I'd done with mine.

Well, some other time then

I finished the burrito, threw the plate in the recycling bin, and headed to the building next door.

The Vibe Building was about twenty times better than mine and housed several big-time law firms, tech companies, and one of the best pizza restaurants in the city. I headed up the stairs to the law firm of Brewer, Talmage & Mack and smiled at the receptionist, an older woman I guessed had descended from Attila the Hun.

"Candy, my sweet Candy. How are we today?"

"You can't be in here, Pete," she said without looking up from the magazine she was engrossed in.

"I just need to talk to ole Jake for a few minutes."

"He's at lunch."

"Huh. That's weird. He said he would be here."

A beat of silence passed and then she looked up from the magazine. "You wanna use one of the conference rooms again, don't you?"

"Oh, well, you know, since I'm already here, if I can get it for just a half hour to meet with someone it would be much appreciated." I leaned on her desk and whispered, "Really nice guy. Poor bastard was hit by a drunk driver. May never walk or talk the same again." I pretended to glance around. "They suspect severe brain damage."

"That so?" she said suspiciously.

I nodded. "Yeah. I just thought, you know, give him a nice office to come to. That's all."

She exhaled. "I want lunch. Right now."

"Okay, great, I'll grab you a burrito from Jorge."

"Oh no, I want a real lunch. I want Sleek's. A ham and cheese sandwich, soup, Diet Coke, chips, and two chocolate chip cookies. Not one, two."

"Sleek's is like twenty minutes . . . okay. No problem. Let me meet with my guy and I'll leave right after."

She shook her head. "You think I'm an idiot? Go get it now."

I glanced at my watch. If I sped the entire way, I could make it back in time. "Alright, ham and cheese, soup, Diet Coke, chips, and a cookie."

She held up two fingers. "Two cookies. If you bring back one cookie, you ain't gettin' in."

"You are a harsh but fair mistress. BRB."

3

Sleek's was packed to the brim, and I had to pretend I placed a to-go order that they screwed up and didn't make so they would put a rush on the food. I got it, ran out, and hurried back down to Brewer, Talmage & Mack. Candy checked the entire bag and made sure to touch both cookies, like I had created an optical illusion or something.

"Okay," she said. "Half an hour."

"You're too good to me. You single?"

She rolled her eyes. "Get inside before I change my mind."

"You're right, you're way outta my league. Query withdrawn."

A giant mahogany table surrounded by high-backed leather chairs took up most of the conference room. A wall of windows looked over the street below.

When Mr. Hamad arrived, we sat down and I undid the top button on my suit. I folded my hands and put a serious expression on my face. A lot of times, all clients wanted was somebody to listen to them. They didn't care if I was good or if I had fifty Bar complaints: they wanted someone to listen without being distracted. It was hard enough to find that in society, among friends, and ten times as hard with lawyers. I could sign almost anybody up just by staring them in the eyes and listening to their nonsense until they felt it was all out of their system.

"So my understanding is you slipped and fell at a Fresh Food Mart, is that right?"

He nodded and proceeded to tell me about the water they hadn't cleaned up near the entrance and his bulging disc that might need surgery.

Surgery. That word was like magic to the ears of a personal injury attorney. I swear it made me tingle. I told him I would be his lawyer.

"That's it? You don't want to ask me any more questions?"

Truth was, I didn't need to. Best advice I ever got about personal injury cases was to sign 'em up before they went anywhere else and then work out later whether the case was good or not. Shotgunning. I could always drop him if it turned out the case wasn't worth much or there were evidentiary problems.

"Mr. Hamad, I'm a man who lives off my word and my gut, and my gut is telling me you're an honest man who was wronged by a giant corporation that isn't going to take care of you. I don't need to know anything else. I trust you, and I hope you can trust me."

He hesitated and then nodded. "Okay."

"Great. Let me get some forms for you to fill out and we'll have everything ready."

I went out to the lobby and took a quick glance at Hamad, making sure he wasn't looking, and then bolted down the stairs and out to my office. I had forgotten my forms so I quickly printed some off and then ran back to the other building and up to the conference room where Hamad was waiting. I placed the forms and a pen in front of him and he said, "You okay? You seem out of breath."

"Oh, just some asthma I'm dealing with. Go ahead and fill all these out and let me know when you're done."

I stepped out of the conference room while he filled out the forms, got a cup of water from a watercooler, and leaned on Candy's desk.

"Why do you do that?"

"What?"

"Call yourself *Game*? Your last name's James."

I shrugged. "I like the way Peter Game sounds. It gives people the impression I'm, I don't know, lively and fun I guess."

"You sound like a douchebag. James is much better."

Says the woman named the most common stripper name, I thought.

I took a sip of water and said, "You like working here?"

She shrugged. "Work is work. It would suck anyplace else just as much."

"There's a cheery thought."

"It's the truth." She looked up at me. "You like what you do? Being a scumbag and chasing after ambulances?"

"Better than digging ditches. Which I actually used to do in college. Only job I could get that had a night shift. That and a convenience store."

I heard people speaking behind me and saw Jake stepping off the elevator with a young associate. All the associates here had that same look. Young with chiseled jaws if they were men, and attractive and buxom if they were women. Business suits that looked like they were handmade that morning. With my hundred-dollar suit and scuffed shoes, I certainly didn't fit in.

"Jake, how the hell are ya?"

He stepped next to me and glanced into the conference room. "Good case?"

"So-so. Might be a nice ten Gs down the line. Fresh Food Mart slip and fall."

He whistled. "They're not settling much these days. They've caught on that people think they're a quick payday."

I shrugged and noticed his eyes, which were always rimmed red from the pot he smoked all day. "Yeah, well, clients aren't exactly raining down on me right now."

He leaned against Candy's desk and said, "You got plans for tonight? Got tickets to a Jazz game."

"Nah, I don't feel like basketball tonight. I got a date actually."

"With who?"

"Tinder date."

"I'm sure that'll turn out well." He looked to the conference room again. "Looks like your boy's ready to go. Shoot me a text if you change your mind."

"Will do."

I went into the conference room and gathered Hamad's documents. I gave him my card and wrote my cell number on the back.

Afterward, with nothing else to do, I got into my car and headed home. I played NPR for a minute but they were talking about the school shooting in Holladay, so I turned it off and drove in silence.

4

Home was a two-bedroom apartment in a place called Sugarhouse. It was a bastion of college kids and those who couldn't really afford to live anywhere else. More than one house had a flag with Che Guevara's picture on it, hanging from the front porch or a window. At least three Bob Marley signs on my street alone. I'd traveled a little bit through South America and it was always those two. The poorer the neighborhood, the more posters of Che Guevara and Bob Marley.

I parked and took the stairs to the second floor. Michael wasn't home, so I kicked off my shoes and flopped onto the couch. I clicked on the television and turned the volume down while I opened my Tinder account and the profile of the woman I was meeting tonight. As was seemingly mandatory, her profile pic was a selfie taken on a cliff in the mountains, with a dog in the background. She loved the outdoors, hiking, biking, and camping. For the amount of people listing those things as their passions on Tinder, you'd think the cities would be empty.

The door opened a bit later and I realized I had fallen asleep on the couch. Michael walked in sporting hair that covered his eyes and a Drake T-shirt, the standard uniform of seventeen-year-olds, and said, "Bring home anything to eat?"

"A 'how's your day' would be nice."

"How's your day? You bring home anything to eat?"

"There's a frozen pizza in the freezer."

"I'm sick of frozen pizza."

I reached into my pocket and took out a twenty. "Grab whatever you want. Bring me one, too." I sat up and rubbed my eyes. "How was school?"

He put the twenty in his pocket and went into the kitchen. I heard the fridge open. "Fine."

"Just fine?"

"Just fine."

He came out with a Coke in his hand and went for the door.

"Hey," I said. "You wanna watch some *Game of Thrones* when you get back?"

"Maybe later."

He left and shut the door behind him. I stared at Tinder for a while, then closed the app and dialed a number. Jollie answered on the second ring.

"Hello, Peter."

"Hey. What're you doing?"

"Laundry. What's going on?"

"I, um, was just calling about Michael. I thought maybe he could visit you in Tahoe this weekend."

"I can't this weekend. Got some hot dates. Next weekend, alright?"

"Um, okay, he was just kinda looking forward to it, Jollie."

"He's almost an adult. He doesn't need his mommy all the time."

"Yeah . . . well, okay. I'll tell him, I guess."

"Okay. Is there something else?"

I shook my head even though I was alone. "No, just um, signed a new client. Just preoccupied with that."

Silence on the other end.

"Hello?"

"Yeah, I'm here. That's great, Peter."

"Yeah." I grinned. "How's everything with you?"

"Oh, you know, same. Some of my photos are in one of the galleries downtown."

"Still dating that philosophy professor?"

"Actually . . . we've moved in together. He and another of my lovers."

This time, I was the silent one. "You're in a relationship with two guys?"

She sighed—it was a sound I'd gotten used to in our marriage. "Spare me the morality lecture, Peter. I'll sleep with whoever I want."

"Yeah, you made that abundantly clear." I didn't know why I kept trying to turn back time, to pretend we still had a relationship, except that she was Michael's mother. And, at one time, I'd thought she was the love of my life. "So anyway, I'll let you go. Have a good night."

"You, too," she said gently, reminding me that there was no point in harboring animosity.

I hung up and sat alone in the apartment for a while, then decided I would get ready and kill time at the restaurant until my date arrived.

5

The date was a bust. I tried two more over the next two weeks, but the results weren't much better.

Today at three I had a mediation on a case that'd been going on for six months. It was out of the scope of personal injury, but the client had gotten my number from a previous client. When business was slow, you took everything that came through the door.

I was representing the wife in a divorce where the husband refused to give her anything. He made over a hundred and fifty grand a year and didn't want to pay a dime in alimony or child support. He'd hired one of those big firms to represent him.

"You sure you want to do this?" Selena said as we waited for the receptionist to announce us. She looked stunning in a dress that came down to midthigh and heels, a look I had asked her to sport. Her hair was freshly done, plenty of makeup, and a pushup bra. Her nails were finely manicured.

"You wanna litigate this thing for the next fifteen months? Because I don't."

She thought a moment. "Okay. Well, I guess I'm ready."

We went into the conference room. Her soon-to-be ex-husband and his attorney, a big guy I only remembered as Something Darren—I wanted to say Bobby Darren but I knew that wasn't it—sat on one end. The mediator, a retired judge whose last name slipped my mind, was looking over his glasses and writing something on a legal pad.

"Mr. Game," the judge said, "glad to see you again."

"You too, Judge."

"Former Judge. You can just call me Will."

"Alright, Will. Mr. Darren, how are you?"

"Good," he said, without standing or offering to shake hands.

I pulled out Selena's chair for her and gently put my hand on her shoulder. Her husband, Randy Lopez, noticed and then glanced at me. I sat down and poured water into a plastic cup, waiting for Will to boot up his laptop.

"You got a little something there," I whispered to Selena.

"Where?"

"On your lip. It's just from the lemon cake." I lightly brushed it off with my finger. "Fine now."

She licked her upper lip. "You sure it's all off?"

"Looks perfect to me."

I glanced over and Will and Randy were looking at me like I was crazy. Darren didn't even notice. He was eyeing Selena's chest.

"Sorry," I said, clearing my throat. "We ready to go?"

"Almost," the former judge said. "I just need to go over some ground rules. We're here as adults, and this process is a way to resolve our issues without the long, costly, and ultimately painful experience of going through court." He glanced at Selena and then at Randy, who had his eyes set on me. "I was a judge for twenty-two years, and I promise you, it will save you so much pain down the road if you're willing to compromise a little bit here."

I put my hand over Selena's and squeezed. "That's what we're here for. We just want Selena to be able to move on with her life and get into the new adventures that are waiting for her." I looked at her and smiled, and she smiled back.

Will glanced from one of us to the other and then cleared his throat. "Yes, well, that's ultimately what we all want. So, Randy, Selena, if you need a break, just say so. This isn't something we need to get done today. We can come back however many times we need to, to get this right. It's much better that you two be happy with the results long term."

Lightly, I lifted my hand and ran the tips of my fingers over hers but kept my eyes on Will, as if it were a casual thing. Selena opened her hand and I tickled her palm.

"Hey," Randy said, "what the hell is going on?"

I looked at Selena and then Will, then Darren, and back to Randy. "Excuse me?"

"What's going on? Between you two."

"Um," I said, glancing at Selena, who also had a confused look on her face. "I'm sorry, Mr. Lopez, but I don't know what you're talking about."

Darren, who still hadn't noticed anything amiss, said, "Randy, save any comments or questions for the breaks or just write them down on the legal pad there for me to see."

Will started again, talking about how mediation works and how it came about and why it was so much better than a court process. I had let go of Selena's hand, but I leaned back and put my arm on the back of her chair. Out of the corner of my eye, I saw Randy staring at us. He was staring so intensely that, when Will asked him something, he didn't respond.

"Randy," Darren said, "can you answer the question?"

"Huh. Oh, what? Sorry."

The judge said, "I was saying that the first order of business should probably be the retirement accounts, as that seems to be the main point of contention. After that we should dip into the real estate holdings and save the business for last, as I feel that will be the most intricate and complex."

"Yeah, that's fine," Randy said.

I watched Will as he continued, and, so slowly you probably couldn't even tell unless you were looking right at me, I gently rubbed Selena's shoulder with the tips of my fingers. She closed her eyes and tilted her head back a little, just enough to show some throat, and I moved my fingers up to her neck and lightly ran them up the skin. She made a soft groan.

"Hey!" Randy said.

I immediately moved my hand away.

Darren looked between us and said, "Randy—"

"No, this is bullshit. What, did you wait a whole month before you starting fucking someone? And the piece a shit lawyer outta everybody?"

I held up my hands. "Whoa, whoa, whoa, fella. I don't know what you think is going on—"

"Mr. Lopez," Will said, "it's not appropriate to begin a mediation with aggression."

Randy looked at us and I could see the light pink of blood rising in his face. Selena had been right: the guy had a short fuse mingled with intense jealousy. No wonder she had pushed for a divorce.

"Now may I continue?" Will said.

Darren said, "Of course, Judge, and we apologize. Mr. Lopez will be more respectful."

I put my hands in front of me on the table and interlaced the fingers to show I wasn't making any moves toward Selena. Will continued and then reached into a box by the table to pull out some documents relating to the retirement accounts.

I waited a good three minutes, enough so that Randy was now paying attention to the documents and what the judge was saying, and only occasionally glancing at me and Selena.

Come on, I thought. *Perfect time. Come on, come on . . .*

Seemingly reading my thoughts, Selena leaned back in her chair and reached her arm over. She put her hand on my thigh and ran it up. I leaned back so that it was more obvious, but we kept our eyes on Will. I glanced over at Randy to see if he noticed, but there was nothing yet. Then, he took a gander and couldn't look away. On cue, Selena began to run her hand farther up my thigh. I looked to her and bit my lower lip and she, lightly and oh so subtly, ran the tip of her pink tongue over her upper lip.

"Motherfucker!" Randy shouted.

Darren's jaw dropped as Randy sprung to his feet. He and the judge were too slow to do anything. The eye of the tiger had been set free. Randy lunged at me over the table and Selena screamed.

6

After being interviewed by the police, I sat in the conference room with some ice on my neck. The bastard had a grip—I'll give him that. Selena, playing the perfect victim, sat outside being consoled by a female police officer while she dabbed her eyes with tissues. I watched as they slapped handcuffs on Randy and hauled him away.

Darren came in, his face drained white, and shut the door behind him before sitting down.

"I don't even know what to say," he said.

"Occupational hazard. Wasn't your fault."

He shook his head. "I mean, I've just never had that happen. What do you think set him off?"

Jeez, this was almost too easy. I was actually nervous Darren might notice. But most transactional lawyers like Darren had OCD, whereas most trial lawyers had ADHD, and so the Darrens of the legal profession were so focused on the minutiae they didn't notice things like how easy their clients were to manipulate.

I shrugged. "Selena told me he's wildly jealous. I'm sure he's just taking out his frustration on a man who's trying to help his ex."

"Yeah, I guess so. I . . . I mean . . . I don't even know what to do from here."

"Well, he's going to be charged with felony aggravated assault for the strangulation. Maybe even attempted murder." His eyes went wide and I had to suppress a grin. "So I don't know. It's going to be hard to do mediation while he's being held in jail. I guess we could do it there. Kinda weird for a mediator to show up at the jail . . ."

"Yeah, yeah . . . what a mess."

"Yeah." I inhaled, as though thinking about a solution. "I mean, look, neither one of us wants to be in this spot. What if, and this is just an idea, we work everything out ourselves? Mano a mano. You and I hash it out and then get both of our clients to accept. I mean, it's going to have to be a bit more favorable to my client than you would like. Frankly, I'm inclined to cancel mediation and take this to court. Once I put Selena on the stand and she tells the judge he tried to kill her lawyer in mediation and that's why we had to come to court, I can't imagine any judge or commissioner being too favorable to your client after that. So, you know, you'll have to compromise on a few things you're not going to want to compromise on, but if you're willing to do that, I think we can get this handled today. And, you know, frankly, if it's taken care of, I'm not interested in pursuing charges. Make sure your client knows that, if it's settled and my client's happy, I'll let the DA know that I'm not looking to have this go any further. I mean, they'll still charge him with something, but with the victim saying he wants the case dropped, they'll at least give him a light sentence."

Darren nodded. "Alright, alright. Should we begin now, then?"

Within two hours, Darren and I had agreed on everything. And by everything, I mean Selena got everything. She got 70 percent of the retirement accounts, one of the cars, the house and half the vacation cabin, alimony for six years, and most of the personal items, and Randy would be taking all the credit card debt. When we walked out of the building, we jumped into the air and she threw her arms around my neck and kissed me.

"Oh," I said, probably blushing.

"You deserve a lot more than that." She grinned mischievously. "Why don't you come over to my house tonight and I'll cook you dinner? And we can see where it goes from there?"

"Selena, um, believe me, there's nothing I'd like more than to go home with you . . . but I can't."

"Oh. I'm not . . . your type, I guess?"

"No, no, no, you are definitely my type. You're every man's type. But I can't. I mean, I can, but I won't. You're freshly divorced and vulnerable. I would feel like I'm taking advantage."

"Yeah, but I want it. I'm asking you to come over."

"I know, but I promise you in six months you'll feel different. I just don't want to take advantage. Tell ya what, in six months, if you still feel that way, give me a ring."

She smiled, kissed me on the cheek, and then said, "Your loss," as she walked away. I inhaled deeply, and then went to my car, wondering if I was crazy.

7

The next day at the office I drafted some documents for a case I was trying to settle with the Utah Transportation Administration. A drunk bus driver had slammed on the brakes so hard that my client flew forward and nailed the windshield. She'd broken her leg and crushed two vertebrae. Initially, the TA denied the claim, saying that my client caused it with her "excessive weight." When someone anonymously let it leak to the papers that the TA was rejecting a suit related to a drunk bus driver because the injured party was fat, the TA immediately issued an apology and offered to settle the case for more than the value. Problem was, my client didn't want to take it. She felt like she'd been so wronged she needed her day in court. It was a rough spot for a lawyer to be in: trying to convince someone who felt wronged that money could make it right. With time, most of them came around.

The receptionist was out as usual, mostly because she knew she worked for the landlord and not the eight people that rented these offices, so I answered my own calls as I drafted the docs. I was in the middle of a phone call when I got a ding on my calendar that I had a client consult in fifteen minutes, at their home.

Not all personal injury lawyers did house calls—the big boys saw it as too lowbrow—but the shotgun lawyers like me had no choice. Some people were too injured to go anywhere and had to be visited while they were laid up at home or in the hospital. Then again, some people, a lot of people, were lazy and wouldn't sign with a lawyer due to the sheer hassle of finding one and going in to fill out documents. You had to hold their hands. I signed up more clients in their homes than I did in the office.

I quickly drafted a representation agreement and ran out the door.

The home was in a quiet suburb of Salt Lake City called Federal Heights. It was a white house with an apple tree in the front yard and a few toys left out: a soccer ball, a toy gun, and some army men.

I knocked a couple of times and then the door opened. A woman answered. Black hair, a button-up shirt, and jeans. From her eyes, I could tell she'd been crying. She had a scar at the base of her neck that looked like someone had cut her once, and I tried not to look at it. On her left ear were about ten or eleven hooped silver earrings. There were none on her right ear.

"Hey," I said. "Peter Game. I have an appointment with a Melissa Bell."

"Yeah," she said, sniffling and wiping away the last tear with the back of her arm. "That's me."

I held out my hand and we shook.

"Um, come in," she said, wiping at her cheeks again to make sure she got everything.

I didn't want to ask what the tears were for. Probably guy trouble. My gender definitely seemed to be the main cause of the female gender's suffering.

The house was nice. A bit cluttered with toys, and the dishes were piled up in the sink, but other than that, it seemed like a welcoming place. Several framed photos of Melissa with a young kid were on side tables and the mantel. Good-looking kid with a wide smile. None of his father. I guessed my initial assumption was right and that daddy was the cause of her tears.

"Rough day?" I said.

"You could say that."

We sat down on the couch. I had the representation agreement and the legal pad under my arm and put them on the coffee table. I had written a note on the legal pad that this was a product liability case. I still agreed with my premise to just sign up all the cases I could and sort them out later, but sometimes I wished I took more notes so I knew what the hell I was supposed to be talking about when I met clients for the first time.

"This is a very lovely home, Melissa."

"Thank you," she said, unable to look me in the eyes.

"Little guy at school?"

She saw me looking at one of the photos. She shook her head. "No, no, he's not at school."

I put one leg over the other and leaned back on the couch. "So we talked briefly on the phone about a product liability issue you were having. Why don't you tell me a little bit more about that?"

"Um . . . it's a . . . Tanguich Rifles."

"Oh yeah? I know them really well. My dad and I would go shooting with Tanguich shotguns. He loved to buy local stuff and they're a Utah company. So did one of their guns malfunction or something?"

She shook her head. "No." She ran her hand through her hair and took in a deep breath. "My boy, Danny. He was shot by a Tanguich gun. A BL-24. Do you know what that is?"

"Um, yeah. I do. I'm so sorry."

She nodded. "I want to sue the company."

"Tanguich?"

"Yes."

I glanced at the photo of the kid. He couldn't have been older than seven. "Was it, if you don't mind me asking, an accident? Did you have the gun in the home?"

"No. The shooting at Holladay-Greenville Elementary. Did you see it in the news?"

I hesitated and then nodded. "I did."

"He was killed in the shooting. He and six other children and a teacher. The man just . . . he just went into the school and shot them. The teacher was protecting Danny and she got shot, too."

My throat dried up and I felt my heart in my chest. The woman was barely holding it together and, somehow, I had to tell her there was nothing I could do.

The law was clear: gun manufacturers were in no way responsible for what people did with their guns. I couldn't even count the number of cases that had been run up to the Supreme Court on this very issue and lost. Also, they were expensive. Only the largest firms could take a case like this, and they never did because the law was so straightforward.

Melissa looked on the verge of collapsing, so I had to be gentle.

"I don't know if I'm the right lawyer for this, Ms. Bell. I mostly handle car accidents, dog bites, slip and falls, things like that."

"You said on the phone you do product liability."

"That's true, I do some, but that's not my bread and butter. Frankly, I look for the slam dunks on those cases. It's expensive to litigate product liability, and solo guys like me don't really have the funds."

She leaned back, wiping at her cheeks again though I didn't see any tears this time, and then folded her arms. "I've talked to twenty lawyers. Maybe more. They all tell me the same thing: that it's a guaranteed loss. They won't even meet with me. You're the first one."

I leaned forward, my elbows on my knees. "I can't even imagine . . . I just . . . I'm so sorry. But I can't help. You need a big firm for something like this."

The veneer of some semblance of keeping it together began slipping off. I saw her hands and, even tucked under her arms and across her chest, I could tell they were shaking. The tears welled up again. I blurted out, "But maybe I know somebody that can help. Give me a day, and I'll see if I can get you a number."

She wiped the tears away again and said, "Thanks."

I rose to leave, and on the floor next to the coffee table I saw a book: *Where the Wild Things Are*. I used to read that to Michael when he was a kid. I looked away and then said, "Um, just give me a day, alright?"

"Alright."

8

I sat at my desk that evening and stared at the ceiling. I kept thinking about *Where the Wild Things Are*. One night I lay in Michael's bed with him when he was nine, and we were about halfway through the book when Jollie, Michael's mom, came in and said she was leaving for a few hours to go out with her friends. I said it was no problem and finished reading to Michael before tucking him in. I didn't see her again for two weeks, and when I did see her, she handed me divorce papers and said she was in love with someone else.

It upset me thinking about it, so instead I called Jake.

"What up, yo," he said.

"I've been staring at my ceiling for like twenty minutes."

"How come?" I heard the crunch of chips.

"You know that school shooting that happened a couple weeks ago?"

"Yeah. My cousin lives four blocks from that school."

"Yeah, well, the mother of one of the boys that died met with me. She wants to sue Tanguich Rifles."

"For what?"

"For the death of her son."

"The guns didn't kill him."

"Shit, Jake, the guy didn't bludgeon those kids with a club. He used one of their guns. But I get it, I know the case law. She's really shaken up and everyone in town's denied her. I was hoping you could do me a solid and talk to her. Maybe tell her you'll look into it a little, something."

He inhaled deeply and thought for a second. "You know I love helping you, pal, I do, but I don't want to touch that. UGAA is the most powerful lobby group in the state, and one of our partners is in the state senate and has their support. If they got even a hint that his firm was considering something like this, shit would hit the fan."

UGAA: the Utah Gun Advocates Association. The most powerful gun lobby group in the state. They had a reputation of owning the Republican Party here, and since 80 percent of the legislature and senate, not to mention the governor and the courts, were Republicans, they had become the de facto ring to be kissed if anyone wanted anything done. When the legislature considered making a crime a felony, they had to get the approval of UGAA first, since felons couldn't own firearms until they got the felony reduced. When they wanted to rezone certain areas, UGAA had to be consulted to ensure the new zoning laws didn't interfere with gun ranges or stores. The UGAA was the boss, and the politicians were the employees.

"Right, I forgot about UGAA. Could you at least meet with her, though?"

"No can do, pal. If the partners found out, they'd lose their shit. You should keep it, though."

"Everyone who's tried to sue a gun manufacturer for this has lost, man."

"Not true. Just the ones that go public. These gun guys, what they're scared of is publicity, not having to pay out money. What keeps them up at night is, if there's enough of these mass shootings, public opinion will change and people will want to take away their assault rifles and shit. So when a case goes public, they gotta fight it as hard as they can.

But if the lawyer goes to them and signs an NDA and keeps everything quiet, they'd rather settle than have another case in the papers. Even if they win."

"No shit?"

A chip crunched. "Yeah, man. Another firm I worked at, they got one of these. Guy got fired and walked into his office that afternoon and shot his boss. One of our partners went in and settled it for three hundred grand. From the time the client—the boss's widow—signed up, to the time we got our check was six weeks, man. And with this being a kid and being all over the news right now, I bet you could ask for two mil and get it."

My heart stopped. I put my hand on my chest because I was scared it wasn't beating. That terrifying feeling of being up on the crest of a roller coaster before it comes plummeting down filled my guts.

Two million dollars.

One third of that mine.

I could pay off all my debts, get a nice car, nice suits . . . I could show that I was successful. I could be successful. That was the type of money that changed lives, that pulled people out of apartments and put them in houses, that made sons proud of their fathers and fathers proud of their sons. That made it so someone didn't have to scrape by every day wondering how rent was going to be paid the next month. A life of ease.

"You there, man?"

"I'm here," I said. "Just . . . wow. Even thinking about it gives me a heart attack."

"I'm not saying you'll get it, but you never know. Go ask for five mil and see what the counteroffer is. Say the kid was a genius or something and his earning capacity would've been ten million over the course of his life, which is what you'd ask for with a jury."

I swallowed and my throat felt like sandpaper. "She said she's called twenty other lawyers. How did no one pick it up?"

"They don't know this stuff, man. These settlements are seriously under wraps. In fact, I shouldn't have even told you. Everyone who worked at that firm had to sign NDAs. And they didn't mess around. One of our secretaries told one of the IT guys about it and she was sued and fired."

I exhaled and closed my eyes.

Two million dollars . . . a third of that mine.

"Umm, well, I better call her. I'll call you later."

"Cool. Remember, though: keep it under wraps. If it goes to the media at all, it's too late. They'll fight you with everything they got."

I hung up and then stared at the phone a second. Maybe Jake was right, but that didn't mean I should take the case. I mean, the gun lobby, especially in a state like Utah, was about as powerful as it got. They had connections to the Bar, the courts, the government, and every company here. Suing them might not be the best strategy. Then again, Jake had never been wrong about things like this. He hated litigation, so settling cases before it got to that point was his specialty.

Two million dollars . . .

For some clients, talking them into taking the money required a trusting relationship between us. A lot of in-person contact was the way to build that. I didn't know if Melissa was like that yet, so I would play it safe and meet with her in person as much as possible.

It was almost nightfall when I got to her house, and the city had a gray haze over it. Either from pollution or from the intense wind that was kicking up all sorts of dirt. The wind blew dust in my eyes and flopped my hair around, and I cursed as I went to the door, wishing I'd just called, or texted.

I knocked and Melissa answered. She was disheveled and immediately ran a hand through her hair, as though embarrassed by how she looked. I waited quietly until she said, "What can I do for you, Mr. Game?"

"Peter is fine. I . . . um . . . I can't promise anything, Ms. Bell—"

"Melissa."

"I can't promise anything, Melissa, but I'll look into the case. I don't have the funds to really fight a case like this. I'm just going to put out feelers and see if anything's there. If they offer to settle this, which I don't think they will—but if they do—that'd be a miracle and we'd have to jump on it. I'm thinking you're bringing this lawsuit precisely because you don't want to take a deal, no matter how good. But I'll tell you what I tell all of my clients: the only thing corporations care about is money. They'll pay out now to avoid a big verdict at trial or a lot of bad publicity, but they also don't like to settle because then someone else will come out next week after another shooting and ask for a settlement, too. So I guess what I'm trying to say is there're no guarantees."

She nodded and said, "Thank you." Then the smile faded and she began to cry.

"Oh, hey, sorry. I just thought—"

She threw her arms around my neck and held me that way for a long time. I didn't know if it was appropriate to hug her back, so I stood there like a lump of clay.

I glanced at some of the toys that were still strewn on the lawn and just said, "Well, um, I guess I have a representation agreement for you to sign."

9

The next day, I paced around my office like a crazy person. I had written and rewritten an email to the in-house counsel for Tanguich Rifles twenty times, and every five minutes I would sit down and write it again. This time, the iteration looked about as good as it was going to get. I read it out loud to make sure there weren't any typos.

> *Dear Mr. Roger Bailey,*
> *My name is Peter Game Esq., and I am representing Ms. Melissa Bell. As you are well aware, Ms. Bell's seven-year-old son, Daniel, was tragically killed in the Holladay-Greenville Elementary School shooting, in which Nathan Varvara used one of your assault rifles to murder seven children and a teacher. Ms. Bell is concerned about her financial situation with the funeral and other expenses as well as everything she has lost with the death of her son. Daniel was a straight-A student with dreams of becoming a physician, which, of course, is heartbreaking to Ms. Bell to not see to fruition.*

We would like to discuss this situation with you in private. I have not, nor will I, contact the media or file anything public with the court at this point. Strictly an in-person meeting between us to see if there is a solution to this situation. I have included my contact information below. Please feel free to reach out to me at any time.

Sincerely,
Peter Game
Attorney for the Plaintiff

I read it again, and then my finger wavered above the mouse as the arrow on the screen hovered over the "Send" button. I closed my eyes and pushed it.

The receptionist, here for once, stuck her head in and said, "Corey called. He has that check ready for you."

"Great."

"Wants to meet you in person. Said to stop by before lunch today."

I rolled my eyes. "Yeah, he likes to humiliate me whenever he pays out. Like he's doing some huge favor."

"What's with you two anyway?"

"I used to clerk for his firm during law school. They thought I was going to work there, announced it in the Bar journal and all that. The nephew of a supreme court justice. That's what they wanted. They didn't give a shit about me. So I quit, and he's been an asshole ever since."

"He's a dick on the phone, too."

"Yeah, well, growing up rich and handsome will do that to you." I rose. "Better go take my medicine."

The firm of Dupont & Ryan was in one of the most upscale buildings in Utah. The type of place that had a fountain in the front lobby and one wall was nothing but a digital screen that alternated between serene forest views and the tops of mountains. I stood in front of the screen and watched some waves rolling into a beach before I took a deep breath and then hit the button for the elevator.

Corey Ozum, who had been a junior partner when I clerked here, had seen me as some sort of prize. When he introduced me, he would say, "This is Peter James, the nephew of Beth James of the supreme court. We got big plans for him. He's as sharp as his aunt." I'd never felt more like a prop in my life.

When I quit and told him I was going out on my own as soon as I passed the bar exam, he threw a stapler at me.

I got off on the tenth floor to the hum of a busy law firm. I closed my eyes a second. I had dreamed of this when I was a law student. Of running around a massive firm, involved in everyone's drama, listening to the partners' closing arguments on big cases, having multiple flings . . . television shows had ruined me.

Truth was, life at a big firm was drafting documents, getting yelled at, and hoping you could avoid interaction with the partners as much as possible. It wasn't about doing good legal work or following your passion: it was about needing a job with all that law school debt, and the firms paid you just enough to get you to come back day after day. Not enough to ever really get ahead, just enough to keep you coming back.

The receptionist was someone I didn't recognize, and she smiled and said hello.

"Hi, I'm meeting with Corey. Peter James."

"Okay, hang tight a sec," she said, perky as can be.

I sat down in one of the plush leather chairs, which seemed to engulf me, and watched some people discussing a case around a cubicle. They spotted one of the partners and dispersed like gazelles seeing a cheetah.

"He'll be a sec," the receptionist said.

"No problem." I leaned back and stared at the ceiling.

And stared some more. I checked my watch: I'd been waiting for forty-five minutes. Every ten minutes the receptionist would say, "Just another sec, I'm sure."

Standing up, I stretched and then went to the bathroom. It had wood paneling on the walls and silver-rimmed urinals. Someone came in behind me and nodded hello. I was washing my hands when he said, "You're Pete Game, right?"

"Um, yeah."

"Yeah, I recognize you from the billboards. Those are hilarious."

"Thanks."

"Get a lot of business from those?"

"I do okay. So you an associate here?"

"No, just a clerk. But they said they're going to hire me after the Bar. Pretty excited."

I nodded. "They tell all the clerks that. Do yourself a favor—send an email to the managing partner saying you're applying for a home loan and they need you to list what your starting salary will be. If they won't say, it means you're not on the list and they're gonna fire you after your clerkship."

He stared at me blankly for a second. Poor bastard.

I left the bathroom and went back to the front entrance. I sat in the same chair and the receptionist said, "It'll be just a sec."

The magazines were about luxury cars, luxury houses, and vacation spots. Dupont was the type of firm that CEOs and celebrities came to when they needed something done. They had eight offices in the US and had once represented a president in a secret paternity suit. No one but the partners was supposed to know that, but Corey had told me one night because, as he said, "You're one of us." I don't know what he meant by "us" but it sent a shiver up my spine.

After another half hour, I sat tossing a tennis ball that had been on a side-table stand—the ball had been used in Wimbledon—to the ceiling, and then I would catch it again with one hand. Finally, the receptionist said, "He's ready for you now."

I put the ball back and rose. Apparently I couldn't be trusted to walk back to the offices myself, so she led me to the massive corner office. It was larger than my apartment and had about six feet of putting green with two holes. Corey was bent over one of the holes, the golf club steady in his hands, his custom-made suit perfect, his silk tie hanging off his perfect neck, which I was sure he had already had surgery on to take care of any wrinkles, even though he was only in his forties like me.

"Hey, Corey."

"Shhh," he said without looking up.

Another few seconds and then he inhaled deeply and tapped the ball. It rolled toward the hole and then bounced out.

"Damn it," he said, shaking his head. "You've always been bad luck, haven't you, Pete?" he said with a laugh. "I'm just kidding." He thrust out his hand and we shook. "How the hell are you?"

"Good. Thanks. I'm just here to pick up the check on the Philman case."

"You like cigars?"

"Um . . ."

"Sit down and have a cigar. Client just got them for me."

"I really just need the check."

"I will not take no for an answer."

I sighed and sat down in one of the leather chairs across from his desk. He sat in his black executive seat, which was jacked up about six inches higher than all the other chairs in the office, to create, as Corey had once said, "An impression of superiority." I couldn't be sure, but I think he'd jacked it up another couple inches since I'd worked here.

He lit two cigars and handed me one. It was wet from where he had put it to his lips.

"How you been?" he said with a smirk.

"Fine. Listen, Corey, I really gotta get going. I just stopped by to pick up that check. Gotta be on my way."

He smiled and stared at me in silence a moment. "Your billboards are something. I see them when I drive by the homeless shelter."

"Yeah . . . well, hey, about that check—"

"You want your job back, don't you?"

"Excuse me?"

"You could've sent your secretary to pick up the check, but you came in person. If you want your job back, just ask me. I mean, we couldn't start you off in partner track again, obviously, but we might have something for you in document review. Stamping files, reading emails, that sort of thing." He smiled widely in grim satisfaction . . . grim for me anyway. "It would be great to have you back here."

"I appreciate the offer, but I'm fine where I am. Could I just please get that check?"

"Oh," he said, holding up a finger, "I almost forgot." He hit a button on his phone. "Mandy, send Kelly in here." He looked at me. "I can't wait to see your face. This is really going to be a surprise."

"Kelly who?"

The door opened, and she walked in.

She looked thinner than I remembered. Her hair was still dark black and came down to her shoulders; her eyes, a deep blue, something she once told me wasn't entirely uncommon in the women of Lebanon, were as sparkling as ever. She wore a suit and heels. On the inside wrist of the hand that held the door handle was a blemish that didn't quite match her natural skin: it was where she had tattooed my name. Now covered with makeup, but not removed.

"Corey, did you nee—"

She stopped when she saw me. Our eyes locked and I swallowed and then smiled timidly.

"He . . . hey," I stuttered.

"Hey." She folded her arms and then looked at Corey. "Did you need something?"

"I just thought you two would want to see each other again. I mean, it's been I don't know how many years since you broke up."

He took a puff of his cigar and leaned back in his seat, his eyes shiny with delight.

I cleared my throat. "Didn't know you were back in town."

"Yeah," she said, glancing at me and then away. "Got back two months ago."

"LA not your fit, huh?"

"It was fine." She looked at Corey again. "Have a lot of work to do."

"Huh? Oh, yeah, of course."

She turned to leave and I blurted out, "It was good seeing you."

She stopped and looked at me, venom in her stare. "You, too," she said curtly before leaving and shutting the door behind her.

Corey chuckled. "That was awkward."

"Did you hire her just to do that?"

He laughed. "You really think too much of yourself. She's a great attorney."

"I know she is. She also doesn't kiss anybody's ass. Doesn't seem like the type of associate you'd hire. Your delicate ego might get its feel-goods hurt by someone like that."

He lost his smile and puffed at his cigar. "Weren't you two going to get married? Yeah, I think I heard that. And then you broke it off . . . with a text message." The smile came back and he laughed. "I mean, who calls off a wedding with a text message?"

I looked down to the floor, my face flushing hot. "Can I just get that check, please?"

He nodded, still laughing. "Mandy has it at the front desk."

I rose and began walking out. "Coulda just told me that."

"What would be the fun in that?"

I opened his door and stepped out and he said, "Oh, and, Peter?"

I turned to him.

"I was just kidding about getting your job back. I wouldn't hire you if the Queen of England was your aunt."

"Thanks, Corey. Delightful as always."

10

I left the parking garage elevator and had to stop a minute. I leaned against a cement pillar and looked at the ceiling, splotchy black from car exhaust. It had been much cleaner when I worked here.

Seeing Kelly had brought up some things I hadn't thought about in a long time. What if you were given a chance for happiness and you didn't take it, and you never got it again? The last words Kelly had texted me were burned into my brain: *Love is too rare to just throw away without a fight.*

Damn . . .

I sighed. I guess nothing could be done about it now. Besides, I wasn't likely to see her again anytime soon.

I went over to my car and felt a sudden impact against my shoulder.

"Ow."

Kelly had punched me in the arm. She cocked her fist and clocked me in the chest.

"Shit, that hurts," I said, taking a step back before she walloped me again.

"Good."

She came at me and I held up my hands. "I give, I give."

She bit her lip and then shook her head. "Dickhead. What did you come here for, just to humiliate me? How did you even find out I work here?"

"What? I had no idea."

"Don't lie to me," she said, cocking her fist again.

I raised my hands again. "Easy. Look, I had no idea you worked here. I came here to pick up a check on a case. Corey was the one who called you in."

"Peter, if you're lying to me and I find out . . ."

"I swear it. I had no idea."

She hesitated a second, and some of the anger dissipated from her face. I lowered my hands.

"You didn't call me when you got back in town," I said.

"Call you? Are you kidding me? Why would I call you?"

"I mean . . . I don't know. Just thought that's what people do."

"People don't call their asshole fiancés that leave them at the altar, Peter."

"Hey, there was no altar involved. It was a full two weeks before the wedding."

She hit me again in the shoulder.

"Shit, knock it off." I rubbed my shoulder. "You been working out or something?"

"Boxing classes."

I sighed and leaned against my car. I stared at a sign on the wall that said to not idle your car in the garage because of the lack of ventilation.

"It's easy to judge someone else. It's much harder to understand where they're coming from."

She stepped closer to me and stuck her finger in my face. "Yes, it is easy to judge someone like you. Someone who doesn't give a shit who he hurts so long as he gets what he wants."

She turned and headed back into the building. The last time I'd seen her, we had spent the day hiking near Park City. We found a large snake and I was too scared to pick it up, but Kelly jumped right in there and held it by its tail.

I remember when we got home we made love and then lay under the sheets and talked about the future. She talked about kids, about how Michael would love having brothers and sisters, about retirement and where to grow old together. I couldn't think of any of those things: my mind was a blank. A black nothingness that I couldn't fill with the imagery of a life lived no matter what I tried. I was only divorced a few years and Michael was a teenager I was raising completely on my own. I felt lost at sea without a ship in sight.

I had kissed her and rolled over, and she gently ran her fingers across my back. The last thing I ever said to her in person was, "Love you. Good night."

The next day, I texted her that the wedding was off, because I was too much of a coward to talk to her face-to-face. That's when she wrote that love was worth fighting for.

Shit, I thought. *I'd hate me, too.*

I got into my car and pulled out of the parking garage. The sun was bright in the sky and the temperature on my car display was 102. I loosened my tie and slipped my suit coat off at a light. The check I had gotten sat tucked in my breast pocket, and I pulled it out and looked at it. Eighteen K, split between me and my client. Not a bad day's work. Even if I did have to put up with Corcy for a little while.

I didn't feel like going back to the office, so instead I drove to the shooting range. I rented a 9 millimeter and bought only one box of ammo. They had some special targets today with the faces of dictators on them. I chose an Idi Amin and went to town, smoking through the entire box of ammo in about fifteen minutes.

Next, I went to a hot dog vendor near the Matheson Courthouse. I watched lawyers going in and out of the building. I could always pinpoint the lawyers because they were the only ones with smiles on their faces. Of course, the smiles weren't real. I'd read a study once that monitored people who attended law school: rates of depression, suicide, mental disorders, and substance abuse skyrocketed after graduation. Of course, I read that study after I was already a lawyer, because life sometimes likes to punch you in the balls.

My cell phone buzzed.

"This is Peter."

"Mr. Game?"

"Yes."

"This is Roger Bailey. I'm in-house counsel for Tanguich Rifles."

I nearly choked on my hot dog. I covered the phone while I coughed up bits of bun and meat, clearing my throat with a swig of soda.

"Are you there?"

"Yes," I said, "I'm here. Sorry, just in the middle of arguments on a medical malpractice case." I paused a second. "Judge, I have to take this, would it be possible to have a five-minute break? . . . I appreciate that, Your Honor. Thank you."

I kept the phone covered, so he wouldn't hear the traffic, and then sprinted inside the courthouse.

"Sorry about that, Roger. You know how it is."

"I certainly do. Well, the reason for my call, I received your email and was hoping we could discuss the matter in person."

"Sure. When did you have in mind?"

"I have a few minutes right now if you're nearby. After your hearing of course."

"Of course. Let me just finish up here, and I'll head down. We're almost done anyway. Would you mind texting me the address?"

"Not at all. I'll be here until six this evening."

"Great, see you soon."

I hung up and exhaled loudly. Then I headed outside and sat on the courthouse steps for half an hour before heading to Tanguich Rifles.

11

I expected the offices for Tanguich Rifles to be on a ranch or a farm or something. Instead they were in one of the sleekest, most modern office buildings I'd ever seen. They were about half an hour outside of Salt Lake in a place called Lehi. They referred to this area as Silicon Slopes because a bunch of tech companies had moved out here in the early 2000s and brought a population boom with them. I hadn't been out here in years and couldn't believe how much it had changed. I remembered mountains and valleys, and all I saw now were office buildings and strip malls.

The Tanguich building was probably ten floors of steel and glass, and I thought they must rent out most of it; no way a gun company needed that much room. But when I went inside, I saw no other companies listed on the building directory.

A beautiful receptionist in a tight dress smiled at me and said, "Good afternoon."

"Hi. Um, I'm here to see Roger Bailey?"

"Certainly. Is he expecting you?"

"He is. Peter Game. Thanks."

I sat down in one of the chairs and felt like I was sitting on the Iron Throne. It was massive and didn't have any give. I chose to stand instead. Up on the wall were photos of the CEO with every president since the 70s.

"Mr. Game, so nice to meet you."

I turned and saw a plump man with a cherubic face. He wore cowboy boots and had a tassel around his neck. We shook hands; he had a firm grip, like he was trying to crush my fingers. "Would you like something to drink?" he said. "A Coke? Perhaps something a little stronger?"

"I'm okay, thanks."

"Then let's head on up."

He swiped a card by the elevator and we got on. The elevator was all mirrors and chrome. He leaned back and smiled at me. "How did your hearing go?"

"What hearing? Oh, the hearing. Right. It went great. Judge is taking it under advisement."

"You know, I have to admit, I do miss the rough-and-tumble of court. As in-house counsel, I'm mostly supervising young attorneys and reviewing contracts and doing negotiations with fine attorneys such as yourself. I haven't been in front of a judge in twenty years."

"Well, you're not missing much. They still think they're right about everything and you're wrong about everything."

He chuckled. "There was this one judge, before your time, named Martin Sabela. If you got him going, boy, watch out. He would turn bright red, he would swear like a cowboy on a cattle drive, and one time he even chased a defendant out of the court, screaming at him the entire way."

"No shit. What happened to him?"

"You can't maintain that level of stress for very long. He died of a heart attack at fifty-six, poor bastard. Anyway, that's one of the reasons I'm in-house now. Much quieter, less stress. Much less opposition. People tell me that being a surgeon is just as stressful as being a lawyer, but they don't understand the process. I tell them, 'Imagine doing surgery while another surgeon yells at you and tries to undo your surgery while you're doing it. That's what being a lawyer is like.'"

"Yeah, pretty close."

The elevator dinged and we stepped off. The floors shone under bright lights, as did the glass walls. Though this floor had a receptionist and cubicles, I didn't see anyone else here.

I followed Roger to a large office with pictures of cowboys and nature scenes covering the walls. He sat down in his massive brown office chair and I sat across from him. He groaned and said, "The knees gave out some time ago. Don't get old, that's my advice to you."

I grinned politely at the joke and waited for him to speak first.

"So, we are here about Ms. Bell and her son," he said.

"We are."

He shook his head. "Such a damn shame. You know, we have this revolving door of mental illness in this country where we let them out as soon as they show a couple of weeks of progress. Then they get onto the street and stop taking their medications and cause all sorts of havoc. I just wish our government spent money on what actually needed money spent on it. You a Democrat or Republican?"

"Oh, I'm not involved in politics. They're all crooks."

He pointed at me. "That's exactly it. They're all crooks. All of them." He exhaled and leaned back in the seat. "I wish you'd brought your client with you. I really would like to offer my condolences in person."

"I could pass them on for you."

He grinned and I grinned back. I got the distinct impression he was sizing me up but he hadn't said anything that would test me, so I thought maybe it was in my head.

"So what exactly does she want from us, Counselor? Money? It's always about money, isn't it?"

"The law doesn't exactly let her hold you guys down and kick you in the nuts, now does it?"

I forced a chuckle and so did he, though his eyes turned to slits, and I saw the first inkling of the disdain he held for me. It seemed almost like he hated me, though he'd never even met me before.

"No," he said with a wide grin. "It certainly does not."

"The law gives her money. That's all she can ask for."

He nodded. "When a parent loses a child, it's about as devastating a thing as a person can go through. They need someone to blame, and unfortunately, we're typically the first in line. The media has done a great job in convincing the public that guns are the problem, without revealing how many lives are saved through good, decent citizens that are armed."

He stared at me again, and this time I was sure of it: this guy hated my guts.

"This little boy was shot to death with one of your guns. I don't know how you feel about that. I'm going to be frank with you, Roger: I've never sued a gun company before, especially for something like this. I'm familiar with the case law saying you guys aren't responsible for shootings, but I thought maybe . . . I don't know. I know you guys are a family business, and I know you're proud of your product and your reputation. I thought maybe you'd want to help this mother out."

"I understand. And I'd love to, I really would, but if we settle one case today, there will be ten more people tomorrow with their hands out. You don't know these people like I do, Mr. Game. They can smell blood in the water."

"What people? Parents who've had children killed by your product?"

His face, for just a moment, flashed disgust and anger, and then went serene again and he smiled. I smiled back. Just two dudes perfectly happy in how much they hated each other.

"You're a bit aggressive, Mr. Game, considering you have no leg to stand on. The law is clear." He raised his eyebrows. "But, you're right, we're a family company and like helping when we can. How about this? We'll pay for the boy's funeral. And then we'll throw in another ten thousand for any incidentals. Keep in mind, now, I have to get approval from my superiors first and there's no guarantee they will allow it, but I'd like to try for that little boy."

"Yeah, for the little boy . . . ten grand, huh? With my third taken out, she'll barely have enough to leave the state for a while on a vacation."

He shrugged. "It's better than zero, which is exactly what you'll get if this progresses any further."

I exhaled and watched him a second. The smug bastard was right: there was no way we would get money for this in court. The Utah and United States supreme courts had basically said it was unconstitutional and immoral to make gun companies responsible for the actions of gun owners. If I filed on this case, it would be thrown out of court at the first hearing, and I might even get sanctioned for bringing a frivolous lawsuit. And Jake's suggestion about asking for five million seemed about as plausible as asking for a unicorn at this point.

"Twenty," I said.

He chuckled. "I knew I liked you. You know when to be reasonable. Very well, Mr. Game, twenty thousand. Though I think you're robbing us now. But we'll let you slide this one time."

He held out his hand and I shook it, and the smile never left his face.

"Now run along and tell your client to take it. I'd like to pay this before my boss finds out. Let's just consider it a favor, from a former trial lawyer to a current one."

"Sure . . . a favor."

12

That night, as I reflected on my meeting with Roger Bailey, I couldn't help but feel the anger rising from my feet all the way to the top of my head. Roger had been nothing but polite, but I hated him so much I wanted to punch him in the face. Every word he said dripped with condescension, as though he were talking to a burglar, trying to negotiate how much stuff the burglar could steal.

I tried to ignore it as I got dressed the next morning. I texted Melissa Bell but she didn't respond, so I headed over there. I parked on the street and went up to the door, realizing I had no idea if she was home, or what she did for a living and what hours she kept. I knocked anyway, and no one answered so I wrote a note on the back of an empty envelope and tucked it between the door and the frame.

As I was leaving, one of her neighbors, an old lady watering her flowers, saw me and headed over. She said, "Excuse me, do I know you? You look really familiar."

"I don't think so."

"No, no, I know I've seen you somewhere." Her eyes widened. "You're that lawyer from the billboards."

"Guilty as charged."

"Oh, I love those billboards. I'm Martha, by the way."

"Peter Game."

"What was that one? . . . 'I wish there were two of me so I could represent myself.' That's what it was. I loved that. Hilarious."

"Yeah, it was okay. Hey, can I ask you something? Do you know where Melissa works? I forgot to ask her."

"Are you a friend?"

"I'm her lawyer, actually. I texted her before I came over but she didn't respond."

Her face took on a sad look as she eyed Melissa's house. "I used to babysit Danny sometimes. You wouldn't believe what kind of a little boy he was. There's another child two houses down—Joshua. He broke a toy and was crying on the sidewalk. Danny ran inside his house and came out with a similar toy and gave it to him. Just gave it to him. What seven-year-old does that for another child?" She shook her head as tears formed in her eyes. "I'm sorry. I can't even think about it without . . ."

"It's okay. Um, listen, if you see Melissa, will you tell her to call her lawyer?"

"Certainly."

I got into my car and sat there a second. The woman went back to watering her flowers, this time wiping tears away from her eyes. I exhaled loudly and texted Jake.

Late breakfast or early lunch?

You got it

We sat at a café in downtown Salt Lake that served upscale food like buffalo burgers and blue-cheese-crumble fries. I hated it, but I knew it was Jake's favorite place so we went there. I ordered a buffalo burger and he got some fish with crazy-looking sauce on it, onion rings, a piece of chocolate cake, and a scoop of ice cream.

"Are you stoned already? It's like ten o'clock."

He shrugged as he ate his cake first. "We all got our vices. Besides, you know I have that neck injury." He took another bite. "You look like shit lately," he said with a mouthful of cake.

"Thanks."

"Getting enough sleep?"

"Not really, no."

"What's up?"

I exhaled and took a sip of my beer. It was warm. "You remember when we were in high school, and right before graduation I was supposed to go on that trip to Europe with . . . what was her name?"

"Amy."

"Amy. That's right."

"Yeah, I remember. I was jealous as hell."

"Did I ever tell you why I didn't end up going?" He shook his head. "A few days before we were supposed to go, she comes over to my house and says she needs to talk. And I mean I had everything packed; never been so excited in my entire life. Anyway, we sit down on the couch and she tells me that she doesn't want to go with me. That she prefers to go with Wayne Graff."

"That doofus who always wore the Megadeth shirts?"

"The same. So I'm heartbroken, right? I'd saved for that trip for like three years, I bought her plane ticket and paid for the hotel. I ask her why she doesn't want to go with me, and she says it would be pointless. She says our relationship is never going to go anywhere and that time is all we got, so we can't waste it doing things that don't lead to anything else."

He stared at me a second. "Amy Holyoak said that? I always thought she was a ditzy stoner chick."

I peeled a little bit of the label off the beer, staring at the bubbles foaming at the lip of the bottle. "I feel like that now. That my life's pointless. That all I do is go in a direction that isn't heading anywhere.

I fantasize about the big case, the one that's going to set me up and give my son the life for him I've always dreamed. I've worked my ass off, Jake. Where's my big case? I think I deserve something for raising a kid all by myself while working every day."

"Hey, man, I've known you since you were ten years old, and I don't remember a time you were ever satisfied with what you had. And right now, you got your own practice, you got a great kid, you're single and don't have to put up with the bullshit of marriage . . . You're living the dream, brother."

"Yeah . . . I guess."

As we ate, he told me about a case he was working. A med mal case where the doctor had cut an artery during a heart procedure and nearly killed the patient. Turned out he was on methamphetamines during the surgery and didn't exactly have the most stable hands.

"So what's going on with that shooting case?" he said.

I took a bite of the buffalo burger and it had a funky, wild grass kind of taste. I poured ketchup on it to drown the flavor. "I met with the in-house counsel at Tanguich. Kind of a prick. Anyway, they offered to pay for the funeral and add twenty grand."

"Twenty? That's it?"

"They didn't even offer that. They offered ten and I countered with twenty."

He shook his head. "They're lowballing you because they know you don't have any experience. Call him back and tell him your client has rejected the offer and ask for half a mil."

"I don't know, man. He didn't seem like he was in the negotiating mood. You sure these guys even settle these things?"

"Think about it: if they didn't want to settle, he would've told you to shove it and file the case. But he brought you in right away and made an offer. They don't like this stuff in the media, I'm telling you. Especially this close to a mass shooting."

I took another bite of the burger and it tasted like ketchup between two pieces of bread. "I don't know, I think my taking this case was a mistake. I'm way outta my league. I might just tell her to take the twenty and get out."

"Not a bad idea. I mean, what've you put into the case? Two hours at the most? Not bad for six grand."

"Yeah . . . hey, guess who's back in town? Kelly."

"Your Kelly?"

I shook my head and took another bite of my ketchup burger. "She's not my Kelly anymore, but yeah."

"No way. I love Kelly. I wish you weren't such a chickenshit and would've married her. You guys would've had some beautiful babies."

"I already got one kid who hates me. Not sure I need any more."

"He doesn't hate you. That's just teenagers. Think of yourself with your dad. I'm sure you were a prick to him."

I shrugged. "You know how I was always trying to make a quick buck? Let's just say he didn't approve, so our relationship wasn't the best."

"I don't remember. Like what would you do?"

"Like that game where we'd throw coins at the wall and whoever's coin was closest got to keep all the coins? I set up those games and had glue on the coins so I could get them right next to the wall. When I was older I'd go to the bakery and get their day-old doughnuts they'd throw out and go sell them to the cops at the station. Stuff like that."

He chuckled. "You're a dick—I lost money to you on those coin games. And your dad was about as straight a shooter as I've met. He must've hated that."

I nodded. "He always told me money's not important. That we've been tricked into thinking it's important, and by the time we realize it's not, it's too late and life has already passed us by. And so he died penniless without a pot to piss in. Lesson learned for him, I guess."

"Yeah, but was he happy?"

My phone buzzed: it was Melissa.

"Hang on, it's my client." I answered. "Hi, Melissa."

"Hey, sorry, I was at my sister's. Um, did you need something?"

"Yeah . . . maybe we should talk in person. You gonna be home soon?"

"I'm here now."

"Okay, I'll be right over. Oh, I'm not interfering with work or anything, am I?"

"No, I took a hiatus from work. I can't work right now . . ."

"Yeah. Well, I'll see ya in a sec."

I hung up.

"This was disgusting, you pay," I said.

"No worries. And thump your chest a little, man. You'll get more money out of them, promise."

13

I texted Michael to see how he was doing and didn't get a response. Sometimes I would go to his school and drop off a doughnut or some candy, but that was years ago. He would run out of class, throw his arms around me, and yell "thank you" and then promptly share the treat with his friends. It put a smile on my face just thinking about it. Then the smile went away when I remembered going to his high school a few months ago to surprise him by taking him out to lunch. He told me I was embarrassing him and to leave.

When I got to Melissa's, the front door was open.

I knocked, but no one came out, and the doorbell had one of those covers on it to prevent people from ringing it. I knocked again and then stuck my head in.

"Hello? Melissa?"

I stepped inside and looked around. The house had been cleaned something crazy since I was here last. The carpets were freshly vacuumed, every countertop gleamed from a scrubbing, every dish put away, every window crystal clear. I couldn't see a speck of dust anywhere.

"Melissa, you here? It's Pete."

I went down the hall and looked into a bedroom, but no one was there. Some stairs led up to the second floor and I took them. Hopefully she wasn't in the shower. The last thing this woman needed was a scare.

Bathroom on one side of the hallway and what looked like a guest room on the other. I went past them. The house was silent and I wondered if maybe she was in the backyard and had left the door open for me. There was one more bedroom and I went over to it for a quick glance.

It was a child's bedroom. Posters of athletes covered the walls. The bedding had superheroes on it, and a four-foot-tall Batman stood in the corner. Sitting on the bed was Melissa Bell. A stuffed animal occupied her hands. A monkey with a Holladay-Greenville Stingers baseball cap. She wrapped both her arms around it, put the monkey to her face, and inhaled its scent. Then she wrapped her arms tighter around it. Tears streamed down her cheeks. She kissed the monkey and gently placed it on the pillow.

I swallowed and stepped back, away from the room. I stood in the hallway for a while and then went downstairs to the living room and shouted, "Hey, Melissa, you here? It's Pete."

"Just a minute."

A second later she came down, her eyes rimmed red, still wiping at the tears on her cheeks. She tried to smile.

"Can we sit down?"

"Sure," she said.

I sat on the couch with her next to me. I leaned forward with my elbows on my knees and my fingers interlaced. I inhaled and said, "I met with the in-house counsel of Tanguich Rifles."

"Already?"

"I like to move quick. He made an offer. It's not ideal, but it's an offer. You have to understand before I give you this offer, that the law is very clear on this issue, Melissa. Gun manufacturers are not responsible for what people do with their guns. That's not just from Utah courts;

it's from the United States Supreme Court down. One analogy a court used was that it's like someone killing someone else with their car, and the deceased's family suing the carmaker. The carmaker can't control what people do with their cars."

"Yeah, but cars are made for driving. Guns are made for killing things. The BL-24 is made specifically for killing people."

I nodded. "That's true . . . and I wish the courts could see it that way, but they don't. The gun is given more protection in this country than anything else. What I'm saying is that it's an impossible battle. So any amount we get is a good amount."

"How much did they offer?"

"Twenty thousand. And they'll reimburse you for Danny's funeral expenses."

She stared off into the distance. "Twenty thousand for the life of my son," she whispered.

"I know it can never make up for it, but it's something." I paused a second. "Can I ask you something? What are you gonna do with the money? I mean, why do you want to sue them?"

"I'm not keeping that money if that's what you're asking me. I'm giving it all to AnyPerson for Gun Safety. It's a lobbying group that fights to not allow people like that man to buy assault rifles."

"Well, I mean, twenty grand, minus my fees, is better than nothing."

She shook her head. "AnyPerson's nothing compared to the pro-gun groups. Those people buy politicians like they're products in a store. They close down anti-gun groups by getting their marches' permits revoked. They get the police in local towns to shut down their offices for ridiculous code violations . . . the anti-gun violence groups, usually just moms that have lost children, are severely outmatched, and all they're trying to do is stop people from getting killed. I want to get them as much as I can."

I leaned back into the couch. "Why don't you work with them? Go volunteer. You don't need to sue someone to make a difference."

She shook her head. "Do you remember Newtown? All those young children that were killed? Do you know the Utah Gun Advocates Association shut down their own Facebook and Twitter after? Why do you think they did that? I bet they were scared their members would leave comments about the children. That you need to break some eggs to make an omelet, and gun rights have to be protected and sometimes children will die. The gun rights people even attacked the parents of the dead children. Imagine that for a second, Mr. Game: the parents of dead children were getting death threats because they didn't want psychopaths to be able to buy high-powered assault rifles.

"The gun people spun it the right way, and now nobody remembers those kids. And they won't remember Danny, either, when the gun lobbies and their politicians are done spinning it. I have to do something. Something . . ."

"You can volunteer, and you can go on the interview circuit, and you can write op-eds for the newspapers—"

"Op-eds?" She scoffed. "We're talking about organizations that control which politicians win elections. No one cares about a mother writing op-eds. The only thing these people will listen to is their hurt wallets. That's it."

"I understand your side of things, I really do, but I'm not sure it's the right way to do it. And I certainly don't think I'm the lawyer to do it."

She nodded. "I understand. I don't blame you. You haven't lost a child so you don't know what it's like. To carry that with you every second you're awake and then in your dreams when you sleep. I hope it never happens to you, Mr. Game. I hope you never have to see your child lying on a metal gurney with gunshot holes in his little body."

I sat there awhile, thinking of Michael. "I do understand, more than you know." I swallowed and said, "I can terminate representation and you can—"

"No, no, you're the only lawyer that would even talk to me. If you think taking their twenty thousand is the best thing to do, I'll trust you. But please think about it. At least think for a day about whether you're willing to fight for me or not. If, at the end of a day, you really think we should just take the money instead of fighting, I'll take it."

I nodded. "I'll think about it."

14

I was starving and remembered I didn't have anything but stale pizza in the fridge, so I walked around the corner to the convenience store and got two hot dogs and two sodas before going into the house. Michael was sitting on the couch with his feet up on the coffee table, laughing into his phone.

"Hey," I whispered, "got you dinner."

He picked up the hot dog and bit into it without a word to me, not even interrupting the conversation enough for a hello.

"Hey, Mikey, can I talk to you for a sec?"

He sighed. "Hang on," he said to whoever he was talking to. "Yeah?"

"I was hoping we could do something tomorrow."

"Like what?"

"I don't know. It's Saturday. I wanted to spend some time with my son. And you're gonna be with your mom next weekend."

"I got plans."

"I know you do, but let's do something in the morning. You don't have any plans in the morning, do you?"

"I guess not."

"Alright. Breakfast. Me and you. And maybe a movie after?"

He rolled his eyes.

"No movie, breakfast and we'll go from there."

He went back to his conversation and I watched him a few moments. When the hell did he grow up? Every time I walked through the door, I expected to see that little kid who was always asking me for toys and candy.

As I was about to go into the kitchen, someone knocked on the door.

15

"You expecting anybody?" I said.

Michael shook his head. I answered the door, and Kelly stood there with her arms folded.

"Hey," I said.

"Hey. Can I come in?"

"Yeah, of course."

I let her in and she saw Michael.

"You remember my son, Michael."

"Of course. What up, poser?"

He smiled like I hadn't seen him smile in a long time and dropped the phone. He rose and they hugged and he said, "Where you been?"

"LA."

"No way? I've always wanted to move to LA. I was planning on it when I graduate."

"What?" I said. "When did this happen?"

"You would love Los Angeles," she said. "It's your scene. Just make sure you're ready to work. It's expensive as all hell there." She glanced at me. "Mind if I steal a few minutes with your dad?"

"Nah. I was about to take off anyway."

They hugged again and said something about following each other on Instagram. When we were alone, Kelly flopped down onto my couch and said, "See nothing's changed here."

"I'm a simple guy," I said, sitting down in the recliner across from her. "Um, you want something to eat or drink?"

"I'm good, thanks. I actually just came by to apologize."

"Apologize? For what?"

"For the way I treated you. I talked to Corey and he said he invited you to come down. That you had nothing to do with it."

I nodded. "I would never humiliate you. Ever."

She sighed. "You mean besides all my friends and family knowing you called off our wedding by text, right?"

I looked down to my fingers and noticed I was fidgeting. "I was stupid and scared, and I hurt the person I most cared about in the world next to my son. I'm so sorry. I wish I could take it back."

"What's done is done. Besides, if you hadn't I never would've met Joey."

"Joey? Who's Joey?"

"My boyfriend."

"Oh. When did that happen?"

"Few months ago. He moved here with me from LA."

"Who is he?"

"He's an actor. Well, aspiring actor."

"Wow. And he has enough to eat from that, huh?"

"He's rich. Trust fund. And gorgeous. And funny, and—"

"Yeah, I get it, I get it, he's Mr. Perfect."

She grinned. "It's good to see you jealous."

"I'm not jealous. Really, I'm happy for you. You deserve to find the right guy and be happy."

"Thanks." She rose. "I'm glad we did this. I don't want to hate someone the rest of my life. It's draining."

"I'm glad we did it, too." I saw the tattoo of my name on her wrist and it was still covered with makeup, though because it was the end of the day, some of it had faded and I could almost see the tip of a letter sticking out.

I tried to hug her and she held out her hand, and then she tried to hug me and I held out my hand, and we chuckled awkwardly. We settled on my patting her shoulder like an uncle.

"Take care of yourself, Peter."

"Thanks. You, too."

When the door shut, Michael came out of his room, dressed in jeans and a hoodie, and said, "Don't wait up, Dad."

The door shut again, and I was alone.

16

I must've flipped through a hundred channels twice and still couldn't find anything to watch. There was some nature show about sharks that looked promising, but the narrator's voice annoyed me so much I couldn't stomach it. So I turned the TV off and lay on the couch in the dark. The moonlight came through the windows and gave the apartment a blue hue. Cars would enter the parking lot downstairs and their headlights would shine on my ceiling and then disappear, leaving only the moonlight again.

I thought about Melissa. That she was alone in her house, too. That she had, only a short time ago, a child asleep in the room next to hers who meant the world to her, and now she only had an empty house.

I had planned to call her tomorrow and tell her I had thought about it and decided she needed to take the twenty grand, but maybe I owed her a little more. Maybe I should at least really think about it.

I sat up and got a pen and a legal pad. On one side of the pad I jotted "Pros" and on the other "Cons" and started writing.

Pros

Could get more money if I threaten a lawsuit

Might get my name in the papers w/ some TV interviews

Ups my standing to potential clients if they see me on TV on a big case

Old classmates would be so jealous seeing me on TV

Kelly would see me on TV

Might get more money. A lot more money.

More money

I paused a few seconds and then filled in the "Cons" list:

Cons

Guaranteed to lose

Might not get any money and will spend a bunch of time

Might not get any press

Will take time away from cases that actually pay

I inhaled and put the pen down. Then I stood and paced the apartment a little. Why was this so hard? I usually decided in a split second whether to take a case or not. There was no reason for it to bug me this much. Lawyers had to treat clients like a means to an end: they were the vehicles that I used to pay my rent and feed my son. If I treated them any different than that, emotions would get all tangled up in it and confuse things. Better to stay objective.

I sat down at my computer in the bedroom and googled the shooting. Several news stories came up:

Seven children had died, four boys and three girls, along with a teacher, Mary Thomlin. Mary had gotten married a month earlier and was back from her honeymoon only three days. The article I read said the gunman, Nathan Varvara, came to the school during recess with a bag holding an Uzi 9 millimeter, a 9-millimeter handgun, a modified BL-24 assault rifle, and a single-barrel pump-action shotgun. He opened fire almost immediately. One witness stated she heard the gunman yell at the teachers to shut the children up as he fired at them.

A video was embedded in the article. My finger hovered over the mouse and then I clicked it.

A reporter's voice came on, describing the scene. Two women held each other, crying. One of them had blood covering her shirt. A man sat on some grass, his face buried in his hands, unmoving. As the camera panned out, I could see blood on the ground and broken glass from where the bullets had struck the building. One police officer, who the camera stayed on for a long time while the reporter described the incident, leaned against his patrol car. His hand covered his eyes, as though he had seen something that burned them. He wasn't moving; it didn't even look like he was breathing. When he shifted his hand, you could see the tears. Dark-black blood had dried across the chest of his uniform.

There was no photo of the gunman but the camera panned to several weapons on the ground. Then the video cut to the Salt Lake County sheriff giving a statement about what they knew about the gunman so far.

Nathan was nineteen years old and had no history of criminal behavior. They didn't know, at this time, how he had obtained the firearms used to commit the shooting. The sheriff said they were currently searching his family's apartment and would report on anything they discovered, like a suicide note. The gunman had turned on police as soon as they arrived. He didn't try to take hostages and didn't try to escape. He had wanted to die.

When the sheriff's update was over, the video cut to a reporter on the scene, speaking about the incident. Several people had apparently captured the shooting on their phones. The news report wasn't going to show it because of the graphic nature. I paused the video and opened another window and googled the cell phone video. Three clips had been uploaded to YouTube. I clicked on the first one.

The first thing I heard was screaming. Women, children, and several men. Then gunfire crackled. So loudly it overtook everything else in the video. A group of children were running away as whoever held the cell phone screamed at them to keep going and ran right alongside them. A male was taking the video, and he was out of breath.

He panned back and I caught only a glimpse of someone dressed in a black shirt and a black jacket and gray camo pants. He was holding an assault rifle: something you'd see on a battlefield. I couldn't make out his face, but the rifle was pointed in front of him as he rounded a corner and kept firing. Something was on the ground near his feet.

The cell phone panned away as the man taking the video kept running. I rewound and paused to see what was on the ground: it was a young boy, with a woman lying on top of him, motionless.

The boy lay facedown, surrounded by blood, with a bike tangled in his legs. I could see blood on his back. It was clear he had gotten on the bike and tried to get away when he was shot in the back. The woman appeared to have covered his body with hers to protect him.

He jumped on his bike to get away, I thought, *and a teacher sacrificed herself to try to save him.*

The boy had messy hair and wore a hoodie. He looked a lot like Michael at that age, from what I could see. And the bike was something I recognized from somewhere. Maybe a model similar to one we had owned. It sent a chill down my back.

I swallowed, my throat dry, but I couldn't take my eyes off the image. I wished someone would knock on the door or call to get me away from it, to get my eyes off the screen, but no one did. My eyes eventually began to burn and I realized I wasn't blinking.

"Damn it," I whispered.

I took out my phone and texted Melissa. My fingers wouldn't move for a good half minute. Then I sent the text, *Screw it. I'm in. Let's make the bastards pay*

A minute later, a text came back to me:

Thank you.

17

"You didn't."

"I did."

"You can't."

"I can."

Jake shook his head. "Peter, you can't, bro."

Whenever he wanted me to know he was serious and that this wasn't just BS, it was actually advice I needed to follow, he called me "bro."

"Why?" he said.

I looked out the windows of his office. An office much nicer than any I had ever had, and certainly nicer than any apartment or house I had ever lived in. The sun was shining in as it came up over the mountains. It was early in the morning, but I had known Jake would be here. He was always here this early and then late at night. The partners rarely looked at an associate's work product. Sometimes they critiqued a memo or something, but only to make the associate think they were actually paying attention to their work. No, the partners based their evaluation of an employee solely on how much time they put in. And Jake had mastered the game. He figured out that they checked up on him in the morning when they got in and at night when they left; as long as he was here during those two times, they thought he was putting in a full day. So the morning and evening were devoted to work and the middle of the day devoted to pot. A perfect setup. Of course, if the partners found out he was high all day and only came in mornings and evenings, they would fire him and maybe even sue him for theft of company money, but that was a chance he was willing to take.

"I have to take the case," I said. "I mean, I don't have to, but I'm going to."

"Again, I have to ask, why?"

I shook my head and sighed. "I don't know, man. I saw Danny on his bicycle at the shooting. He'd jumped on his bike to get away . . . He looked just like Michael. I can't even imagine how scared he must've been when he realized what those gunshots were and he saw his friends dropping. And imagine what Melissa thought when she got there and realized her boy was one of the dead. You don't have a kid, you don't get it. But things like that keep parents up at night. Every day I sent Michael off to school, I was terrified something would happen to him. I can't even imagine what it would feel like if something did."

"It's a damn tragedy, one of the worst I've ever seen in my life, but that doesn't mean we sue, Peter. Sometimes there just isn't anyone to hold accountable."

"This guy had a military rifle. He had a *military rifle*, Jake, and he used it to kill children like they were cattle. Someone has to be responsible. Someone made these weapons to kill, and then when they're used to do exactly what they're designed to do, everyone holds up their hands and says, 'Not me, not my fault. I can't control what people do with them once they buy them.' It's gotta stop somewhere. There's gotta be that first case that tells these people they can't keep doing this."

He hesitated. "The world isn't about what's right and what's wrong. It's about what is and what isn't. And this isn't a case you can take. You will spend a ton of time, money, emotional energy . . . You name it, you're gonna bleed it. And for what? A guaranteed loss at the end? And probably a Bar complaint? These guys will make a lesson out of you." He leaned forward, his elbows on his desk. "Just do what I say: tell them you need more money or else you'll have to file suit. If they offer even a dime more than twenty grand, you jump on it. But I really think they'll offer two hundred grand to half a mil at least. We're talking about kids here."

"Yeah, I know . . . I know. I just . . . okay, okay, I'll do that before I do anything else. I'll tell them my client is hesitant to take the offer, and if they could offer more money that might be enough to convince her. I mean, ultimately I'm in this for the money. I'm not losing sight of that. It's always about the money."

"See," he said, slapping the desk. "That's the Pete I know. Practical."

I shrugged. "Yeah, practical."

18

The first thing was to talk to Roger Bailey. I wanted to meet with him in person again but this time he insisted on a phone call. When he answered, he was on speaker, and I got the distinct impression that someone else was in the room with him.

"Counsel, how the hell are ya?"

"I'm good, Roger, thanks. Listen, the reason I wanted to talk was that I spoke to my client, and she's hesitant to take the offer. She thinks it's a little low."

He chuckled. "Yeah, they always think it's low." He sighed. "Too bad, I thought maybe this one, just this once, would actually be thinking about her kid rather than the money. But I guess they always just think about the money."

I ignored him and said, "So what do you think about a little bump? I mean . . . if you offered half a million, she would take that in a second."

"Half a million? Why on earth would I offer half a million dollars on something no court in America would find us liable for?"

"Out of the goodness of your heart?" I said.

Silence. And then laughter.

"Boy you are one rascally sonofabitch, ain't ya? I like you, Peter. I really do, and I don't like a lotta lawyers." He paused and the phone seemed to go dead: he was covering the receiver while he talked to whoever else was in there with him.

"I can't offer half a mil, not on something like this. But I'll tell you what, and this will take some clearing with the bosses, mind you, but I think we can offer a hundred thousand dollars. More money than your client will ever see at one time in her life."

I rubbed the side of my head. I had been ground down with a headache today that just wouldn't go away. "I'll take it to her, but she really had her heart set on that half a million number. I mean, it's her child she lost. We can't insult her with a hundred thousand dollars for the loss of her child."

"We could just offer nothing and say do your best. I've done that before, you know."

"I know. Well, I'll take this to her, but if you can talk to the bosses or do what you gotta do to get it up, let me know."

"I will."

I hung up. If he wanted to offer me ten million right there, he would've had the authority to do so. Negotiating between attorneys was always this little dance that had to be done just so. We had to pretend we didn't really have the authority to do something we clearly had the authority to do, so that we could make it seem like a big accomplishment when we finally did it.

I sat there for a second. I had a client consult in an hour. I took my phone and texted the client, rescheduling the meeting for tomorrow. Then I grabbed my suit coat and headed out.

Holladay-Greenville Elementary looked like a school from the 1930s. The bricks were old and the roof cracking and falling apart. I stood in the parking lot a long time before I went inside.

The air was cool, and I was surprised at how low the ceilings were. I wondered how it was that elementary schools seemed so large when I was a kid and so much like a small box now.

I went to the front office. The woman behind the desk was watching a video of something on YouTube. She smiled at me and I smiled back and said, "Hi, um, this is gonna sound weird, but can I just look around the school? I'm an attorney and I'm working on a case that involves the school, so it'd be helpful to have a look around."

"You want me to let a full-grown man wander around an elementary school?"

"Well, when you put it that way, no." I grinned awkwardly to a police officer sitting in the corner behind her. "Um, look, I'm representing one of the mothers of a child who was killed here. Could you have someone show me around? Maybe the officer there?"

She froze for a few moments, and then cleared her throat. "I can show you around. Let me get my jacket."

When she came back out, she had a pink jogging jacket on and zipped it up. She led me outside without a word and we went around the building.

"Is it Melissa?"

"I'm not really at liberty to say."

She glanced back at me. "You don't look like a lawyer."

"No?"

"No. You look like a car salesman. Somethin' like that."

"It's an honest living, selling cars."

We got around to the back near the playground and she stopped. She put her hands in her pockets and stared out over the grass field and the playground equipment. Her jaw clenched, and I could see the muscles in it, the striations as she ground her teeth together.

"Were you here?"

She nodded but didn't look at me. "Yeah I was here." She closed her eyes and exhaled deeply. "I still can't sleep. I was a hundred feet away and not a single bullet flew toward me, but I still wake up screamin' in the middle of the night. Why you think that is?"

I hesitated. "I don't know."

She looked back out over the playground. "He started over there."

We walked the fifty yards or so and stopped at the playground. She pointed to a length of the chain-link fence. "Used to be a hole right there. That's where he got in. He came over to the playground. There was some kids there, but he didn't shoot at them at first. Then he walked that way. There was five or six teachers and aides over there watching the kids. He had a big bag with the guns in 'em so no one did nothin' at first 'cause we couldn't see 'em. I saw him, too, but I thought he was just a kid from the high school. Sometimes they cut through here."

She began walking and I followed behind. We went closer to the school, and as we got nearer, I could see the bullet holes in the walls.

"He was standin' right where you are when he started shooting."

I looked out over the playground. I couldn't have been more than twenty feet from it, and maybe sixty feet from the school.

"Tell me what happened next."

"I seen him bend down and open his bag, and then he came up with this gun. Big rifle. I still didn't scream or nothin' like that. You don't ever think somethin' like this is gonna happen, so I didn't even know what was going on. I thought maybe it was a toy gun." She stopped and her eyes welled up. Her hands were trembling. "Then he fired that first shot. The rifle. It sounded like thunder."

"Where did he shoot?"

She pointed toward the school. "At two teachers over there. Hit one, but they lived. They ain't back to work yet but they're alive." She swallowed and held her hand to her mouth for a few seconds, as though physically choking back something that was pushing its way out. "The kids started screamin', most of them, and runnin'. Some of them didn't know what was going on and they kept playing." She started sobbing now. "So when he turned to shoot them, they were just playing because they didn't know no better . . . they didn't know no better."

I looked at the playground equipment. Several of the pieces had bullet holes in them. Children would come play here again, would see those holes every day, and still play, because that's how children were. Some of the adults would never come back here, though.

I let her wipe at her tears a minute before I said, "What'd he do then?"

"After shooting at the kids on the playground, he started walking toward the school. The teachers coulda got away if they wanted to, but not one of them did. All of them stayed to get the kids. Lotta kids are alive right now because the teachers stayed and led them where they needed to go."

"So he was chasing them?"

She shook her head. "No. He never ran. He just walked slow . . . real slow, and just kept shooting. Anyone that got away he didn't go after. He just picked the people that stayed behind. Another teacher, Jody, was over here."

"Jody's alive, too, right?"

She nodded. "She had a little girl underneath her. He fired three times. Jody almost bled to death, but she didn't let go of that little girl. Not for one second. Her heart stopped for four minutes in the hospital, but the doctor said she fought to be alive. He said he ain't never seen someone fight so hard to live. I think 'cause she has three of her own daughters at home to take care of."

I stared at the spot on the grass and said, "What'd he do next?"

"Some kids was runnin' around that corner and he started walking there, past the school. He just kept shooting . . . He shot inside the school, outside the school, everywhere. He stopped when the gun was empty and reloaded it. And then he started shooting at people running away. He coulda shot more if he ran after them, but it was like . . . he was waiting."

"For what?"

She shrugged. "I don't know. He just looked really calm . . . and then he saw me. I was near the corner. I'd run there after helping some kids get inside the building, and he saw me, and you know what he done? He smiled at me. It was the most awful thing I've ever seen. I still see it at night in my sleep. That smile . . ."

Some children came out of a classroom and walked over to a separate building. That's when I noticed the police officer in the hallway. He was staring out the glass doors at us, his arms folded.

"What did he do then?"

"Our school officer was shootin' at him and he was shootin' back. I don't know what happened after that. I was just tryin' to get as many kids inside the building as I could. The police was almost here by then anyway. You could hear the sirens. So he went out right there on the grass and then took all his guns out. He put 'em down on the ground in front of him and checked all of 'em."

"And you watched all this?"

She nodded. "When I got all the kids inside I didn't want any to come runnin' back or something so I stayed in case one came out of the building."

"What'd he do when the cops got here?"

"He was real calm. Didn't try to run or nothin'. The first few cops that came stopped over there near the fence. When they got out of the car, he started shootin' at 'em. Just like that. Didn't wait or nothin'. Just started shootin'. But them cops weren't shooting back. Someone told me later they didn't want to hit anyone in the houses behind the school so there were other cops clearing everyone out. So he just kept shooting at 'em. And then this big car comes, like a big van. But really big, like a semitruck, and all these police jump out. They're the ones that have the—what'dya call 'em?—the armor and the big rifles."

"The SWAT team."

"Right, yeah, the SWAT team. They came and they circled around, and two of their guys went up to the roof. That's how they got him. He started walking toward them firing, and one of the SWAT guys up on the roof shot him. Just one shot, got him through the neck and made him fall down. Then the other cops rushed in." She paused. "Some of them started cryin' when they seen the kids."

I glanced at the police officer. "Where did Danny Bell get shot?"

She pointed near the school. "Right over there. He was on his bike. Mary, the teacher that died, covered him with her body. She wasn't as lucky as Jody. She died right on top of him." She was silent a moment and lost in thought before she said, "She didn't let go neither." She looked at me and wiped the few remaining tears away. Her hands dug into her pockets and came out with some gum; she put a piece in her mouth. "I gotta get back to work," she said. "You let me know if you need anythin'. I want to help Melissa all I can."

"I will. And thanks for showing me around."

I waited on the grass until she left. There were so many bullet holes everywhere . . . it was hard to count them, much less think about repairing them. I wondered how many of them would stay permanently. Things could get scarred just like people did, and it would remind people that the past actually happened.

Then I walked over to where Danny Bell had been shot and Mary Thomlin had died trying to protect him. I sat down on a bench in front of the spot and stared at the pavement.

19

It was evening when I showed up at Melissa Bell's house. She opened the door wearing jeans and a blue blouse. She grinned when she saw me. Her eyes weren't rimmed red today. It was as if knowing we were going after Tanguich had given her purpose.

"Hey," I said.

"Hi. Come in."

I went inside and sat down. *Where the Wild Things Are* had been picked up and the rest of the house cleaned again, spotlessly so. She sat down on the couch and I sat next to her. I cleared my throat and said, "I got a little better of an offer from them. A hundred grand. Minus my fees, that's about sixty-six K for you."

"They went from twenty to a hundred just like that, huh?"

"They want this story in the press as little as possible. When I file a suit it will be in all the media outlets. It's worth something to them for that not to happen. They don't want a court case dragging out for years, even if they are guaranteed a win. Like I said, public sentiment is important to them. The only thing they fear is enough people getting fed up and deciding to do something about all . . . this."

She looked down to the couch and ran her fingers over the material. "Do you know what the last thing I said to my son was? I told him to be careful biking to school. That there were cars and people drove angry or drunk and he could get hurt."

I let her stay lost in thought a few moments before I said, "What do you want to do? Sixty-six K is a lot to donate to the AnyPerson folks. I mean, what do you really want to see happen?"

She nodded. "Here's what I want, Peter: I want them to donate at least two million to AnyPerson to fight to protect us from this type of thing happening again. I want scholarships set up for victims of gun violence, and I want a memorial for the kids who died. And, this is the most important part, I want a public apology. I want them on television apologizing for allowing this to happen so that they could make a few bucks on the life of my child."

I shook my head. "I don't think that will ever happen, Melissa."

She looked at the floor and was silent a long while. "What do you think I should do?"

I hesitated a second . . . moment of truth. I kept trying to think of what an easy paycheck this would be: about five hours of work for thirty-three K. Easy peasy. I tried to think about that, but I couldn't. Every time I tried, an image of a young boy with a bicycle tangled between his legs would come to me, and an image of my own son after that. Michael could've been that boy on the bike.

"I . . ."

She grinned. "You don't want me to take it."

"I didn't say that."

"No, you did. Good, because I don't want to take it either. I want them to feel scared. Let them sweat for once, like the rest of us do every day."

I opened my mouth to say something and then closed it. "I'll, um, get the paperwork started."

20

I contacted Roger and told him my client had turned down the offer. He immediately invited me out for a chat, this time insisting that it be in person. I called Jake and said, “You have to come with me.”

“I’m in a deposition. I can’t run out.”

“You have to. This is their ‘we’re gonna scare the shit outta him’ meeting. I need someone else there with me.”

He sighed. “I can’t do it. The partners will have my ass if they find out.”

“Well, thanks anyway.”

“Sorry, pal.”

I hung up and tapped the phone against my lips, then I dialed again. Kelly answered on the second ring.

“Hello?”

“I’m surprised you kept the same number,” I said.

“It’s easy to remember.”

“I, um, hate to ask this of you, but I need your help with something.”

Even though she probably hadn't gotten over hating me, Kelly said she would help. Not for me, but for the mother who'd lost her child. She showed up outside of Tanguich Rifles wearing a business suit and looked about as beautiful as I remembered, with raven hair and caramel skin. For a second, just a second, I got jitters in my stomach like I used to get when I saw her.

"You have no idea how much I appreciate this," I said.

"It's fine, Peter, really." She looked at the building. "I love these anyway. They don't want you to file suit so they'll make you feel like filing it would be the biggest mistake of your life. These corporate guys are such assholes."

"Well, assholes or not, we need to have at least one chat with them before starting litigation. Maybe they'll give me what I want."

"Which is?"

"Well . . . Melissa wants two million dollars, donated directly to AnyPerson for Gun Safety, and a public apology to the parents, and a memorial set up for the kids, along with scholarships for kids who have been affected by gun violence, and probably enough money to the injured teachers so they never have to worry about working again."

She chuckled. "You'd be better off asking for a pot of gold at the end of a rainbow."

I adjusted my tie. "Thanks for the vote of confidence." I looked up at the building. "And seriously, thanks for coming out to this with me."

She grabbed my tie and fixed it, since I always got it lopsided, and said, "It's not for you, it's for your client. You ready?"

"No, definitely not. But let's go in anyway."

This time Roger didn't come down to greet me. He made us take the elevator up with a security guard. When we got to his office, the door was closed and the security guard indicated we would have to wait. We sat down in two chairs against the wall. It sounded like about five people were in the office talking. The security guard left.

"So what's he like?" I said.

"Who?"

"Your boy toy."

She raised a brow. "What do you care?"

"I don't. Just making small talk."

"You were never one for small talk."

I leaned back and put my head against the wall and looked up at the ceiling. The hallway was rimmed with cherrywood. "My dad would kill me if he knew I was doing this. Suing Tanguich Rifles. He loved his guns."

"The first time I met him he was carrying."

I chuckled. "Yeah, I don't even know if he noticed it anymore. We got busted at the airport once because he forgot he had the gun on him." I tried to peek into the office through the glass on either side of the door. "He hated me being a lawyer anyway, so it wouldn't have mattered. You know what he wanted me to do? Something blue collar. He said a man's paycheck should be exchanged for his sweat. He thought that was the only honest labor."

"You believe that?"

I shook my head. "No one's honest. Not really. Besides, all he did was scrape by every day. Not for me, thanks."

The door opened and a slim man with a bright-white balding head said, "In the conference room, please."

I followed him, three other men, and Roger to the conference room. I tried to say hello to Roger but he didn't even look at me.

We got there and I sat, Kelly next to me. She kept her back straight and folded her hands in front of her on the massive table and stared each man right in the pupils.

The room was bigger than any conference room I'd ever been in. At least thirty leather seats, several phones, and a projector. I glanced at Roger, who still wouldn't meet my eyes. One of the other men, the skinny bald one, said, "Roger?"

"So, Mr. Game, we have been discussing the rather . . . interesting . . . proposal you emailed me last night, and have decided that it's ludicrous. Particularly the portion about a public apology, for something we had no control over and strongly condemn. No one ever has won a claim like you're considering filing. You should be aware that should suit be filed, we will immediately seek sanctions from both the court and the Bar, and file motions to dismiss the claim. We will seek attorney's fees, and any other remedy available to us under the law."

"Yeah, I get it, you'll make an example of me. Well, my third-grade teacher, Mrs. Garrett, tried that. She had me stand in the corner holding stacks of books at chest level. When the books would drop, I'd get an extra fifteen minutes. There's nothing you can do to me worse than Mrs. Garrett, so let's cut the BS and get down to it: how much is the maximum you're willing to give us to go away?"

He grinned. "You are an uppity little prick, aren't you?"

"Roger, I'm hurt. You just told me the other day you liked me."

Kelly chimed in. "Guys, please, you can compare penis size later. Give us a final number and we'll take it to our client. If it's reasonable, she'll take it, if not, we will file suit. And not just file suit, we will scream to anybody willing to give us an avenue to scream about how your guns were used to kill children and you don't care. I'm guessing the CEO won't be too happy about reporters barraging him and asking for his take on being called a child murderer."

Wow. I stared at her a second. I'd forgotten that she was a pit bull. I'd only seen her tangentially in court, since our work together was limited, but every time was like watching a caged animal set loose on prey. I guess you had to be that way in a profession so dominated by males that women weren't even allowed into it until sixty years ago.

The skinny one said, "Who are you again?"

"Kelly Baun. I'm working with Mr. Game."

Roger said, "I thought you were a solo guy."

"Just work big cases together," I said. "Two sets of eyes are better than one."

The skinny one sighed and said, "Mr. Game, you are hopelessly out of your league. We have the resources to bury you with this case. You will not have a second in the day to do anything else. A solo practitioner like yourself, taking a case like this, would mean your business shutting down, your clients going elsewhere, your advertising turning off. Perhaps losing your office space or apartment, leaving you unable to take care of your son—"

"What did you say?"

"Excuse me?"

"How'd you know I have a son? Have you guys been looking into me?"

Kelly placed her hand on mine, indicating not to get emotional. "What is the final number?" she asked.

The skinny one looked to Roger, who nodded. "Three hundred thousand dollars. With an NDA and a few other stipulations, of course. Acceptable by ten o'clock tomorrow morning. If Roger doesn't hear from you by then, please go ahead and file suit because negotiations will be concluded."

I swallowed and looked at Kelly. "Well," I said coolly, "that's certainly something to consider. We will take that to our client."

I rose, and Kelly and I left. No one offered to shake hands. I glanced back as I was leaving, and Roger was staring at me like he wanted to gut me with a fishing knife.

21

I waited until we were out of the building before I said, "Holy shit!"

Kelly grinned. "I thought you wanted millions?"

"That was before I knew they'd offer three hundred. I mean, Jake told me they would but I didn't believe it."

"Well, your client should take it. They're right: they could destroy your life if you file this case."

I stared at her. "You were awesome in there. Seriously."

"Boys' clubs always act tough until they see a woman with balls."

I went to hug her and she pulled back a little, so I stopped. "Sorry," I said. "Old habits."

"Goodbye, Peter," was all she said.

As she was walking to her car, I called out, "Hey, I hope he makes you happy. I really do."

I watched her leave and knew I wished like hell he didn't.

When I got into my car, I thought about going right to Melissa's and telling her it wasn't going to get any better than this. That she had to take this deal and forget about the suit.

I texted her. *There's another offer. 300K*

what do you think, came the reply a second later.

it's your decision

i trust you Peter. What do you think? Do you think this will teach them anything? Will it make them think about my son and that his life didn't need to be taken? Will it help get more of these weapons off the street so another parent doesn't have to go through this?

I typed and deleted about ten text messages. It was no use: she was right. Three hundred K to them was pocket change. Nothing would be different, and they sure as hell weren't going to give that check with an apology like Melissa wanted. I hesitated, and then sighed as I typed, *I think we should tell them to shove it*

Tell them then

I put my phone back into my pocket, called myself an idiot, and then headed to my office. I had to figure out how the hell I was going to file suit against one of the most powerful companies in the state, backed by the most powerful lobby in the state, backed by the Utah State Bar connections they had, who were all backed by national gun lobbies and even bigger gun manufacturers that wanted to make sure no case like this ever went to verdict.

Shit, kid, you got yourself in it now.

22

The first thing that happened in any lawsuit was that the plaintiff drafted a complaint, a document outlining why they should get the money they were asking for, and sent it to the defense. Basically, it was a way to say, "Hey, jerk off, I'm about to file this with the court unless you give me something."

Since they'd already made pretty clear that they weren't going to budge on any numbers, I decided I wasn't going to send Tanguich the complaint. I would draft it and file it with the court. But drafting it had to be done carefully: legal writing and research, which required vast amounts of concentration and detail orientation, were not my strong suits and never had been. I was always the big-picture guy.

It quickly became apparent after twenty attempts that I wasn't going to get the complaint perfect. I could draft complaints in my sleep, but those were for fender benders and slip and falls in small courts. Opposing counsel and judges barely read them. Everything I filed in this case would be reviewed by a team of lawyers who all went to Harvard and Yale, and they would find every little mistake, down to a misplaced comma, that they could bring to the attention of the court to get this case tossed. I needed help.

I went to Jake's firm. Candy was there, filing her nails. She looked up and rolled her eyes. "You can't use our conference room right now. They got a mediation going."

"I'm not here for that. Is Jake around?"

"He ran downstairs. He'll be back up in a minute."

I leaned against her desk and tapped my fingers on it a few times. She kept filing her nails. "You can stop doing that anytime," she said.

"Oh, sorry."

"What are you nervous about? Not that I care."

"I'm not nervous about anything. What makes you say that?"

"Because you're fidgeting."

"People fidget without being nervous."

"Fine, don't tell me. Then let's see how many more times you get to use the conference room."

"Alright, alright. Man, you're worse than my ex-wife." I glanced around to make sure no partners were near. "I'm filing a lawsuit against Tanguich Rifles for that school shooting."

She smirked. "You could say you're outgunned, I guess."

"Ouch. Are puns really appropriate right now?"

Jake stepped off the elevator. I ran up to him and said, "Walk with me." I took his arm and we headed down the hallway. "I need your help, man. I'm filing that suit, and I need about as perfect a complaint and follow-up motions as I can get."

"I can't do it," he whispered, looking around.

Someone walked by and we both smiled like idiots at her as she passed.

"I don't expect you to do it. You're worse at them than me. I need one of your well-paid Harvard interns to do it for me. And you owe me, man."

"Pete, I'll get fired. How's that gonna help either of us?"

I exhaled and leaned against the wall. "I need help."

"You know who'd be great at this? Kelly."

"She already helped me once. I doubt she wants to get involved any further. Plus she's got her man and her own career to worry about. Corey wouldn't dig her helping me with anything."

He thought a second. "You need your own clerk."

"This late in the game? I need someone brilliant. It's too late to find that now; it's the middle of the semester. All the good students have been scooped up already."

"Don't know till we try, right? I'll call the career services people at BYU." He glanced around. "Dude, are you sure about this?"

"Do I look like someone who's sure about anything?"

23

I texted Michael that I wanted to have lunch, and I could tell he didn't have any money because he said yes. I picked him up at school and we drove down to Alberto's and got two burritos. We sat on the steel benches and he drowned his burrito in salsa.

"Want some burrito with that salsa?" I said.

"Funny, Dad."

"Well you don't talk enough. I gotta get the conversation going." I hesitated. "Um, listen, pal, I wanted to tell you something . . . Your mom called me the other day and said she can't watch you this weekend. You'll have to go down and see her another time."

"What? Why?"

"I don't know, work I think."

He shook his head, looking off at the table next to us.

"Listen, I know you were looking forward to a weekend in Tahoe, but maybe we can do something outdoors. Camping or something."

"You hate the outdoors."

"Not true. I hate bears. They're satanic murdering sons of bitches. But if we go somewhere south, with more desert, there won't be any."

"She is so full of shit."

"Hey, watch your mouth. That's your mother." I took a bite of the burrito and put it down. "I'm sorry, pal."

"Whatever," he said, picking up his burrito and taking a bite. "I don't care."

I stared at him awhile, and then started eating again. "It was good seeing Kelly, huh?"

"Yeah. I wish you woulda married her."

"Ya think? You'd have been cool with having a new mom?"

He chewed for a second. "You're not happy. I think she'd make you happy."

"What're you talking about? I'm happy."

"Come on, Dad."

I watched him a few moments. Children had a way of seeing through you, I guess, that no one else did. "Yeah, she would've made me happy."

"Why did you run out on her?"

I took a deep breath and said, "Sometimes, pal, the fear of failing at something is stronger than wanting to succeed at it."

"That sounds like bullshit. A fancy way of saying you were scared."

"I was scared. I mean, I didn't know how it would work with us living with someone else—"

"If she would leave you like Mom did."

My guts seemed to drop into my feet. "You talk too much. Eat your burrito."

24

There were two law schools in Utah: The University of Utah and Brigham Young University, and no two schools could hate each other more. BYU was a Mormon school, and the U went the opposite direction, so the students at the U felt that BYU looked down on them as heathens and BYU felt the U hated them for being religious. Jake had gone to BYU and I went to the U. We decided to hit BYU first to find my legal clerk.

Clerkships were funny things: law students were desperate to get them because they thought they led to jobs, and law firms loved to have them because they were cheap labor. In recent years, they'd even become free labor as the market became saturated and law students began offering their services without pay.

We reserved a room at the library for the twenty interviews we set up. Jake sat next to me and said, "I hated these interviews."

"I never tried to get one," I said. "Old Aunt Beth had my clerkship with Corey arranged by the time I'd finished my first year, after I turned her down to clerk at the supreme court."

"Yeah, how come you didn't use that connection more? I totally would've if she were my aunt."

I shrugged. "I don't know, felt weird. That's kinda the reason I left Corey, too. Just felt slimy using my aunt's name for everything. Took a job at the Salt Lake County public defender's office for a year after Corey and then left that, too. Thought I could make it on my own." I chuckled. "Joke's on me, I guess, right? Now I'm literally chasing ambulances like Beth warned me about when I told her I was leaving Corey."

Jake used some eyedrops to try to alleviate his permanently veiny red eyes.

I picked up a résumé. "So who's our first candidate?"

"William Harold, top one percent of his class, nearly straight As, recommendations from two professors."

Jake got up and stuck his head out to the waiting law students sitting around in chairs in the center of the library. "William?"

A skinny white kid came in and sat down. He didn't offer to shake hands or even smile.

"Um, hi," I said.

"Hello."

"I'm Pete Game, and this is Jake."

"Hello," he said again.

I looked at his résumé. "You've really got an impressive résumé here, Will."

"William."

"Okay, William. You've really got an impressive history here. I mean, you won the St. George Marathon. What was that like?"

"I ran faster than the other runners and I won."

We sat in silence a few seconds.

"Um, was it hard?"

"No."

Silence again. Jake and I glanced at each other.

"So, how much would you expect in salary, William?"

"I don't know."

"Ballpark."

"I don't know."

"Can you just give me a range that you're expecting?"

He thought a second. "No."

I leaned back and watched him. "Well, lemme ask you this. Hypothetically, if you were to work on a case suing a gun manufacturer for a shooting that took place using one of their guns, I mean, what would you think about that type of case?"

"Can't be done."

"What can't be?"

He shook his head. "It would be a waste of my time and the time of the attorneys working on it. Causation would be impossible to prove. It has been in nearly fifty years of precedent."

"Yeah, but hypothetically, how would you approach a case like that?"

"I wouldn't."

"Again, hypothetically."

"Hypothetically, I wouldn't work on a case like that. It's a waste of time." He paused. "Is there anything else? *Big Bang Theory* is paused on my laptop."

"Um, no," I said, looking at Jake. "No, I think we'll reach out to you when we've decided."

"Thank you."

He got up and left like a robot.

The next eight interviews were no better.

Whenever I would ask the question about suing a gun manufacturer, the students would talk about its impossibility. One guy laughed and said he was a member of the UGAA and had been hunting since he was four and would refuse to work on such a case. The closest we got to approval was a young gal saying "Interesting" and nodding her head.

"Why do you ask them that question?" Jake said between interviews.

"What? About what they think about the case? It's all they're going to be working on. They should care about it."

"They're law students. All they care about is not starving and getting a clerkship to put on their résumés."

"No, man, I don't want somebody just doing things half-assed. I want someone who believes in this."

"You don't believe in this."

I shrugged. "I went to the school. I saw all the bullet holes and where the bodies were. I don't know. It seems pretty monstrous that a kid could go and get an assault weapon like it was nothing."

He shrugged. "I got guns, and it's all in how you use 'em."

"And that's exactly why I need a clerk who's going to go balls to the wall on this. Someone who's passionate about it is going to go all out and find me something to hang my hat on." I rose. "I'm gonna piss and then get the next applicant."

When I got back, the next applicant was sitting near the door. He was wearing a Pink Floyd T-shirt that looked like his father's pajamas on his abnormally skinny frame and was chewing on a candy bar. I wouldn't have thought he was applying except he had a résumé in his hand.

"Hi," I said.

"Hey."

"You applying for the clerkship?"

"Yup." He took a bite of the candy bar. "I like your billboards."

"Thanks. Um, come on in. I'm Pete by the way."

"Craig."

We went inside the room and I said, "Jake, this is Craig."

"Hey," Craig said.

He sat down without shaking hands and took another bite of his candy bar. Jake picked up the copy of his résumé that he'd placed on the table and I took the one he had submitted beforehand.

"So, says here you have a degree in mathematics?" Jake said. "That's an interesting undergrad to have. What made you go to law school?"

"I want to go into patent law. I looked at the data, and the number of people with science degrees that go to law school is miniscule. Basically I'm guaranteed a high-paying job after graduation."

"That's a good way to do it. Do you find the law interesting at least?"

"No, no I don't."

Jake went to say something and then stopped and said, "I'm sorry, I have to ask, is that a pentagram necklace around your neck?"

"Yes. I'm a Satanist."

Jake chuckled and then stopped when he saw Craig was serious. "A real Satanist?"

"Yeah."

I said, "And you go to Brigham Young University? Don't they require you to be religious?"

"I am religious. I got a recommendation from my priest like they wanted. I also sued them when they denied me the first time."

"It's a private school, though. They can deny whoever they want."

"Doesn't matter. Just filing suit and claiming they discriminate against other religions was enough to get their attention. They let me in after that. It's something I'm used to. Religious discrimination is alive and well if you're a Satanist." He bit into his candy bar again. "Besides, this place is funded by tithing money Mormons pay to the church. I love the idea of a Satanist's education being subsidized by Christians."

He chewed awhile.

"So," I said, "what do you think, hypothetically, if you had to work on a case suing a gun manufacturer for a shooting that happened with one of their guns?"

He bit into the candy bar again and said with a mouthful of chocolate, "You're talking about the Holladay-Greenville shooting, right?"

"No, it's hypothetical."

"Well, hypothetically, I think that's fucking awesome."

I grinned. "Really?"

"Yeah. Never been done before. So much of the law is just rehashing the same nonsense. Doing something new would be pretty bitching. Besides, they got it coming."

Jake said, "But as a Satanist you don't really care about stuff like mass shootings, do you?"

"Of course I do. We're not monsters. We just put ourselves before other people. Much better philosophy for living in the modern world than loving everybody without any conditions, you ask me."

"Out of curiosity," I said to him, "how much are you expecting to get paid?"

"Whatever. I just need some experience on my résumé, and the patent firms are all filled up before the school year even begins. Don't care if you pay me or not."

He finished his candy bar and the three of us stared at each other in silence a few moments.

"So are we done?" he said.

"Yeah, yeah, sorry. We're done. Um, we'll give you a call."

"Thanks." He rose. "Oh, and I got a four oh GPA, first in my class. And I could brief any clerk on the Supreme Court under the table, so, you know, keep that in mind I guess." It seemed he was struggling with something and then he forced a smile and left.

"Man, that guy gives me the creeps," Jake said.

"I liked him."

"You liked the Satanist out of everybody we interviewed?"

"He had, I dunno, spunk. Reminded me of me."

"He worships the devil, Pete."

I waved my hand dismissively. "Worshiping an invisible grandpa on a cloud or a dickhead in a fiery pit, it's all the same bullshit to me. Besides, how many people would've hidden that from us? He came right out with it, flying his pentagram and everything."

Jake flipped through the stack of papers in front of him and found Craig's writing sample. We'd asked each applicant to submit a small piece of legal writing for us to analyze. Jake read it and then put it down. "Shit."

"What?"

"It's brilliant. It's like freaking legal poetry, man. That guy's either insane or a genius. Or both."

25

We finished the interviews and then decided that Craig was the obvious choice. Jake was still hesitant, given the Satanism stuff, but I thought life was hard enough without judging other people for their choices to make themselves a little happier.

I went over to the student dorms. I didn't have to guess which one was Craig's: there was a picture of a bald dude with pointy eyebrows on the door next to a vinyl decal of a goat's head. I knocked and Craig answered.

"Hey," he said.

"You're hired. What hours can you work?"

"Got some classes in the afternoons; that's it. I can mostly ditch 'em, though."

"Mornings it is." I gave him one of my cards. "Be at my office tomorrow. We're suing Tanguich Rifles for the Holladay-Greenville shooting. My problem is causation. I gotta come up with some way to make a jury see that they're the cause of what happened. Be thinking about that tonight." I looked to his door. "By the way, who's the bald guy?"

"Anton LaVey. Founder of the Church of Satan."

"Really? You couldn't go with like a baseball player or a chick in a biki—never mind. Just be at the office tomorrow morning."

When I left, I texted Michael to see how his day was going and got no response. I thought about how a suit this work intensive would affect the time with my son, what little there was.

As soon as I filed this lawsuit, it would be full-court press time. Tanguich would do everything in their power to stop me, including bribing witnesses if possible. I'd once had an insurance company hire a witness in a big case I was working on for Corey, just so the witness wouldn't testify against them. When money was involved, there was no limit to how far people would go to protect a dollar.

There was one thing I had to do before all their investigators and attorneys rained down fire and brimstone on everything.

The Varvaras lived far from the school. The shooter, a nineteen-year-old high school dropout, had lived in a two-bedroom apartment with his parents. I had searched for interviews with them and found they hadn't granted any.

The apartment complex was run-down to the point that the buildings looked like they could fall over. Bricks were chipped and crumbling; the asphalt on the parking lot was sunken in and cracked; multiple windows were broken out and had either been left that way or had been covered by draped blankets to prevent anyone from seeing in.

I found the Varvaras' apartment and parked in front. I went up to the door, and hesitated a second. It hit me that, like Melissa, these people had lost their child.

I knocked. A moment later, a middle-aged woman answered. She looked Eastern European and wore a style of clothing I didn't immediately recognize. Maybe something Russian. An older man was seated on a couch watching television.

"Hi, are you Georgina?"

"Yes," she said with a thick accent.

"My name is Peter Game. I'm an attorney-at-law. I'm working on a case involving your son. Do you mind if I come in? It will only take a moment."

She blinked a few times and then looked down. "Yes."

She opened the door and I stepped inside. The place was dark, the windows blocked with exquisitely made rugs. The furniture had plastic coverings, and the old man sipped tea out of a white teacup. The cup he was holding had a large chip in it. He didn't pay any attention to me.

"What do you need?" Georgina said as she went past me and sat on the couch next to her husband.

"I, um, just needed to know some things about your son."

The husband looked at me now, and then his eyes drifted back to the television.

"We told the police everything," she said.

"I know you did, and they'll be sending me their reports, but I wanted to ask you directly. Sometimes people aren't comfortable with the police and they forget things." I grinned. "Cops affect the memory."

Neither of them moved or spoke so I cleared my throat and said, "Where did Nathan get his guns?"

"He buy them from somebody. A friend."

"Do you have the friend's name?"

"We only know his name, David. Nothing else. They friends from work."

I wanted to take out my phone and start typing notes, but these people were barely talking to me as it was, and they might clam up if they saw me making a record of what they were saying.

"Where did he work?"

"At hamburger place down street."

"Burger Barney's?"

She nodded. "He work part-time."

"Mind if I sit down?" She shook her head. I sat across from them and leaned forward. "When did you last see your son?"

For the first time, I saw a flicker of emotion. Just a tremor in her lip and a glance down, but it was enough to let me know the wound was still wide-open.

"He come home from work and went to his room. Then he have a bag with him. He take the bag and leave. Don't say goodbye."

"Did he say anything before then? The day before maybe, or did he text you anything before the shooting?"

She shook her head. "No." She paused. "He wasn't bad boy. Just shy. He don't know how to talk to people. Quiet boy." She folded her arms against herself and watched the television a few moments before saying again, "He wasn't bad boy."

"I'm sorry for all this. I can't even imagine what it's like to lose a son, much less in this way. I mean, did you have any indication that he was capable of something like this?"

Basically, I wanted to ask about his mental health issues but had to word it carefully. It wasn't something parents of children with psychiatric problems liked discussing with strangers.

"No. Nothing at all. He was seeing doctor and was on medication."

"What kind of medication?"

"I don't know. They are in his bathroom. He have schizophrenia."

No surprise there: I figured it was either that, borderline personality disorder, or schizoaffective disorder. All things I had come across in my time working at the public defender's office. "Nathan was schizophrenic?"

"Yes."

"You're sure?"

"Yes. We take him to psychiatrist and told he have schizophrenia. That he would always have it. The medication make better but it will never go away." She paused again and glanced to her husband. "We looked at his medication after . . . after. He don't take it for two weeks."

I knew that story. Medication, any medication but especially the antipsychotics, had horrific side effects that no one would want to go through: hallucinations, involuntary muscle tremors, seizures . . . you name it, the antipsychotics did it. People who had to take them wished for nothing but to get off them. So when they were feeling better, had more clarity and a grasp of reality, they began easing off or eliminating the medications entirely. Of course, as soon as they did that, the symptoms returned and then they didn't have the clarity to get help. Most homeless people were homeless because of that exact vicious circle.

"When was he diagnosed?"

"Since seventeen. They said it was early to show symptoms. Most people begin show them at twenty-five or thirty, not seventeen. But that's when he begin show them. He hear things. He told me he knows they're not there and he tells himself this but his brain believes they are there. Sometimes, I find him on floor shaking and talking to no one."

"Did he ever display any interest in guns before?"

"No. My husband fought for Serbian Army. He hate guns now. We don't have guns here. We don't think Nathan knew how shoot a gun."

I nodded and rose. "Well, I'm going to leave you my card. If you think of anything else that could help me, please let me know."

"Who are you again?"

"Pete Game. I'm helping the mother of someone who was . . . who was hurt by Nathan."

She nodded and followed me out, shutting the door behind me. I looked at the tiny apartment. Who could suspect that one of the people here would become a true monster, one you would read about in history books? I sighed and got into the car.

26

Burger Barney's wasn't far. It was the type of place taken out of the 1950s that still had the red-and-white-checkered tablecloths. I ordered a cheeseburger combo, and when the girl behind the register was taking the money, I said, "Is there a Dave here? A buddy of Nathan's who used to work here?"

"Oh, ah, yeah. Why?"

"I just need to talk to him for a second. Is he here?"

"No, his shift starts at five."

I checked the clock on my phone: that was in twenty minutes. "Okay, well, I'll wait for him. Thanks."

I got my food and a Coke and sat in the corner while I ate. The burger dripped grease like it was bleeding the stuff but it hit the spot. And they had poured pepper and salt over the fries, which made me drink down two full sodas before my stomach hurt and I had to loosen my belt a little and lean back in my seat.

The people coming in here were mostly young kids and couples. Some sheriff's deputies, probably staff at the jail, sat in the corner at a table by themselves and one of them kept eyeing me. He looked oddly familiar. After a few minutes he rose and came over. Huge guy, probably six foot with a flattop and a red, rough-looking face to match. He smiled a wicked smile and tucked his thumb in his belt.

"You remember me?"

"No, sorry."

"I remember you. You were an attorney at the public defender's office some years ago."

I nodded and took a sip of soda. "Yup, that was me. Why?"

"Peter, right?"

"Right."

His smile went away. "You filed a civil rights suit against me for police brutality."

Right . . . Now I remembered him. Officer Dane Howick. My client had been a really attractive model who got pulled over by Howick and another cop. Though she didn't have the odor of alcohol or show any signs of impairment, they took her out and had her perform field sobriety tests. At one point Howick grabbed her and said, "Oh, thought you were going to fall." You could see clearly on the video that he grabs her ass and gives it a squeeze. The model slapped him, and they instantly tackled her, held her down by her throat, and wrapped plastic ties around her wrists and ankles before tossing her in the patrol car. Of course, they had to perform a full search on her while she was hog-tied, to ensure there were no weapons, and the search took a full four minutes.

"The ass grabber," I said. "Yeah, I remember you now."

He put his hands on the table and leaned his face close to me. "I was suspended for a month without pay for that shit. Then they sent me down to the jail, and I gotta guard the pieces a shit in there now. They said they can't have me back on the road 'cause I got that on my POST file."

"Well, next time don't be so handsy. And why the hell would you pull that crap knowing the dash cam was on?"

He didn't say anything.

"Oh shit." I chuckled. "You thought the video was off. Oh, man, that must've been a little shock when you found out I had a copy."

He breathed heavily out of his nose, his pupils glaring into mine.

"What, Howick, what're you gonna do? Hit me? You want another settlement and suspension, go ahead. I can take a punch. I'd love to personally sue you and the county, so go ahead and make your move."

He straightened up. "Watch your ass."

"Or what? You'll grab it?"

He turned and went back to his table. The other deputies glared at me and I smiled and waved.

Just then a young kid walked in, probably in his late teens, with shaggy hair and wearing a Burger Barney's uniform. His name tag said "Dave" and I rose to grab him before he got to the back.

"Hey, Dave, right?"

"Yeah."

"I'm Pete Game. I'm an attorney-at-law. You mind if we talk outside really quick?"

"I'm supposed to clock in."

"It'll just take a second."

He came out with me, and we stepped a few feet away from the door as he took out and lit a cigarette. He reeked of weed.

"You're Nathan's friend, right?"

His eyes went wide. "I already told the cops I don't know where he got the guns. It wasn't me."

"That's good, you should tell the cops that. Because they might try to charge you with something for getting him the guns. Now, I'm a lawyer and I'm representing the mother of someone killed by Nathan. I'm suing the gunmaker, which means I need to know exactly how he got the guns. So you need to be truthful with me. Because see, the cops aren't going to go very far with this. They'll poke around a little bit, but if you say you didn't sell him the guns, and he gave you cash, it's impossible to disprove you, right? But I'm not going to do that. See what I'm going to do is hire my private investigator to follow you around for the next few months. No matter where you go or what you do, he'll be there. He gets paid by the hour so he'll want to stay up all night just watching you and then switch out with one of his employees when he's too tired. Think of that: For months, you're not going to be able to do anything. No booze, no selling, no pot—"

When I said "no pot" his eyes turned the size of golf balls and his jaw comically fell open.

"I can't say anything. They'll get me."

"Not if we play it right. Now, look, just tell me where you got the guns and how the deal went down, and then let's brainstorm and come up with a way I can use that information and keep you out of it, okay?"

He thought a moment and then nodded. "Okay."

"Where'd you get the guns?"

"From a dude named Jamal. He's a scarecrow."

"What the hell's a scarecrow?"

"It's a dude that buys guns. You know, he goes into a store and buys a bunch of guns for people who can't get them. Like, people that have been to prison or whatever. So, like, he goes in and buys a bunch of guns and then calls it in and says they were stolen and then just sells the guns to anybody who needs them. A scarecrow."

"Scarecrow . . . do you mean straw man?"

"No, man, a scarecrow. That's where I got 'em from."

I'd come across, briefly, straw men, or what I guess were now called scarecrows, before. Since felons or people convicted of domestic violence couldn't buy guns—something the gun lobbies were constantly trying to overturn—if they wanted a gun and didn't trust a street dealer, they could buy from a straw man who bought the highest-quality guns from a reputable gun store.

"So how'd Nathan get them?" I said.

He shook his head and looked away. "I never . . . I mean . . . if I had known he'd . . ."

"I'm not blaming you, Dave. If it wasn't you, he would get the guns from somewhere else. You can throw a rock down any street and find someone selling a gun."

He nodded and tossed his cigarette to the asphalt and stepped on it. "He said he wanted to learn how to hunt and he wanted a BL-24. I asked him why he needed a BL-24 to hunt with. You can't hunt with those things. I'm a hunter and that shit just tears the meat apart. Makes it unusable. The only thing you need that shit for is to shoot people or shoot bottles out in the desert. He said he still wanted one, just to have it. He knew I knew Jamal so I just hooked them up. Made a couple hundred bucks. And it wasn't me that sold him the guns, just hooked him and Jamal up."

"Where'd he get the money?"

"I don't know. Probably saved it. He was always working double shifts and holidays."

"You do a lot of this sort of thing?"

"No, man. That was the first. And the last damn time. I'll stick to pot."

I thought a moment. "When was the last time you saw Nathan before the shooting?"

He blew out a puff of smoke. "I don't know, man. Like two days before, at work, I guess. He seemed normal, ya know? Just like . . . how he always was. That's some shit, though, ain't it? That people can act one way on the outside but they're just totally different on the inside."

27

I sat in my office late at night. Michael said he was sleeping over at his buddy Jarod's house, and I didn't mind. I liked Jarod.

Dave had given me a good "before" picture of what happened and the chain of custody of the guns. Dave refused to give me Jamal's contact information, but I didn't need him right now. Besides, Dave had let slip that Jamal worked at the local community college as a maintenance worker, and it wouldn't be hard to track him down.

I scrolled through a few tabs I had open, researching gun crime statistics and Tanguich Rifles.

Tanguich was started by a man named Hank Buck, which I figured either had to be a fake name or, man, did that guy pick the right business to go into. Hank was the grandfather of the current CEO of the company, Charles Buck.

The biography of Hank on the company website described him as an outdoorsman who felt most rifles just weren't right for him, so he decided to craft his own. He made his first rifle in his barn with his own hands and his second for a neighbor who loved firing it. Only when word spread in the small town of Fruitville did he begin forging them for sale.

Yeah, right. I'm sure that's how it went down.

The company had a government contract supplying rifles and sidearms to various law enforcement agencies around the country, and had even picked up a military contract with the nation of Sierra Leone, supplying rifles to the government there. I'm sure Hank would be proud.

I leaned back in my chair. My neck hurt and I twisted it from side to side. My problem, the problem of every case like this that had come down the pipeline, was causation.

There were two types of causation in a negligence lawsuit: proximate cause, and cause in fact. Cause in fact had the fancy Latin name of *sine qua non*, which meant "without which not." It was basically something that, without it, the injury wouldn't have happened. This is what people think of when they think something caused something else.

But then there was proximate cause. This was a much wider gray area, and the area shotgun lawyers lived in. It was something that was sufficiently related to the injury for the law to consider it the cause. So maybe it wasn't *the* cause, but it started the dominos falling.

That's where we had to be for this case. I had to somehow come up with a believable link between the gun manufacturer and the shooter, more than just Jamal the scarecrow randomly picking their brand at a gun store.

My phone rang. It was Kelly.

"Hey," I said. "What are you doing up in the wee hours of the morn?"

"Research."

"Sounds like a blast."

She sighed. "It is, let me tell ya. I forgot how much I hated being a lawyer."

"Yeah? You weren't practicing out there in Cali?"

"No, I was a director at a nonprofit."

"No shit?"

"Yeah. Little art gallery that tried to raise awareness about art in the community. Just dealing with artists all day. People who don't just try to get through the workday but who actually love their work and are willing to suffer for it. I mean, a lot of them lived really shitty lives, but they were happy doing their work."

"Happy artist, huh? I don't think that's a real thing."

"We all have our demons, but they at least enjoyed getting up in the mornings."

"You don't?"

She hesitated. "This is crossing into the personal and I don't want to get personal. That's not why I called."

"Then why did you call?"

"I talked to Jake. He says your client turned down the offer and you're getting ready to file suit?"

"It's true. I'm a madman."

"What's your basis?"

"They made the guns; there's got to be something there."

"Peter, there's not. Precedent couldn't be more against you. I mean, you file that complaint and it's an automatic Rule Eleven sanction for filing a suit you know is frivolous, and a Bar complaint on top of that. Why risk it?"

"I don't know."

A long pause. "You want my help, don't you?"

"Yes!" I nearly shouted. "I mean, you know, if you got the time or whatever."

She chuckled. "Why didn't you just ask me?"

"Because the other day at Tanguich, for just a little bit, it seemed like you didn't hate me. I didn't want it to go back the other way and thought it might if I called you again."

Silence on the other end. "I don't know, I'm pretty booked over here."

"Yeah, I know. I don't expect it. I got a clerk, and maybe I can convince Jake to pitch in here and there when he's not stoned. We'll be fine."

"How about I think about it?"

"Sure. Yeah. Anything you can do would be awesome. You're the best lawyer I know."

It was true. She had a mind for this stuff I hadn't seen elsewhere. She knew hundreds of statutes off the top of her head, the origin of why they came about, even the legislators who proposed them and why. She could spout to any judge the legislature's intent when they passed a certain bill or why the bill was incorrectly written and what the legislature really meant to say. And it seemed like she could pinpoint the flaw in an opponent's argument within a second and attack it like a pit bull.

She had graduated from Yale with both an MBA and a JD and had had her pick of where to go and what to do, but she chose Utah of all places because she loved the outdoors. In fact, half our relationship had been spent hiking or skiing, both of which I hated but did with a smile on my face for her. She was an associate at Corey's firm while I clerked there and we hit it off and became friends. After my divorce, she was the one who was always there for me. Getting together with her just seemed . . . natural.

"Listen, even if you don't help me, just coming with me to that Tanguich meeting was huge. I really appreciate it."

"Good night, Peter."

"Yeah, see ya."

I hung up and stared at the phone a second. Before I could put it back on the desk it rang. It was Melissa.

"Hey," I said. "I was just—"

She was sobbing uncontrollably. "I was . . . I was just going on a walk to clear my head and I said that I didn't want to talk to them and they asked about Danny and I just lost it and they kept—"

"Whoa, whoa, Melissa, slow down. Slow down. It's okay. Take a deep breath. Come on, deep breath."

"I just, I just can't do this. I can't do it. I see him everywhere and this makes me think about it—"

She stopped and began a deep cry and I said, "I'm coming over."

28

When I got to the house, the door was open. I heard crying inside. Melissa was on the couch, bent over, her face in her hands, loudly weeping. I came in and stood there a moment before saying, "What happened?"

She looked at me, her face wet with tears, and jumped up. I thought she was going to hit me, but instead she threw her arms around me and buried her face in my shoulder. She was crying and convulsing so badly I thought she might faint.

I stood frozen awhile, and then got it together enough to put my arms around her. I don't know how long I let her cry but it was a long time. When she pulled away from me, I said, "Let's sit down." We sat and she wiped the tears away with the back of her hands. "Tell me what happened."

"This lawsuit. Someone called me about it and said that it's too bad I'm interested in money in exchange for the blood of my son, and that Danny would be ashamed of me."

Anger rose in me like a volcano. I had to swallow just to get it back down. "Someone called you and said that?"

She nodded, wiping away more tears.

"What else did they say?"

"They said he would be ashamed of me. That I'm trying to make money off his blood." She closed her eyes. "They said it was my fault. That I couldn't protect him and what kind of mother can't protect her child?"

"Let me see your phone."

She took it out and handed it to me. There was a call to me, and then the number below that said "Private."

"Is it this one?"

She nodded.

Son of a bitch. The only people who knew about this were Kelly, Jake, Craig, and Tanguich's team. I could take a good guess as to which of them had called.

"Melissa, what happened is not your fault, and you are not taking advantage of his death to make money."

She shook her head. "No, they're right. They're right. This is wrong. We need to stop. This is wrong." She put her hand over her mouth, as though trying to physically push back the sobs. "They're right."

"No, they're not. They're just trying to break you."

"I'm already broken!" she screamed.

She slumped down like someone who had lost control of every muscle in her body. I put both my arms around her and held her.

Eventually Melissa calmed enough that she went to the bathroom and washed her face. When she came back out, she sat down across from me and said, "I'm so embarrassed. I'm sorry you had to see that."

"You have nothing to be embarrassed about." I leaned forward. "Melissa, they're trying to shake your resolve. What you're doing is right. You don't want this to happen to any other parent, and you're doing what you can to prevent it."

She nodded. "I know. I know. But to hear someone say . . ."

"I'm gonna take care of that. They're not gonna call you again. Okay? You trust me?"

She looked at me. "Yes."

I nodded and looked around. "What does Danny's father have to say about all this?"

She rolled her eyes. "Bastard didn't even pull the car over when I called him. He was on some date. He just said we would talk about it later. We haven't talked about it. As far as he's concerned, Danny and I died a long time ago."

"Do you have any family you'd like me to call?"

"My parents come by all the time. I'm really fine now. That just threw me."

"I know it did."

She looked at me and grinned. "I don't know what it is about you, but I completely trust you. You were the first person I thought to call."

"Yeah, I just have that face I guess." I rose. "Do you need anything? Have you eaten?"

"I'll be okay," she said, forcing a smile.

"Alright. Well, I'll bring by a copy of the complaint as soon as we have it drafted. I like my clients to see those before we file."

"Sure. I'm home most of the day." She took a deep breath. "Thank you."

I nodded. "Just remember that you're doing this so it doesn't happen to another mom. They can't shake you if you remember that."

I left and then sat in my car. Anger weighed me down like an anchor chained to my feet. I hit my steering wheel and started the car.

I got up early the next day, went straight to Tanguich Rifles, and drove slowly by the executive parking. Roger's space was near the front. I parked in it.

I tried to read the news for a while but it was always the same thing—violence, hatred, incompetence, violence, shallowness, violence, sex, violence, and then kittens—and so I listened to music and leaned my head back and tried to imagine something positive.

A few minutes later, someone honked behind me. I saw a silver Mercedes off to the side with Roger in the driver's seat. I got out and stormed over. He rolled down his window, looking frustrated.

"You need to set an appointment if you—"

I grabbed his tie and pulled him near me. "You son of a bitch!"

He pulled away. "Are you crazy?"

"To a mother?" I grabbed his tie again and he slapped my hand away. "To a mother! Do you have any damn decency? Do you have any morals at all?"

"I don't know what you're talking about. And you sure as hell aren't one to talk about morals. How many clients you ripped off, Counselor, huh? How many thirty-percent fees you taken on cases for the injured and poor when you've only put in an hour's work?"

"That's business and within bounds. This is different."

"Again, I have no idea what you're talking about, but if I did, how is it different? Anything to win, right? You think we didn't look up everything about you? You put a fake client on the stand to be identified by a witness. You think we're not going to use that in trial? By the time we're through with you, the jury won't believe a damn word you say. Now get that piece of shit out of my parking space before I have it towed."

I took a step back and stared at him. Nothing. He didn't feel anything.

I grabbed his windshield wiper and ripped it off.

"You damn idiot, that's worth more than your suit!" he shouted.

I went to my car and threw the windshield wiper into the back seat, got in, and left.

29

Craig sat in front of me in my office eating a candy bar. Baby Ruth. He chewed it with zeal but slowly, as though he was trying to make it last as long as possible. I wanted to see how long he could keep it up if I was silent, and we went almost three minutes. He would just stare at me and chew. The kid was unshakable.

"What's with the candy bars?"

He shrugged. "Everyone's got their thing that's gonna kill them, right? Some people it's drugs, or sleeping around, or booze, or eating too much, or gambling . . .whatever. Mine's candy bars."

"How many you eat a day?"

"Probably six or seven. I have only one, what you'd call, real meal, a day. Usually just some cereal."

"That's not healthy, kid."

"Nothing is." He unwrapped a little more of the bar. "So why you all in a shitty mood this morning?"

"How can you tell that?"

"I'm good at reading people."

I smirked and leaned back in my chair, putting my feet up on my desk. "You know what those bastards did last night? They called my client, a mother that's lost her child, and told her it was her fault."

"How do you know?"

"I confronted their in-house counsel this morning. He pretty much admitted it."

"Whoa."

"I know. I knew these guys would do anything to protect themselves but I thought it would have limits. I guess it doesn't."

He took a bite of his bar but his eyes never left mine. The spark of joy that he got from each bite was almost unsettling.

"So what're you gonna do about it?" he said.

"Nothing we can do. Private number and they'll deny it up and down."

"Private number doesn't mean anything."

"What'dya mean?"

"I got a hacker buddy who could see where that came from in five minutes. Nothing's protected anymore."

"Wow."

He stuck his finger in his mouth to loosen a bit of chocolate between his teeth. "Do, lak, aht ew meed knee ta do."

"What do I need you to do?"

He nodded and removed his finger and wiped it on his jeans.

"I need the complaint drafted. I'm no good at legal writing."

"Cool."

"When do you think you can get it to me by?"

"Five days."

"That's pretty precise."

He shrugged. "Tomorrow."

"What?"

"*Star Trek.* Scotty said to never tell the captain how long something's really going to take because then you seem like a miracle worker when it takes just a fraction of the time. But screw it, I'm too tired to lie. I can have it done by tomorrow. Just need to sleep for a few hours."

I nodded. "Well, alright. Let's see what you can do. Grab a notepad and let's go over the claims."

30

The next morning, Craig brought the complaint to my office rather than emailing it to me. He sat across from me, chewing on a candy bar, while I read. This time, a Mars bar. Apparently the time of day determined what type of bar it would be.

"Damn," I said, putting the complaint down. "This is damn good."

"Thanks."

"Like, really good. Amazingly good. Brilliant even . . . but it's wrong."

"What about it is wrong?"

"Negligent entrustment is kind of a stretch. That's used to sue gun stores for selling to psychopaths and bartenders handing car keys over to drunks."

"It's all we got."

I sighed. Damn it, he was right.

When the gun epidemic in this country began in earnest in the 80s, people started suing the gun stores that were selling to the shooters. The legal theory was negligent entrustment, which basically said they gave something to someone who they knew had a strong likelihood of injuring someone else. The big case was against Kmart, when a cashier sold a gun to a visibly drunk person.

The problem was that Congress passed something in 2005 called the Protection of Lawful Commerce in Arms Act, or the PLCAA. They didn't like the fact that gun store owners were being held liable for selling guns to people who walked out and murdered someone five minutes later, so they passed this act to ensure that no one, not retailers, advertisers, or manufacturers, could be held responsible for a shooting.

I pulled up the act on my computer while Craig chewed away. They'd packed it tightly with legalese to confuse the issue and make sure anyone from the public reading it wouldn't read too closely. Basically, it granted immunity to anyone selling guns no matter what the other person did with them. It had a few minor exceptions, and the only one that looked relevant to us was negligent entrustment.

"I can't believe how broad this is," I said.

He shrugged. "I'm guessing you knew it was an impossible case when you took it."

I nodded. "Yeah, I guess. Well, screw it, negligent entrustment it is. What's the case law look like?"

"Not good. Retailers sometimes get popped, because they're usually little gun store owners who don't have the money or connections the manufacturers do, but no manufacturer has ever lost. Nineteen out of every twenty of these cases filed are dismissed before a trial, another ninety-five percent of them are lost at trial, and then the few cases that are won have been overturned on appeal." He took another bite of his bar. "Literally, there is not a single case on record I could find going back a hundred years with facts like ours where the plaintiff has won. The gun people are just too careful and too powerful."

I stood up and paced the office. "There's got to be something, though. We gotta find it. This guy had a military weapon, designed for killing, and bought it from a scarecrow. So, could the manufacturer have reasonably foreseen that a scarecrow could buy their guns and get them into the hands of people who couldn't buy them on their own because of felonies or mental illness?"

He shrugged. "You gotta talk to the scarecrow."

I nodded. "That's one way, I guess. If the gun store owner somehow knew he was a scarecrow, I guess we could hold him liable, but that's not what Melissa wants. That's not going to help prevent another one of these or put a dent in the gun lobby's armor like she wants." I shook my head. "We gotta find a way to link Tanguich with Varvara's purchase of the guns. There's gotta be something. Something's there that I'm not seeing."

He rose. "So I stayed up all night drafting that. I'm gonna hit the hay for a few hours and then I have a couple classes, but I can come back this afternoon."

"Huh? Oh, sure, yeah. No need to come to the office if you don't want to."

"Nah, I like it. It's like . . . I feel like a real lawyer." He was about to leave when he said, "Thanks for the job, Peter."

"You're welcome. Hey, that's a helluva complaint, I'm not kidding."

After he left, I thought a few more minutes and then decided I had to reach out for help.

The restaurant was in a crappy location, so they went high-end to make you think they were being chic. I took the crumbling stairs down to the basement and walked into smoke and wine scents that burned my nostrils. They called it a restaurant, but really it was a bar with a few tables set up for food. I had never been in here but Kelly was chatting with the bartender and laughing as though she lived here.

"Hey."

"Hi," she said. She looked to the bartender and said, "This is Tommy. He's the owner. This is Peter, my ex-fiancé."

"No shit? You're crazy to let Kelly get away."

I nodded and they chuckled.

"I got us a table," Kelly said.

We sat against the wall away from the bar. Their menu had like six items and Kelly ordered foie gras. I asked for soup since everything else sounded inedible.

I pulled out the complaint from the manila folder I was holding and handed it to her.

"I really appreciate this," I said.

"Reading over a document isn't a big deal. Don't mention it."

I looked around while she read. At least ten people were in the bar and loud as all get out from the booze they poured down their throats. It wasn't even noon yet and they were pounding shots like it was New Year's in Vegas. Most of them wore suits with shoes that looked shined to a sparkle.

"Wow," Kelly said, setting the document down.

"Good, right?"

"It's more than good. A complaint is usually just filler, boilerplate almost. I've never seen one like this. I mean, he did legal archaeology on the cases he's using as precedent for negligent entrustment. Did you say a law clerk did this?"

"Yeah."

She shook her head. "It's beautiful, Peter."

"Alright, he's a genius, but what about the claims?"

"They're crap. The PLCAA negates all this. It grants them almost complete immunity."

"Almost, not quite." I leaned forward. "Now hear me out—the BL-24 is a military-grade weapon, right? I mean, it's meant for the military. So what if we argue that by allowing these weapons that are meant to kill enemy soldiers on a battlefield, by allowing them to get into the hands of psychopaths and gangsters, they're committing negligent entrustment? They have a duty to make sure their guns don't kill innocent people, and they're violating that duty by allowing a weapon like this to be sold to the public. So we're not saying they should be held responsible for what people do with their guns, just what they do with *this* gun because it's a military weapon."

She thought a second. "Well, that's certainly something."

"It's better than walking in there empty-handed and shrugging to the jury."

"Oh you won't make it to the jury. A 12(b)(6) motion will dismiss this case within the first month or two."

I grimaced, which caused her to chuckle.

"You would pull that face when I didn't feel like having sex."

I couldn't help but turn the grimace into a grin. The thought of sex with her always had that effect on me. "You remember that time we got stuck on the Ferris wheel in Vegas? That was my favorite. Just under the stars, me and you, the city lights shining like gems underneath us. I think about it a lot."

She slid the complaint back to me and her face went stern. The levity that had been there completely disappeared. "If you're determined to go forward, this argument is probably your best bet."

I nodded. "Yeah."

She got her purse and rose. "If you need any help . . . maybe I could pitch in here and there. Not for you, but because I think this is fascinating. I can only write so many commercial agreements."

"Corey won't have a problem with it?"

"He lets me do what I want. He'll be fine."

"Thanks. You're better to me than I deserve. I mean that."

She grinned and said, "Good work on this. I think you might actually make it to the 12(b)(6) hearing with a straight face."

I watched her leave, and just then the food came.

"Will she be returning?" the waiter said.

"I don't think so."

31

I paced in my office. Jake sat in the corner returning some emails, and Craig was playing a game on his phone and swearing every time he died. I must've circled my desk twenty times before I decided I needed a Coke.

The vending machines weren't far and I grabbed three Cherry Cokes. As I was heading back, Patricia, an accountant who rented an office near mine, saw me and smiled and said, "What're you doing here so early?"

"It's like nine."

"I know. I've never seen you here at this time."

I chuckled. I guess it was probably true, and she didn't say it with any malice. "Waiting for a phone call."

"Oh yeah? Big case?" She put money into a machine and pushed the button for a Diet Coke. "I've been kicking around going to law school, you know."

"Yeah? How come?"

"I don't know, change of pace. I love the process, too."

"That sounds like you don't really know why."

She laughed. "That's true."

"Well, ninety percent of the people there don't know why. Don't let that stop you if you want to do it."

"Maybe I could come follow you around sometime, see if it's something I really want to do?"

"You're not going to want to follow me anywhere for a few months. I'm about to get my ass handed to me on a case."

"Really? Then why don't you drop it? Isn't that what you told me? That you only take winners?"

I stared at her a second. "Better get upstairs. Nice seeing you again."

When I got to the office, neither Jake nor Craig had moved, so I assumed there'd been no call. I checked the clock on my phone.

"He should've gotten it last night."

"He'll call," Jake said, not looking up from his phone. He pulled a brownie out of his pocket, saw me glare at him, and slipped it back.

"I mean, I know he gets there at like eight. He should've called then, right? First thing."

"He'll call, relax."

I handed them their Cokes and then proceeded to pace again. About halfway around my desk, the phone rang.

All three of us looked up, staring at it like it was some alien spaceship. I glanced to Jake, and then Craig, and then back to the phone. It kept ringing.

"You know you actually have to answer it to hear anybody," Craig said.

I swallowed, and picked up the receiver.

"This is Peter."

"Counselor." Roger's voice slithered into my ear. It was calm and smooth. Not friendly like the first time we'd met and not aggressive like the second. It was measured, like he was trying to say as little as possible and checking every letter before it came out of his mouth.

"Hello, Roger. How's it hanging?"

Jake looked at me and shook his head and I shrugged. I had panicked.

"I read your complaint. Interesting tack to take."

"Yeah, well, don't have much choice. Gotta come up with something that hasn't been tried before."

"Certainly . . . certainly."

He inhaled deeply and there was silence on the other end. Jake whispered, "What's he saying?"

"He's just sitting there," I said, covering the receiver with my palm. "Um, so, Roger, are you there?"

"I'm here. I'm afraid this has gotten out of hand, Counselor. The CEO, Mr. Buck, and I spoke about the complaint. He was rather . . . livid, that I wasn't able to nip this in the bud."

Ah. That's what this was about. I'd gotten him chewed out by the boss.

"Offer more money and maybe we can."

"No, I don't think we'll be offering any more money. And also, I don't think you and I will be speaking again. We've referred the case over to our trial team. You'll be dealing with Mr. Brennen Garvin from now on. I suppose you two should meet."

"Alright, happy to. He out of Salt Lake?"

"Oh, no. Mr. Garvin works for Dell, Garvin, Strutt and Lamb."

"Why does that sound familiar?"

"They defend senators and movie stars, Mr. Game."

"That supposed to intimidate me?"

"No, no, I'm just stating a fact." A small pause. "I should go. We won't be speaking again. Good luck to you, Mr. Game. I hope you get everything that's coming to you."

He hung up and I replaced the receiver.

"What'd he say?" Jake asked.

"Sounded like he got chewed out for not being able to settle this before the complaint was filed. Said they referred it to their outside litigation team."

"Yeah? Anyone I know?"

"Um . . . what was it? Brandon Garvin. Or Brandon Darving. I don't know, I was super-nervous, could barely pay attention."

"Wait, Brennen Garvin? Do you mean Brennen Garvin? Out of Dell, Garvin, Strutt and Lamb?"

"Yeah, that's him. You know him?"

Jake rose and came over to my computer. He googled Garvin's name. The first link was an interview with him in the *New York Times*, with the title, "What's It Like to Be a Super-Lawyer?"

The next link was to the website of his firm, and then one to his personal page at the firm, and then to a list of "Richest Attorneys in the United States."

"Look at this," Jake said.

Craig had come over and was staring over my shoulder. He smelled of chocolate, though he hadn't eaten a candy bar while he'd been here, and that made me ponder whether chocolate just naturally came out of his pores.

Jake flipped to a list of cases handled by Garvin. Everybody was there. Tech giants, A-list celebrities, multibillion-dollar companies, several banks, and . . .

"I didn't even know you could defend Finland."

Jake nodded. "Regulatory compliance. EU stuff. There's like five attorneys in the world that are trusted to do it, and he's one of them. The dude is a legend, Pete. The partners at my firm would step over their mothers to have a lunch with this guy. You sure that's what Roger said? Brennen Garvin?"

I nodded. "What's he doing on a case like this? This is small potatoes for a guy like him."

"Not really," Craig said. "I mean, if one of these companies loses and precedent is set, that precedent can be used by any other plaintiff suing a gun company because they lost a child or spouse to a shooter."

Jake said, "I bet they pool their money. National manufacturers and lobbies helping out the little guys. No way Tanguich could afford a lawyer like this."

"Pull up a picture of him."

Jake pulled it up. Garvin was tall with a square, good-looking face and brunette hair. His skin was tanned and his teeth unusually white. Even his eyes seemed to glimmer compared to the background of the photograph, which had been dimmed to emphasize the subject.

"Wow," Craig said, pulling out a candy bar. "The dude is damn good-looking. Way better looking than you, Pete."

"Thanks, Craig."

32

When Jake went back to work and Craig left for class, I sat at my desk and read about Brennen P. Garvin.

The guy had more awards than I thought possible for a lawyer. Of his past five clients, two had been politicians, one a prince, one a CEO, and the last one a tech company that was accused of stealing technology from start-ups.

On the law firm's website were photographs of Garvin shaking hands and joking around with everyone from Fidel Castro to the Pope.

I thought a few moments and then logged into the criminal cases database. I ran his name through a nationwide search and got zero hits. The one advantage criminal lawyers had in this area was we were given access, for a monthly fee, to a system that was able to bring up expunged or destroyed records. It also had a function linked to the juvenile courts to look up people's juvenile histories. Most lawyers didn't even know about it because you had to be a public defender or a prosecutor to access it, but I still had a valid passcode from my days at the PD's office. I put my feet up on the desk as I waited for the results.

Bam.

Brennen P. Garvin of New York City, New York. One count of domestic violence assault four years ago. The case had been dismissed within two weeks and then expunged. I wondered how he got a case dismissed in two weeks, and which poor prosecutor had been fired for daring to file charges against a guy like this.

The police reports were in there and I read through them. His wife had called the police, saying she was locked in the bathroom and that Garvin was trying to break through the door. On the dispatch tape, Garvin could be heard screaming, "I'm going to kill you, cunt!" I went back to the website; one of the photos was of him with his wife and four kids. Everyone all smiles.

My phone rang. I recognized the number but didn't remember who it belonged to.

"This is Peter."

"Peter, this is Ash, Michael's principal."

"Oh right. How are ya, Ash? Been a while."

"Yes, it has. I'm doing fine, thank you. Um, listen, Peter, the reason I'm calling, we had a bit of an incident down here."

"Yeah? What'd he do now? Cherry bomb in the toilet or spray-painting a penis on the locker room wall?"

"I'm afraid it's a bit more serious than that. I think it best if you come on down to the school so we can talk in person."

"Ash, now you have me worried. What the hell is going on?"

Silence a moment. "We caught him having . . . relations, with someone underneath the bleachers in the gym."

My mouth fell open. My son had always seemed asexual to me. Instead of girls in bikinis hanging on his wall it was *Doctor Who*. "What?"

"It wasn't sex per se, but they weren't fully clothed either. They were discovered by one of the janitors."

"I mean, you know, so he's fooling around with some girl underneath the bleachers. I mean, we've all been there, haven't we, Ash?"

Silence.

"What?"

"It wasn't a girl."

We didn't live in an upscale neighborhood, but I'd always been impressed with how the high school made do with what little they had. The teachers were overworked and underpaid like all teachers, but worse, Utah had one of the highest student-to-teacher ratios in the nation, and West Valley High had one of the highest student-to-teacher ratios in the state. But I'd never felt like they ignored anyone, though they certainly never called unless it was serious.

I went to the principal's office, where Michael sat in front of the desk, his head hung low.

"Ash, can I have a minute alone with my son, please?"

"Of course. I'll be right outside if you need me."

When he'd left, I sat down in the chair next to my boy. His hands were trembling and I could tell he'd been crying.

"Is it true?" I said.

"No. Dad, no it's totally—"

He looked up at me and stopped. He knew that I knew he was lying. We stared at each other for a few moments and his head hung low again.

"I mean, were you just experimenting or are you . . ."

"I'm not a fag."

"Hey, I didn't teach you to use words like that. Look at me . . . Michael, are you gay?"

He began to cry and couldn't look at me. I put my arm around him.

When he stopped and began to wipe away his tears, I said, "Why didn't you ever tell me?"

He shook his head. "I was going to. Before I moved out." He ran his hands through his hair. "Fuck! The whole damn school knows now."

"So what?"

"It's not like that here, Dad."

"You listen to me. Whether you are or not, whoever you are or are not, it doesn't matter. You are perfect the way you are. Gay or straight. There's nothing to be ashamed of. I just wish you'd told me sooner, Michael. I can't imagine what it's like to carry around something like this by yourself."

"I can't . . . I didn't think I could talk about it with anybody."

"You can talk to me about anything. You should have come to me."

He began to cry again and I put my forehead against his. I wished I could take his pain. When he was a kid, I would wish it when he was sick, and I wished it now.

"Does your mother know?"

He nodded. "Yes."

Ouch. That hurt. I guess boys always go to their mothers first. I tried not to show my disappointment.

He wiped at his tears. "I don't think I can come back, Dad. I mean . . . I can't come back here."

"Buddy, there will always be people who mock you or look down on you for something. The way you give them power is by running. So you don't run. You face them head-on. Never, ever, be embarrassed of who you are."

He nodded, and then threw his arms around me. It surprised me. He hadn't hugged me like this since he was ten years old, and all those memories came flooding back. The tucking in at night; the sick days where I'd stay up pacing the house, unable to sleep because he'd have a fever or strep; the injuries and drives to the hospital; the nights he'd come to my room and sleep in my bed because he missed his mother and didn't understand why she wasn't home anymore . . .

I closed my eyes and felt the warmth of tears on my cheeks.

33

Michael and I went to dinner that night at a nearby pizza joint. He seemed shaken, but somehow lighter. He even laughed a couple of times. We talked about sports and video games and college, anything but what had happened earlier. Only when we were leaving the restaurant did he say, "Dad . . . um, just . . . thanks."

I nodded. "You're my son, Michael. Do you understand me? There's nothing you can't share with me. I never want you to feel you have to hide anything from me, okay?"

"Okay."

He saw some friends on our way out and stopped to chat with them. While I waited for him in the car, I dialed his mom.

"Hey, Peter."

"Did you know about Michael and not tell me?"

Silence. "Know what?"

"Don't lie to me."

She exhaled. "He told you, huh?"

"Not exactly. They caught him with another boy underneath some bleachers."

She laughed. "He sounds as adventurous as his mother."

"Hey, gay or straight, I don't care, but he was about to have sex underneath some bleachers. Does that not bother you, raise some red flags?"

"Oh, Peter, they're just kids. We were kids once."

I exhaled and leaned back in the seat. "I kinda always knew. I mean, not really, but kinda."

"I know. I did, too. Since he was three years old I knew."

"And you just happened to not want to share this information with me why?"

"He didn't know how you'd react. Fathers are weird about these things with their sons. So I told him it would be better if maybe we waited awhile before telling you."

"*You* told him."

Now it made sense. This had been a power play. She could be the one to confide in. The cool parent who understood everything. And I was the ogre who would throw him out on his butt.

"You did that on purpose. You told him not to tell me so you could seem like the more understanding parent. For hell's sake, Jollie, he's almost an adult. We don't need to fight over him anymore."

"I wasn't fighting." For just a moment, the poison in her voice that I remembered came back. I chuckled to myself.

"I'll talk to you later."

"Wait, wait . . . I don't want to fight. I wanted to talk to you about something."

"Go ahead, I guess."

"I was thinking that, you know, I'd like to spend more time with him before he graduates and goes off into the world. Have you given any thought to him moving out here?"

"No way he'll leave his friends. Especially not now. He's going to need them."

"He'll make new friends."

"No way."

"Why not?"

The real reason was that I didn't want her influencing him. But all I said was, "It's too much of a sudden change."

"Well, I'll talk to him about that."

My phone beeped. I didn't recognize the number.

"I got another call. I'll talk to ya later."

"Mr. Game?" a calm, cool voice said when I answered. It sounded deep and hoarse. Like the voice an old oak tree would have.

"Yeah. Who's this?"

"This is Brennen Garvin."

I was silent for what seemed like a long time, but he didn't say anything. "I didn't think you'd be calling so soon."

"I take it then you know who I am."

"Yeah, I know."

"Good," he said, slowly, as though making sure I understood. "I'd like to meet."

"Yeah, okay, I got tomorrow afternoon free."

"No, I think I'd like to meet in a couple of hours. I just arrived at the airport and would like to check in at the hotel beforehand, but am free afterward."

I checked the clock on my phone. "It's past six. Workday's over, man."

"Our workdays are never over, are they, Mr. Game?" He paused. "I think it best we meet right away, just you and I. Before we get our teams involved."

Our "teams." My team was made up of a Satanist and my friend who thought weed brownies were a nutritious breakfast.

"Um, yeah, well, I got something going on with my son and I'd like to spend some more time with him. How about ten tonight? That too late for you?"

"Ten it is. Let's meet at the Marriott bar."

"Alright, ten at the Marriott."

I sat staring at my phone when Michael got in the car.

"You alright, Dad?"

"Yeah. Why?"

"You look like you've seen a ghost."

34

I spent the evening with my son. We took a long walk around our neighborhood and grabbed a couple Slurpees. He talked about everything: when he knew he was gay, what it felt like to kiss a girl, how he tried to convince everyone he wasn't gay, and the friends of his that would leave him once they heard what had happened at school. It was the most we'd talked in years.

When we got home, he said he was tired and just wanted to go to bed. I stood by his bedroom door after he'd been in there awhile and watched him sleep. Something I'd been doing for his entire life. I couldn't even picture this room empty and him away in Tahoe with his mother or off to college.

I remembered my appointment then and checked my phone. It was past ten.

Rushing to the Marriott downtown, I almost got clipped by a truck, and a couple pedestrians flipped me off, but I got there in ten minutes. I parked at the curb and went inside. The bar was dark and musty and filled with wood paneling and framed photos of celebrities skiing and hunting. Sitting at the end of the bar, nursing what looked like whiskey, was Brennen Garvin.

The thought that went through my head was Craig saying how much more handsome he was than me. Stupid Craig.

He was also, apparently, a giant. Though he was sitting down, I guessed he was almost seven feet tall.

"Kinda late to be wearing a suit, isn't it?" I said.

He smiled, revealing perfect teeth in a large mouth. With hands the size of soccer balls, it looked like he could crush my head at any second.

"You're late, Mr. Game."

"Pete is fine."

"No," he said, taking a sip of whiskey, "I think we should keep it formal."

"Okay, *Mr. Garvin*, what did you want to talk to me about?"

"First, some drinks."

"I'm fine, thanks."

"Nonsense. We can't talk business without whiskey. It would be rude."

"Really, I'm fine."

"Two whiskeys," he said to the bartender.

The bartender came over and poured them. Garvin held up his glass and I held up mine and he tapped it and said, "To being cordial." He uttered it with such a grin that I got the impression he was anything but. I placed the glass down.

"It's rude to do that, you know," he said without looking at me.

"I don't feel like drinking. What did you need to talk to me about?"

He sighed. "I read your complaint. It was nice work. I assumed it would be some boilerplate bullshit you downloaded from the internet. Lawyers just don't take pride in their work like they used to. It's nice to see someone who does." He smiled widely. "You clearly didn't write it. I'm curious who did."

"What'dya mean *clearly*? You have no idea what I wrote and didn't write."

"On the contrary, I read every motion, complaint, answer, and brief you've ever written. One hundred and fifty-six. Not a bad number over a relatively short career."

Was it that many? I had no idea.

"How's your wife?" I said.

It was the first crack I saw in him. A slight, really slight, curl to his lip before it smoothed again and his smile returned.

"You're hoping for a settlement. It won't happen now that I'm here. I have a certain reputation to maintain. Settling winnable cases would tarnish that reputation."

"Yeah? And how do your clients feel about that? A settlement could save them a lot of money."

"My clients know that I will do what's in their best interest. Can you say the same?"

Something about this guy reminded me of a snake. The way the words slithered smoothly from his mouth, his calmness, his creepiness. A general creepiness with no source I could pinpoint.

He reached down and pulled a document out of a bag. It was easily two hundred pages. He slid it to me and I took a quick glance. It was the answer to the complaint. The answer was usually just a general denial of all the claims we, as the plaintiff, were making. Saying the case is BS and should be tossed out. I'd never seen one more than thirty pages long.

Each claim was refuted by case law and logical arguments. There was no general, "We deny this claim." It was a perfectly reasoned argument backed by precedent for every single assertion in the complaint.

Then he handed me another document. It was a counterclaim, stating they were in turn suing my client and me personally.

"Seriously?" I said. "You're going to start with the bullshit already?"

"You have filed a frivolous claim, harmed my client's reputation, and cost them considerable expense."

I had no doubt that *he* was the considerable expense.

"There will be a story in the *New York Times* about this case tomorrow, which will further harm my client's reputation. They might be reaching out to you for an interview," he said.

"I can't control what the media does or doesn't do with public information. No way the judge buys your lawsuit."

"Perhaps. Or perhaps not." He sipped his whiskey again. "Did you know that Australia and New Zealand banned firearms after mass shootings, and they haven't had mass shootings since? Why do you suppose that is? I'm curious as to your thoughts."

"Make something harder to get and people will use it less."

He nodded. "That is correct. We are the gun-murder capital of the civilized world. Study after study has upheld that lack of guns would lead to fewer deaths, and yet we don't act. Do you want to know why? Because we are in love with the *idea* of guns. You can fight guns, you can take them away, you can destroy them or ban them, but how do you fight an idea? How do you fight something ingrained in a person's mind? You can't, Mr. Game."

"I don't have to change everybody's minds. Just the eight jurors that are going to sit in that courtroom." I took my whiskey and finished it. "Thanks for the drink. I'll see you in court."

I turned and left. When I got to the doors, something hit me: How in the hell did he know the *New York Times* was going to run a story on this case tomorrow? The story would certainly cause damage to Tanguich Rifles, what they were alleging in the counterclaim.

Son of a bitch planted the article to purposely cause damage to Tanguich so that he could sue me for it. Someone willing to hurt his client on purpose just to hurt me . . . that was someone willing to slit my throat in my sleep.

I glanced back and he lifted his glass in salute.

35

The next day, Craig and Jake were in my office and I let them read through the answer and counterclaim. Jake kept saying, "Damn it . . . damn it . . . man, shit . . . damn it." Craig took it in passively and when he was done, sat back and thought a second.

"He's got a point," Craig finally said. "You knew this lawsuit was frivolous when you filed it."

"Not frivolous, just novel. I get that no one's ever won before, but someone has to be the first, right? I'm guessing car accidents started with people losing all the time until someone won that first case."

"Not sure a judge is going to buy that," Jake said.

I shrugged. "So they win, so what?"

"*So what* is that they're asking for damages."

"I got malpractice insurance."

"Not after you get sued. Your provider will pay and then drop you, and good luck getting someone else to cover you. Not to mention, if the insurance doesn't cover what they're asking for, you're going to be personally liable."

I exhaled and began pacing around my desk. "So the question is, is it worth it? The payout on something like this could be massive. I mean, like, the biggest verdict in Utah's history massive. The downside is I could owe them a bunch of money. Shit, I owe a bunch of money to people anyway. I owe two hundred K in student debt. What're they gonna take from me? My crappy car? They can have it."

"They can garnish your wages for the rest of your life. The complaint says damages to be determined, but I bet they ask for one or two million in damages, easy."

I looked at Craig. "What do you think?"

"Are you ever going to be able to pay back your student loans?"

"Probably not."

"How much can Tanguich garnish?"

"Twenty-five percent of every paycheck in Utah."

He shrugged. "I mean, eventually your student loan provider will garnish your wages, too. Does it really matter if someone else does it on top of them? If they just take the twenty-five percent, I mean?"

I considered it and then said, "I don't want to back down. Not like this."

Jake tossed the answer on the desk. "Will you at least call Kelly and have her look it over?"

Kelly came down to my office at lunch and read the counterclaim. She read it in less than five minutes. Her reading speed was something almost supernatural. She placed the document back on my desk and stared out the window awhile. Her tattoo of my name was covered completely today.

I knew she needed to process everything, kind of digest it as though she'd eaten a meal too fast and her stomach needed to catch up. I sat quietly. Craig and Jake were gone so it was just the two of us. I could smell her perfume, the same one she had worn when we were together.

"It's a coin flip based on the judge," she finally said. "You just have to show some rational belief as to the possible success of your suit, and they'll lose their counterclaim. A few judges are beholden to the gun companies, so they'll find for them; a few hate the gun companies; and a few are neutral. I think you did the right thing filing this at the West Jordan District. Three of the six there dislike guns, and one of them used to work at the ACLU. Two are hard-core gun advocates, and one's a Libertarian. Those three will be against you from the start. All the federal judges would've been against you."

"So fifty-fifty shot, huh?"

"Looks like it."

She flipped through a few pages again. "I'm going to prepare a response for you. They need to see that you'll match them claim for claim and I don't think your clerk is ready for this."

"I wasn't going to ask, but, man, would I appreciate that."

She nodded. "Garvin's ruthless, you know that, don't you? He started his career on foreclosures, and there's a story of him laughing because he took the home of a veteran who accidently underpaid a single payment by forty-six cents." She paused. "When you met him, did he keep trying to get you to drink?"

"Booze? Yeah, actually. Kept pushing it, saying we can't do business without whiskey."

She nodded. "It's a tactic of his with lawyers he hasn't dealt with before. At the first meeting, he'll take them to some bar—he doesn't need to, you know, he's got a giant house in Deer Valley here—but he takes them to a bar and gets them to drink as much as he can. Then when they're leaving, he calls the police and reports a drunk driver."

"No way." I felt my eyebrows rise; in a morbid way, I was impressed. How did I not think of something like that?

She nodded. "The lawyer now has a DUI pending and Bar sanctions and can't concentrate on the case. They usually settle somewhere down the road for pennies just to be rid of it. He's a monster, Peter."

"Yeah, well, the world's filled with monsters."

She stared at me a second. "How are you doing?"

"I'm fine. Why?"

"You seem distracted."

I hesitated. I guess she had a right to know. In some ways, she was probably Michael's favorite person. "Michael, um, came out of the closet recently. It's kinda thrown me."

"Really? Why? You didn't know?"

"No, I didn't know. Did you?"

"Of course."

"How?"

"The fact that he kissed a boy on our trip to Florida was a clue."

I thought back. We had caught him kissing at Disney World once.

"That was a boy?"

"You couldn't tell?"

"No. We were kinda far away and you know my eyes aren't great. I just . . . I thought it was a girl he'd met."

She laughed. "Sometimes we see what we want to see, I guess."

"Holy shit. You're right. That was a boy, wasn't it? I had no idea. That's why he didn't tell me. He probably thought I was insane to not even bring it up after I saw it."

She leaned back in the seat. "He's a good kid. Give him some time and he'll be fine."

"I just feel bad for what he's going to go through."

"Every generation sees it as less of a big deal. By the time he's thirty, no one will even care." She looked around at my office. "You know you could lose this, right? And they would basically own you for the next thirty years."

"I got nothing for them to own. Probably worth a spin of the wheel."

"So is that what this is to you? A gamble for a payday?"

"No. I mean, not really. Shit, I don't know. It's all so damn confusing."

She inhaled deeply and rose. "I'll have the response done in a couple days."

"I thought you were swamped? If I didn't know better, I'd say you actually care about this case."

She folded her arms. "I have my reasons for helping. Don't look a gift horse in the mouth."

"Believe me, I'm not. I'm going to set a date with the court to get our discovery schedule. I'll get you a helluva lot more than a couple days for the response if you want."

"It's all I need. I prefer to get things done quickly." She paused. "Joey wants to meet you."

"Really? Why?"

She shook her head. "He says you were a big part of my life he knows nothing about and that he should know every part of my life. Dinner, on Friday."

She said it like a statement rather than a request. Since she was saving my ass, I didn't feel I could tell her no.

"Alright, dinner."

"Bring a date so it's not so awkward."

"Ah. Yeah, I'll find someone."

She nodded again and glanced down at the papers. "I hope you know what you're doing. This is really going to damage you personally and professionally if you lose."

36

I couldn't concentrate and felt anxious and claustrophobic, so I left the office early. I thought maybe I should update Melissa. I texted her and she said to come over.

When I got to her house, she was washing dishes. I knocked even though the door was open.

"Come in."

I went around to the kitchen and she smiled. "Nice suit."

"This old thing? I think I've had it since college."

"You've been the same size since college? Wish I could say that. Every year the scale becomes my enemy just a little bit more. Sit down, I made us dinner."

"No, I couldn't. I just came by to check up on you."

"Nonsense. I made it for two. We can't let it go to waste."

"Well, I guess if it's already made. What can I do to help?"

She placed some tomatoes in front of me with a knife and an apron. "You can start cutting these."

"Oh man, you trust me with a knife, huh? Last time I was in the kitchen with one of these the tip got stuck in my palm. I'm not what you'd call super-coordinated."

"Well you're sweet and that makes up for it." She picked up the knife and held it out. "Now cut, mister."

I started cutting, trying to make sure I would leave tonight with all ten fingers. Melissa began humming, and I was glad to see her feeling this way. What was that saying, time heals all wounds? Maybe it was true. I hoped it was.

"Anything interesting in your day?" she said, stirring a pot of meat sauce.

"Well, that's one of the reasons I came over. Tanguich filed what's called an answer and then a counterclaim. It means they're suing us. Like you and me personally."

"Really? What do they expect to get?"

I shrugged, and slowed down cutting when the knife almost nicked my finger. "Money is what they're asking for. Really, what they want, though, is a public statement. They want it in the press that whenever you sue them for something like this you're gonna get sued in return. Where do you want these tomatoes?"

"In the pot."

I slid them from the cutting board into the pot, and she stirred them. "That smells awesome," I said.

"The vegetables are fresh from the garden. Have you seen the garden?"

"No."

"We went through a rough patch a couple years ago when I lost my job, and the garden was basically what fed us. So I kept expanding it. I don't even buy produce anymore. That and my apple and pear trees give us everything we need." She stopped. "Sorry, everything *I* need."

I stared at her, her eyes never lifting from the pot. "You don't have anything to be sorry about."

She took a deep breath and said, "Have a seat. It's done."

The table was solid oak and the chairs were uncomfortable as hell, but the food smelled so good I barely noticed. Melissa laid out a salad with olive oil and vinegar, pasta, garlic bread, and the sauce. She sat down and spooned it onto a plate for me and then for herself.

"Do you want to say it?" she said.

"Say what?"

"Grace."

"Oh. Um . . . you better."

She folded her arms and her head lowered. I did the same, though my eyes were open and I kept staring at that luscious sauce.

"Dear Lord, please bless this food to nourish and strengthen our bodies. We thank thee for all we have and for all we will have and are grateful this day to have good friends in our lives to share thy bounty . . ." She stopped and swallowed. "Please bless Daniel . . ." I saw her body move a bit, a small tremor of emotion. "Please bless Daniel, that he knows how much I love him . . . and that he knows his mother will see him again one day. Amen."

She opened her eyes and blinked away a few tears. Then she unfolded her napkin and took out a fork and I did the same. I bit into my food and decided it was damn well the best pasta I had ever had.

"So I don't really know anything about you," she said. "Are you married? Kids?"

"Divorced. One son. He's seventeen."

"Divorce is fun, isn't it?"

I chuckled and some food came out of my mouth. "Yeah. Right up there with colonoscopies and visiting the dentist."

"You know my ex is a dentist, right?"

"No way."

She nodded, taking a bite of pasta. "Yup. I helped put the prick through dental school and then as soon as he was out and had some money coming in, he was gone."

"I've always wondered who goes to dental school. Like, who wakes up and says, 'I'm going to be eighty percent of the population's worst experience of the year and torture them while they're strapped down in a chair'?"

"Sadists maybe. You seen *Little Shop of Horrors*?"

"Oh, man, I love that movie. Steve Martin and Bill Murray make me pee my pants."

"*I think I need a root canal. I definitely need a long, slow root canal.*"

I laughed. "That guy can seriously make anything funny. He and Richard Pryor were my favorites."

"I met him once. Pryor."

"Get outta here."

She nodded. "It's true. We were both waiting for a cab. He was there first and it was kinda raining, just like a sprinkle, and he let me have the cab."

"Wow. Did you say anything to him?"

"No. What could I say? It's Richard freaking Pryor. I just stumbled into the cab like an idiot."

I shoveled in some pasta and said, "I met Andy Warhol once."

"Are you kidding me?"

"It's true. We were at a 7-Eleven and he walked in. Probably just driving through or something."

"What did you say to him?"

"I said, 'Hey.'"

"That's it?"

"That's it. One of the greatest artists ever and I said 'Hey' and then slinked away to the Slurpee machine."

She chuckled. "I love it." She took a bite of food. "So why the law? Did you just kinda fall into it?"

I shook my head. "I wanted to be a lawyer."

"Really? I've known a lot of lawyers through my work as a social worker. I don't think I know any that said they wanted to be one."

I poured some red wine into a small glass and took a long drink. "My dad was a real blue-collar guy. Didn't have a pot to piss in. There were a lotta dinners of peanut butter with no bread at my house if you know what I mean. Sometimes we got government assistance, but my dad was proud and usually we just suffered through the tough spots. Anyway, I have this aunt, Elizabeth, who was on the supreme court. But before that she was a big shot at one of those fancy firms. So on holidays, while we were barely crawling by, we'd go up to Beth's house and my cousins would be in their pool, and showing me photos of their trips to New Zealand or whatever. I was pretty young, but I knew I didn't want to have the life my dad had. I wanted to be my aunt Beth."

Melissa had put her fork down and was staring at me. "So did she help you become a lawyer?"

"She called the school and made sure I got in and lined up a clerkship job for me. Honestly though, she was really smug about it. Like she was making me the man I was and I owed her for it, you know? That I was just riding her coattails. So I quit the job after graduating from law school, worked as a public defender for a year, and then went out on my own. Because screw good sense. Besides, corporate clients kind of suck. I like representing the little guys."

She picked up her fork again and took a small bite. "That doesn't seem like the talk of someone who only cares about money, like you told me you do."

"Did I say that?"

"Basically. Only slam dunks, remember?"

I stared at her in silence a minute. Her phone rang and she excused herself. I inhaled and stood up. Strolling around the house, I looked at photographs and decorations. The bathroom was just around the corner next to the bedroom and I went in to urinate. After I was done, I was washing my hands and noticed something on the shelf above the toilet: at least ten amber medication bottles. I debated a second, and then looked at them. Hydrocodone, Percocet, Ambien, and Lortab. In two little plastic bags were some white pills I couldn't identify. I guess I knew why she was so happy. I sighed and arranged the bottles the way they were before leaving.

"I have to go," I whispered to her while she was on the phone. "Thank you for dinner."

She stepped close to me and gave me a hug. I just stood there. When she pulled away, I thought about mentioning the meds, but decided not to. I couldn't judge her, even though it was worrisome. I'd seen so much addiction with my clients. One accident, one bottle prescribed, and within a month they were full-blown addicts. Six months down the line, the meds would either dry up or they'd start costing too much, and heroin would be where they'd turn after some internet research. The difference between heroin and oxycodone was the difference between Coke Classic and New Coke.

I stared at her house a second. Maybe what she needed was some sort of endpoint. Some point in time where she could say "I can heal now," and that would take care of the pills. I didn't know. But if there was a chance I could help her with this case, I was gonna take it.

I sighed and drove away.

37

The court called me at eight in the morning. I reached for my phone from the bed and knocked it and the nightstand over. I fumbled out of bed and answered the call while lying on the floor in my boxers.

"Yeah, this is Peter Game."

"Counselor, it's Kristen in Judge Roberts's court."

"Hey, Kristen. What's up?"

"Judge Roberts would like to set a scheduling meeting to get a discovery calendar. Can you be here this morning?"

"Um, sure. Gimme an hour."

"Will do."

I hung up, stretched, and then went into the bathroom and stared at myself in the mirror. Sometimes I looked so much like my father it was creepy. Guilt usually accompanied that realization because I knew he wouldn't be proud of what I was doing. He didn't feel his sister was earning an honest living defending the rich to make them richer and wanted me to be an electrician or a plumber. He did see me graduate from law school before passing away, and all he said was, "There's no such thing as a fast buck. Easy money always has a hard price."

Easy.

Yeah. Right.

I showered and dressed in a blue suit. I only had a handful of ties and none of them appealed to me right now except a snowman one that Michael had gotten me for Christmas. I put on a white shirt with the Christmas tie and grabbed a Pop-Tart before heading out the door.

The West Jordan courthouse was a behemoth of a building compared to other courthouses and housed civil and family courts, juvenile courts, probation offices, and of course the criminal courts. The bailiffs wanded me through and one of them asked, "How's business?"

"One day at a time."

"Hear that."

Judge Jim Roberts was a portly man with a face that always looked like he'd just pulled it out of a hot oven. Sweaty, greasy, and pink. Rumor was he'd had gastric bypass surgery twice but refused to let it take and now had decided to give up on dieting and exercise. I knew all this because I tried to know everything there was about every judge I was in front of. What a judge's biases were and whether that judge had much of an attention span influenced a case far more than any law in any book.

I happened to also know that Judge Roberts was a gun nut and went hunting at least two or three times a month. Deer, elk, rabbit, birds . . . didn't matter. The dude just liked killing. Which meant I had one helluva battle ahead of me convincing a guy like that that gunmakers needed to be held responsible for their guns.

I got into court, and Garvin was already there. He stood towering over the judge's bench, and the two of them were laughing about something. They saw me and stopped and Roberts cleared his throat and said, "Counselor."

"Judge."

I looked over to the defense table as Garvin returned there, and I sat down at the plaintiff's. Garvin had a few other people with him, attorneys from what I could tell, and one of them was giving me a serious

A-hole smirk. Someone from Tanguich Rifles was required to be there, too, and it looked like it was the COO. A pudgy little guy in a black suit with a red pocket square.

"I have read through the complaint and answer, Counselors, and just wanted to clarify a few things. Mr. Game, my understanding is that you are holding the manufacturer to a standard of gross negligence in the sale of their guns, even though that is not the recognized standard per statute, is that correct?"

Here we go. First question and already getting shafted.

"Yes, your honor, I think you'll find that the complaint lays the groundwork for our assertions rather well. Something that we'll be happy to explain in detail when Mr. Garvin no doubt files his 12(b)(6) motion."

The judge nodded. "Let's take a quick break and chat in chambers, shall we?"

It was unusual for a judge to do that. If they wanted something off the record, they just turned off the microphones and video cameras in the courtroom and had us come to the bench and whisper.

Judge Roberts motioned for us to follow him and I noticed that Garvin didn't look surprised by this move at all. Like he had been expecting it.

I followed him around the bench and to the door, which blended into the wall like it wasn't there. We followed Roberts around the corner to where a bunch of cubicles were smashed together, filled with secretaries and clerks and interns. I nodded to a few I recognized while Garvin strode past them without a glance.

Judge Roberts's chambers were massive. Far bigger than any judge's chambers I'd ever seen. Like an apartment almost. He took off his black robe and hung it on a coatrack while he said, "Damn thing itches like crazy. Hard to find high-quality robes." He turned to us. "Have a seat, gentlemen, relax. Let's talk informally for a bit, shall we? Drinks?"

Garvin got up and went over to a mini-fridge as though it were his office. He took out three bottled waters and handed the judge and me one each.

"How you been, Peter?" Roberts said. "I don't think I've seen you in my courtroom for at least a year."

I nodded, placing the bottle of water on his desk unopened. "Yeah, haven't been getting out this way much."

Garvin sat silently, his giant frame fitting uncomfortably in the chair. He didn't look at me but instead watched the judge.

"Well you do good work, Peter, there's no doubt about that. I remember one of your closing arguments on a soft tissue case to this day. You had that jury eating out of your hand. Excellent work."

Why did I feel a "but" coming on?

"But, this is something else entirely. I'm nervous for your client, Peter."

"For my client, huh?"

"Indeed. You're dealing with parties here that can bury you in litigation with the snap of their fingers. I've seen entire practices of solo practitioners destroyed by cases like this. I was speaking to Mr. Garvin this morning and we thought—"

"When this morning?"

"Excuse me?"

"When this morning were you speaking to him without me present, Judge?"

The judge glanced at Garvin, who calmly took a sip of water.

"Just before you came in. Just common chitchat. Nothing to get your feathers ruffled over. Anyway, what I was saying was that I think this is the type of case that can be settled. It's clear, and this is off the record of course, that the law is on the defendant's side. To pursue this will harm you, harm your client, and hurt the cause your client cares so much about. I'm sure Mr. Garvin is more than willing to settle this claim for a fair amount."

"And what amount did you two discuss ex parte, Judge?"

He chuckled. "No need to be standoffish, Peter. We're all friends here."

"Really? 'Cause it seems like you two are friends and I'm the mark you're trying to hustle."

His face went slack and his pink cheeks began turning red. "I've been more than friendly with you, Peter. I'm trying to help you. If you're unwilling to be helped, then perhaps my efforts aren't worth it and you can fight this out in my court."

Garvin just took another sip of water, staring at the judge.

"You got nothing to add?" I said to Garvin.

He smiled at me with that giant mouth and pearl-white teeth but didn't say anything.

"Alright," Roberts said, "if there's no convincing you, there's no convincing you. Let's head back out there and put the schedule on the record."

As we headed out, I stayed close to Garvin and said, "How do you know him?"

"What makes you think I do?"

"Come on."

He grinned and buttoned the top button on his suit as we went back into the courtroom. I took my place at the plaintiff's table again and the lawyers at the defense table were staring at me. One of them flipped me off underneath the table.

Roberts took his seat on the bench with a groan and said, "Are we back on the record? . . . Good. We're here on the matter of Melissa G. Bell versus Tanguich Rifles et al., and a discovery schedule will be provided to both parties. Ms. Bell is not present today, but I assume plaintiff's counsel is moving to waive her appearance, is that correct?"

"Correct, Judge."

"Then we'll move forward today with the discovery schedule. I'll place a pretrial conference on the calendar thirty days out to check in with both parties, and please keep the court apprised of any settlement agreements. Okay, anything else?"

"One matter, Your Honor," Garvin said, standing up and seemingly almost bumping his head on the ceiling. "Defense would move for a protective order in this case barring the plaintiff, plaintiff's counsel, or any party associated with the plaintiff from discussing this matter with the media. As you know, significant damage has already been done to my client's reputation just by the filing of this lawsuit, and I think any further damage needs to be mitigated until the conclusion of this pending proceeding."

"Seems reasonable to me. Counsel?"

I stood. "Judge, she should be allowed to give interviews if she wants. This is a high-profile case that's going to get a lot of media attention and frankly it should."

"So that it can taint the jury pool," Garvin said.

"No, because this is what my client cares about. This type of case has been litigated a thousand times. Everyone already knows what it's about. There's no reason to bar my client from speaking publicly about it."

"Except that it's costing my innocent client tens of thousands of dollars. Why, a story just appeared in the *New York Times* about it."

"A story planted by Mr. Garvin to hurt his own client."

"That's slanderous."

"You're slanderous. And I want a protective order against Mr. Garvin to prevent him from planting any more stories that hurt his client in order to drive up damages in their countersuit."

"These are wild accusations, Judge. I can only assume Mr. Game has been drinking this morning to bring these out in open court."

"Like you were drinking when you beat your wife?"

"Mr. Game!" the judge bellowed. "That's enough. I'm imposing a pretrial protective order preventing Ms. Bell, her representatives, and any third parties associated with her from speaking to any media about this case. Will you accept service of said protective order on your client's behalf?"

I glanced at Garvin and then took a deep breath and said, "Sure."

"Good. Now, I expect an orderly discovery process. I don't want my courtroom to become a zoo. Do I make myself clear?"

Garvin said calmly, "Of course, Judge."

Why did I get the feeling the judge had meant, "I expect a clean fight," and that it only applied to me?

38

Interrogatories were the first step in civil litigation. They were a pain in the ass. Hundreds of questions, most of them useless, trying to gather enough information to see if you could trap someone into admitting something they didn't want to admit. But when I opened Garvin's interrogatories a few days after our court appearance, I couldn't believe it.

There were 368 pages of questions for Melissa alone. I'd never seen that many for a single person, or even a group of people. It would take us days to answer all of them. Some of them were relevant; most of them weren't.

Craig sat across from me glancing through them, and Jake was in the corner flipping through some other ones.

"Wow," Jake finally said. He tossed some of the papers back on my desk. "You're gonna need a bigger boat."

I leaned my head back. "So, what, more interns?"

Craig took a bite of today's chocolate bar and said, "I know a few people at the law school who would love to help with something like this."

"Good, get them, because between this and the depositions and the document review, we're gonna need all hands on deck. I don't even want to think about how many boxes of discovery they're going to send us."

The door opened and the receptionist walked in. "Just got this."

She handed me a manila envelope. "Thanks." I opened it. Inside was a thick stack of documents: Garvin's motion to dismiss the case.

"Motion to dismiss. Thought he'd at least wait until our first deposition."

Jake leaned back in the seat and undid his tie. "Sounds like he's not going to play nice."

I went over to Kelly's office with the motion to dismiss. Corey was there, talking to one of the receptionists, and he saw me and came over. The grin on his face was almost comical. Almost. If I didn't know how much he hated me, it could pass for a real gesture.

"What can I do you for, Peter?"

"I just need a minute of Kelly's time."

"Seems like you need a lot of her time lately. Maybe I should be billing you for it?" He slapped my shoulder. "Just kidding. She's in the conference room with a client. Have a seat and I'll grab her when she's finished."

"Thanks."

I sat down in a chair, and played on my phone.

Then I played some more, and some more. Then the vending machines, the bathroom, and more games on the phone. An hour passed.

Screw it.

I went into the conference room. No one was there. I checked Kelly's office and she was sitting behind her desk drafting something on the computer.

"Hey," I said.

"Hey. What're you doing here?"

"Just needed your opinion on something. Were you in the conference room with a client a bit ago?"

"No, been in my office all morning. Why?"

"No reason."

I sat down and slid the motion to dismiss to her. She read it over quickly and then said, "'Bout what we were expecting, isn't it?"

"Yeah. I guess. The court called and scheduled the hearing for a couple weeks from now."

"I'll draft the response and be there."

"I didn't ask that."

"I know. But I will anyway."

I nodded. "I appreciate that. Seriously."

She sighed and leaned back in her seat. "So it says here Roberts is the judge. That's a tough break."

"You're telling me. They talked ex parte about settlements before I even got to court." I thought a second. "What do you think about a motion for recusal?"

"On what grounds?"

"I don't know yet. Garvin wouldn't tell me how they know each other. I was thinking of getting my investigator to look into it."

She shrugged. "Couldn't hurt. But it's risky sending an investigator after a sitting judge."

"This whole thing is risky. Sunk costs. I'm in it already, might as well go all the way."

She glanced down at the document. "They're really gonna hammer the PLCAA and say that you're completely barred from taking this case forward. Make sure you're familiar with it. Unless you'd like me to argue it."

I shook my head. "No. This is my case. It has to be me." I stood up. "I, ah, I like this. Discussing cases with you again, I mean."

She hesitated and said, "I do, too."

Yes.

"I'll see ya."

As I was walking out, she said, "Peter, don't forget we have dinner with Joey tonight."

"Oh, right. Almost forgot. Okay, I'll be there. Can't wait."

I'd rather shove an ice pick in my face, but what could I do? I'd promised her.

Before leaving, I went down the hall to Corey's office. He was on the phone, his feet up on his expensive mahogany desk, staring out his floor-to-ceiling windows. A bust of some prestigious judge stood near the door on a marble pedestal right by the two-hole putting green. I whispered, "Corey." He looked at me, and as soon as he did, I tipped the bust over and then hurriedly left the firm.

39

I'd spent six hours on the interrogatories. I had Melissa on speakerphone and she hung in there with me and we got through as much as we could.

"Are they usually this long?" she asked.

"No, not at all. These guys are going to fight hard. You gotta remember, if we win we set new precedent, so a lotta powerful people want to see us fail." Silence on the other end before I said, "How you holding up?"

"I'm fine." She cleared her throat and said, "Do you mind if we stop now? I'm losing my voice."

"Not at all." I checked the clock on my cell phone. "I got a dinner thing anyway. I'll call you tomorrow morning and we can polish off some more of these."

After hanging up, I texted a few women I'd been on dates with. No one was available and dinner started in forty minutes. I looked out my office and saw Craig talking to the receptionist. I grabbed my jacket and said, "Craig, you're coming to dinner with me."

"Um, okay. Where we eating?"

"Doesn't matter. Just sit there and look pretty."

We got to Gustavo's fifteen minutes late and I spotted Kelly sitting at a table with a guy wearing torn jeans and a beige jacket with a little blue-and-white scarf. He had curly hair and some scruff. Some guy you'd see in the stylish section of Rome or Florence.

"Wow. That's a good-looking dude, Pete. Almost as good-looking as Garvin. Don't know if you can compete with him."

"Always appreciated, Craig. Come on, let's get this over with."

I grinned and Joey smiled at me.

"Peter," he said, holding out his hand but not standing up. "So good to finally meet you. Kelly's told me a ton about you."

I shook his hand, which I think had lotion on it, and said, "Yeah, nice to meet you, too."

We sat down and Kelly said, "Who's your friend?"

"This is Craig. He's my intern."

"Oh," she said. "Hi, Craig."

"Hey. You think they got candy bars here? I mean it seems like kind of a fancy place. Don't think they'd have 'em."

"How many restaurants you ever been to that have candy bars?" I said.

He stared off into space, lost in thought, and I turned to Joey and said, "So you moved all the way out here from Los Angeles, huh? Different world, isn't it?"

"I don't know. People are pretty much the same everywhere." He looked at Kelly and said, "But I'll go wherever this little lady takes me."

How adorable.

"I do miss good beer, though. I can't imagine Utah will have much in that way."

"Actually we have some of the best beer in the world," Craig said, pushing his glasses up higher onto his face. "See, alcohol covers up the taste. When you use as little alcohol as we do, you have to actually make the beer taste good. I've had beer in Belgium and Germany and nowhere is as good as Utah. Weird as it sounds."

"What were you doing in Belgium?" I asked.

"Satanists' conference."

Kelly looked from one of us to the other. "I'm sorry, did you say Satanist?"

"Craig here is a full-blown member of the Dark Prince's army."

"Really? How long have you been one?" Kelly asked.

"Since I was thirteen. My parents let me choose whatever religion I wanted, but they said I had to choose one. I began researching the different churches and this is the only one that appealed to me."

"Not exactly what your parents had in mind I'm guessing," I said.

He shrugged. "What are parents for if not to piss off, amiright?"

We stared at him a second in silence and then Kelly said, "So, Peter here is working on a very big case I'm helping out on," she told Joey. "We're trying to hold a gun manufacturer liable for a crime committed by a consumer with one of their guns. We came up with a pretty novel argument for it."

Joey looked at me. "Really? That sounds fun."

"I guess if getting my ass kicked was fun it would be. Anyway, what do you do, Joey?" I said.

"You know, kinda cliché story. I moved to LA to be an actor and it just never really took off. I do a few theater productions, though. Some plays here and there."

"Huh. That sounds cool."

"It's not ideal but not the worst."

He placed his hand on Kelly's back and I thought I felt vomit rising in my throat. I wondered how soon I could get out of there.

Then Craig said, "I mean, I know it's a fancy place, but aren't these fancy places supposed to always cater to the customer? Like if I ordered a Butterfinger, they should go out and get me one if they don't have it, right?"

I stared at him a second and he rubbed his nose and said, "I need to take a piss."

40

I spent most of the week preparing for the motion to dismiss—the 12(b)(6) motion. Garvin was arguing exactly what we thought he would: that the PLCAA barred any type of lawsuit like this from going forward and the judge had the legal obligation to dismiss it.

After dinner with Kelly, I had also paid a little visit to my private investigator. He called this morning and said he had something for me, so after work, which consisted of filling out more of the stupid interrogatories Garvin had sent, I headed over to his office.

My investigator rented a space beneath an adult novelty store. Stairs led down to his offices behind the shop, and there wasn't any sign or address marker indicating anyone was there. He said he was just being lazy about it, but I'm sure it was so the cops couldn't find it if they needed to. His methods weren't exactly on the up-and-up.

I knocked and waited. Nothing showed on the outside, but there was a camera somewhere staring at me. The door buzzed a second later and I walked in.

The place reeked of pot. The magazines on his coffee table in the meeting area were mostly porn mags. A few gun mags on top of that. Off to the side he sat behind his desk, typing something up.

I sat down across from him and he slid an ashtray with half a burned joint over to me.

"I'm good. You got a beer?"

"In the fridge," he said, without taking his eyes off the screen.

I rose and grabbed a bottle. "Chris, you gotta get better offices, man."

"This suits my needs. People who know don't care, and the people who care don't know. Check this out." He opened some files on his computer. They were pictures, mostly of people having sex.

"What is that?"

"Case I just closed up today. I had to go undercover in the swinger scene, homie." He lit the joint and inhaled a long puff. "There was these two business partners. They owned a bike shop. One partner was getting ready to take off and leave the business, and the other one was gonna screw him. My client, the one that wanted to take off, wanted dirt on the other guy he could use against him. I followed him around for a while and found out he and the missus were swingers. So I hired myself an escort and signed up and went in. Crazy stuff, homie. Cops was there, judges, religious leaders. All there just bangin' away."

"I'm in a hurry, man. You got something for me?"

"Hold up. Shit, lack a patience is the problem with the world today." He reached down to his bottom drawer and said, "Hell, you get a few billboards and some green and suddenly your shit don't stink." He pulled out a file and gave it to me.

The first page of the file was a black-and-white photo of Judge Roberts stepping out of a car. Several photos followed, each capturing a single step. The photos were clear and crisp, and each photo captured the face at a different angle. For a stoner, Chris was the Picasso of spying.

"Where's he going?"

"Keep flipping."

I shuffled through a few more photographs. He went up into an apartment building, and Chris followed him. He went into an apartment on the second floor and I could tell Chris was hiding around a corner in the hallway. The next photo looked like it was taken from the fire escape. It peered through some blinds that weren't drawn all the way. The Honorable James Roberts was getting naked with a young lady who was not his wife.

"No way."

He blew out some pot smoke. "That's where I always start. Always the affairs. They say half of all men are having affairs or have had an affair, but that's bullshit. That's self-reporting and most men aren't gonna say they're out there bangin' some strange. I'd put it at eighty percent. Eight outta ten dudes have cheated on their wives. I usually don't even need to dig further than that."

"What's her name?"

"Emily P. Barley. She's a former clerk of his. He bought flowers afterward for his wife. Dude feels bad about it. You can use that."

I nodded.

"What you tryin' to get outta him anyway? It's gotta be solid if you're risking a federal offense for blackmailing a judge."

"I'm not blackmailing him. I just want him to know that I know. I won't say anything more than that. And all I want is him off a case. He's too friendly with the defense, and no one will tell me how they know each other. I even tried to bribe his clerks with gift cards and they said they didn't know."

"Well you got what you need in there."

"How much I owe ya?"

"Four grand."

"What? For five hours' work? That's crazy. You normally charge me half that."

He shrugged. “You want quality work you pay quality prices. Besides, if you was some housewife checkin’ up on her husband I woulda charged you ten. Consider it a friends-and-family discount.”

I took out my credit card and handed it to him. “You truly do have a heart of gold.”

“Damn straight,” he said, as he ran my credit card on his phone.

41

The hearing came quickly. Far quicker than I thought it would. I'd been trying to spend as much time with Michael as I could, and for those periods I would forget about the case. We went to a ball game and were eating hot dogs when his mother called. He spoke to her for a few minutes and then when I asked him what that was about, he just said she'd been calling lately to talk about moving in with her. I wasn't happy about it, but giving him a hard time would only encourage him to leave.

The night before the hearing, I paced around my apartment reading the cases pertaining to the PLCAA when someone knocked on my door. I assumed it was a friend of Michael's since they would come over at all hours without letting anyone know first. When I opened the door, Kelly stood there in sweats with no makeup.

"It's eleven o'clock," I said. "I thought you never stay up past ten?"

"Things change. I need to come in."

I stepped aside and let her in. She wrung her hands a second and then said, "I'm nervous."

"About what?"

"About the motion to dismiss tomorrow."

"Why? You're not even officially on the case. If we lose, I'm the one whose name is gonna be on all the news websites."

She folded her arms, staring down. Suddenly I was aware of how dirty my carpet was. Funny that you never really notice how dirty something of yours is until someone else is there to see it.

"What?" I said. "What is it? You look scared."

"I am scared." She rubbed her arms though it wasn't cold. "I was in a mass shooting once."

I stared at her. "What?"

"I never told you. It's not something I ever talk about."

"Well . . . what happened?"

She shook her head. Her tongue jutted out just a little from the side of her mouth, a tell indicating she was lost in thought and couldn't be reached right now.

"We were at a shoe store at a mall. We were immigrants and my mom didn't have much so we were in the back at the clearance bins. I was complaining of course, embarrassed that we had to buy clearance at an already cheap store. Now that I look back on it, I can't imagine how it hurt my mom. She would scrimp and save for weeks to get me a new pair of shoes, and I would tell her I was embarrassed because they weren't brand name. Anyway, we heard this loud bang. I thought it was fireworks at first. Everyone in the store was looking at each other and asking if anyone knew what it was. Some people didn't even stop shopping because they didn't think it was anything. One man knew. He ran out the back door as fast as he could."

I watched her a minute. I'd never seen her this scared. Her hands trembled and she kept flicking her tongue out of her mouth.

Tears flowed from her eyes now. "He started at the front of the store. We were frozen. I mean, just frozen. And then my mom grabbed me by my hand and dragged me out of the store. The back door was right next to the clearance bins."

She wiped away a few tears.

"My mom ran around to the back of the mall and to our car. We never looked back. She just took off. Never gave a police interview or anything." She paused. "She never brought it up again, but when I was older I looked into it. The gunman was a former employee of the store and had been sleeping with one of the cashiers, who dumped him. So he grabbed a rifle and went down there. He shot four people, and luckily three survived." She grinned through her tears. "Bad shot I guess."

I sat down on the couch. "Why didn't you ever tell me?"

She sat next to me, her hands clasped, probably to keep them from trembling. "People sometimes look at you different when they know you've been through something like that. And if you just keep quiet about it long enough, you don't really remember it most days. It affects you in other ways, but most days I don't have to think about it."

"Did you actually see the shooting?"

She nodded. "He came in right by the register and lifted his rifle and fired at the woman behind the counter. She screamed and toppled over and there was blood everywhere. I can still hear that scream in my sleep sometimes. Even thirty years later." She looked at me. "I don't . . . I don't want to lose tomorrow."

"Hey, no one wants to lose less than me, believe me. And I got a few tricks up my sleeve."

"Are you going to file the motion to recuse Judge Roberts? I mean, I know he's the one who decides whether or not to recuse himself, so it's a long shot, but it's worth a try."

I grinned. "Oh, I think the judge might see things our way."

42

The next morning I made toast with butter and jam, and Michael and I ate on the way to school. Usually he just got out of the car and didn't say anything, but today he said, "See ya, Dad."

I beamed like I'd just won father of the year, and then I headed for the West Jordan courthouse.

I got waved through and went up to the third floor. The courthouse was busy, I mean packed way beyond what I was sure any fire department would say was a safe amount of people. Kelly sat outside the courtroom on one of the benches, speaking with Melissa. I stood there a moment and watched them. It seemed like they were connecting and I didn't want to interrupt. Besides, I hadn't decided what the hell to do with this new info I had on Judge Roberts wetting his whistle with his former clerk. Last night I was certain I would use it, but now I thought it was a bad play.

If I brought it up to him in any way, and I mean *any* way, he would immediately accuse me of blackmailing him and get his bailiffs to arrest me and the DA to press charges. Then he'd call the Bar next. Or, he would cower, afraid that his wife would find out. Still, I had a feeling all cheaters knew they would eventually get found out; they just didn't care. Or maybe they wanted to be busted and get it out in the open? Guilt was a helluva thing. It could physically weigh you down and wear out your body and mind.

I decided in the end it was too risky. I wanted him off the case, but getting arrested and losing my license to practice law wasn't worth it.

Damn it. Four grand down the drain.

I walked up to Kelly and Melissa and said, "Looks like you two have met."

"Melissa and I were just discussing what's going to be happening today and what our chances are."

"Not good," I said.

Melissa nodded. "I knew what this was going into it. If this is where it ends, then this is where it ends." She took my hand. "If this is really it, then thank you for everything you've done."

The bailiff stepped out of the courtroom's double doors and said, "Judge is ready for you."

Garvin and his team showed up five minutes late. Four other attorneys were with him now instead of the three who were at the last hearing. Like gremlins, they were multiplying.

I sat at the plaintiff's table with Melissa. Garvin didn't even look at her. The attorney who had flipped me off last time flipped me off again by rubbing the side of his temple. Either this guy was one of the biggest dickheads I'd ever met, or this was an actual ploy, like Garvin's DUI scam, to get into my head. I took a deep breath and looked away, trying to ignore them.

"This is so scary," Melissa whispered. "This room. There're no windows, everything's made of wood. The carpets are plain and dirty . . . Is it meant to be scary? So that people behave?"

"I don't think so. I think it's just government hiring the lowest bidder. It's probably a good thing not to have windows. I had a jury trial last year in a courtroom that had windows, and the jurors were so bored they kept staring out of them. Didn't hear a word anybody said."

She chuckled.

I hesitated a bit and then said, "Hey, um, you holding up okay?"

She shrugged. "It's day by day."

I nodded. "Okay. Just, if you need to talk to anybody or anything, I'm a pretty good listener."

This softened her up some and she put her hand on mine, giving it a squeeze.

"All rise, the West Jordan Third District Court is now in session, the Honorable James Barlow Roberts presiding."

"Be seated."

Roberts sat down with a groan. He looked to Garvin and his table. Though they didn't say anything, they didn't have to. My case was lost. Roberts had already made up his mind. It had been a long shot he'd deny the motion to dismiss after hearing the facts, but now we wouldn't even get that chance.

Shit.

"Everybody ready to proceed?"

Garvin said, "We are, Your Honor."

I sat staring at the judge. Should I throw the surveillance photos in my bag at his face while screaming, "You're out of order!" Should I hold them up to the clerk and ask that they be introduced as evidence? Should I nail them to the courthouse door Martin Luther style? What the hell did someone do with photos of a judge cheating on his wife?

"Peter," Melissa whispered.

"Huh?"

"He's waiting for you."

I looked back to Roberts and his eyes were on me. I said, "Yeah, we're ready."

"Good."

It was normal for the plaintiff to go first since we had the burden of proof in a civil case, so I stood up, buttoned my top button, and said, "What Mr. Garvin is going to argue is that the PLCAA bars this type—"

"Mr. Game, I have reviewed both the plaintiff's and defense's briefs as well as your response to the defense's brief and I'm ready to make my ruling."

I glanced toward the audience at Kelly, who shook her head, a look of absolute amazement on her face. I wasn't amazed. Judges were an insecure group, and over time, everyone calling them "Your Honor" got to their heads and they started to believe the hype that they were kings. Ultimately, they were the last form of tyranny in the United States unless they had a strong moral center, which, really, how many of us did?

"Judge, we have a right to be heard on this. If for nothing else than to make notes of record for an appeal."

He held up his hand and turned to the clerk and said, "Kill the recording." She nodded and he said, "Mr. Game, don't try to pull one over on me. You're not appealing this and we all know you don't have enough to get past this motion. Truth be told, you knew there's no way you would get through a motion to dismiss but you filed anyway. The only reason I'm not going to report you to the Bar and impose sanctions is because of the enormous sympathy I feel for your client."

"You can't do this, Judge."

"I can do whatever I want."

"Spoken like a true defender of the Constitution."

"You better watch your mouth."

I couldn't help it. The rage inside me was too much. He was making accusations against me on an issue he'd probably decided right when he'd heard about the shooting and knew there'd be a lawsuit or two.

"You watch your mouth. How dare you sit here and say you sympathize with my client and then you won't even let her be heard? That's all we were asking today. We weren't telling you to rule for us or else; we just said hear us out. But you couldn't even do that."

"Mr. Game, you are about five seconds away from being held in contempt."

"You need a hearing to hold me in contempt. Or did the gun lobbyists not teach you about that at the retreats you all go to?"

"Mr. Game!"

"Cheater!" I shouted, pointing my finger at him.

The courtroom went silent.

My eyes must've gone wide, because when I glanced back at Melissa and Kelly, Kelly's mouth had fallen open. In the back of the courtroom I saw Craig and wondered how long he'd been sitting there. I looked at his shirt, at his glasses, at Kelly's red lipstick . . . at anything but the judge.

When I looked back to Roberts, he was pale and quiet and staring at me. Really staring at me. The way someone stares at people when they're trying to read them. I didn't move. He stared into me so hard that I felt physically uncomfortable. And then the moment came. It dawned on him as surely as if he'd read an email announcing it in all caps: I knew.

I swallowed and tried to say something but my voice cracked.

"In chambers, now!"

He rose and stormed back there. I looked to Garvin, who wore genuine confusion on his face. He really didn't know what was going on.

I took a deep breath and went back to the judge's chambers.

43

When we got back to chambers, Roberts stood in front of his desk with his arms crossed. His face was a hard pink from the anger bubbling up into it like lava.

"Wait outside, Garvin."

"I think I need to be—"

"Get the hell out, now!"

Garvin, rather than getting upset, folded his hands in front of him and smiled. "I would be careful who you take that tone with, Judge." He glanced at me, and then he left and shut the door behind him.

When he was gone, Roberts said, "What are you trying to do?"

"Nothing."

"Don't lie to me!"

I shrugged. "I don't know what you're talking about, Judge."

He took a few steps closer to me, until he was right in my face. "You want money, huh? You think you can blackmail me? How the hell did you even find out?" He stopped and his eyes went wide. "Did you have me followed?"

"Judge, I don't know what you're talking about." I closed my eyes a second and then opened them again. This was it: the moment of truth. "I was planning on losing this motion and then filing a motion to recuse you from this case. I mean, it's clear you know Garvin somehow and have a relationship. But as far as what you're talking about, I have no clue. And if I did, I wouldn't know what to do with some hypothetical information that could be used to blackmail you. I would never, in a million years, use some hypothetical information like that." I paused. "I was just expecting to ask you to recuse yourself."

He grunted and swore under his breath. "Just wanted me to recuse myself, huh?"

"Yeah. I was going to file a motion to recuse you. That's all."

He nodded. "Get out of my chambers."

I left and entered the courtroom. Kelly gave me a quizzical look and mouthed, *What happened?*

Hell if I know, I mouthed back.

The judge returned and sat down. He looked at me and then at Garvin and then back to me and said to his clerk, "Let's get back on the record."

When the microphone and video were back on, the judge cleared his throat, tried to force a look of serenity onto his face, and said, "The plaintiff has made a motion for recusal. After consultation in chambers, I have decided to grant the motion."

Garvin's lawyers huddled around him and started whispering. Garvin finally stood up and said, "Your Honor, we would object to your recusal. The court hasn't even laid down the foundation as to why—"

"As we discussed in chambers, and as you so honorably reminded me before I sent you back out here, Mr. Garvin, your firm and you personally helped fund my wife's campaign for city council and then state senate. I had simply forgotten that, as the connection is so far removed. But it would be improper for me to stay on the case now that it's come to my attention."

Garvin huddled with his team again, and then said, through what seemed like clenched teeth, "Objection withdrawn."

Roberts looked to me and said, "I'm setting a meeting for tomorrow morning with the new assigned judge. Any dates and a new discovery schedule can be worked out with him. You're all excused."

He rose and stormed out of the courtroom.

I sat down next to Melissa and she said, "What just happened?"

I shook my head. "You wouldn't believe me if I told you."

After we left the courtroom, I asked Melissa to be there again tomorrow. Kelly came up from behind us and waited until we were alone.

"What did you do?"

"What?" I said. "Why do you assume this was something to do with me?"

"I didn't until just now. When you're guilty of something and someone accuses you of doing it, your voice goes really high."

I cleared my throat and said in a low voice, "I don't know what you're talking about."

She nodded. "I'll assume what just happened was a result of Roberts actually remembering something I'm sure he remembered the second Garvin filed on the case. But from now on, if you want my help, you need to be straight with me."

"Yeah."

"I'm serious, Peter."

"Yeah. Straight. Razor straight."

She put her hand on my shoulder, and said, "I'll see you tomorrow."

The touch sent a little shock through me, and I watched as she walked away and got into the elevator.

"You two were almost married, I believe," I heard a bass voice say. I turned to see Garvin standing in front of me.

"You're pretty quiet for a giant."

He grinned. "Whatever happened in there just now, it's not going to help you. It'll just delay the inevitable and drag out your client's hopes. Hope is a terrible thing. The longer you have it, the more it hurts when you lose it."

44

When I got home after court, Michael was there with another boy.

"Hey," I said.

"Hey, Dad. This is Paul."

I tried to smile, feeling like the quintessentially awkward dad. "Hey, Paul."

"Hi."

We passed a few seconds in silence. "I'll, ah, just be in the bedroom."

I went to my room and shut the door. I kicked off my shoes and lay back on the bed and stared at the ceiling fan that was slowly twirling above me, sending down barely a wisp of air. I thought of Kelly and how good she looked today, of the touch she gave me. Though nothing had changed between us, I felt closer to her now that she'd revealed her traumatic experience. I had forgotten what her touch felt like. I wondered if every lover had a different touch. Was every person really a unique snowflake that could make someone feel a certain way, or were we just hairless apes, here for a brief period, all trying to procreate, and then we vanished to dust?

The thought, for some reason, made me laugh. *No time for philosophy, old man.* I now had another judge to convince to let us go forward with this case. But at least we had a shot. That's all I wanted: Not a guaranteed victory, not an apology, not the odds in my favor. Just a single shot. I exhaled loudly and closed my eyes, and sleep slowly crawled over me.

45

I woke up when it was still dark and checked the clock on the nightstand. I had an hour until court. I found Michael eating cereal at the breakfast table. I sat next to him and rubbed my face.

"Hey," I said.

"Hey. How's the case?"

"Crazy. How are you doing?"

He shrugged. "School sucks and someone spray-painted the word "faggot" on my locker, but other than that, great."

"Michael—"

"I don't really feel like talking about it, Dad. I gotta go anyway."

He grabbed his backpack and by the time he got to the door, I said, "Hey. I love you."

"I know, Dad. I'll see ya tonight."

I showered and dressed, wearing my American flag pin and a tie with a bald eagle on it. No idea who the judge was, but who could hate an American eagle? My stomach was too upset to eat anything so I gulped down some orange juice and left.

The courthouse was packed again, and just getting through the metal detectors took nearly half an hour. They made me take off my belt this time, and I had to do the embarrassing waddle that all lawyers grew accustomed to where I'd shuffle to the side of the line and put my belt back on with one hand, my other hand holding up my pants so I didn't moon everybody.

Kelly was already there, again sitting with Melissa on a bench outside the courtroom. This time they were laughing together.

"Ladies, glad to see everyone's having a good time while I was getting strip-searched."

"Kelly was just telling me about how you guys were almost married."

I looked at Kelly. "Really. That seems a bit personal to tell a client, doesn't it?"

"Oh, don't worry, Peter," Melissa said, "I'm sold already. I won't be getting another lawyer because you broke up with someone by text. But seriously, who does that?"

I looked at Kelly again. "Cowards do that. Cowards who don't know what they have."

Kelly and I stared at each other a second and then Kelly said, "We better get in there."

I was about to follow them when Craig stepped off the elevator. He wore a T-shirt with a goat's head on it and a button-up shirt over that, unbuttoned about halfway. He took out a Baby Ruth and said, "You ready for this?"

"Sure. Nice shirt, man."

"Thanks." He opened the Baby Ruth and offered a bite to me. "It's good luck to have a bite of chocolate before a big event."

"No thanks," I said, opening the door. Then I stopped, turned to him again, and took a giant bite of the candy bar before going inside.

The tension in the courtroom felt like a brick sitting in my throat. The clerk wasn't speaking, the bailiff was playing on his phone, and Garvin and the goon squad were whispering and smirking at me. Melissa sat down at the table and Kelly, to my surprise, sat next to her. I came up to the table and said, "Kelly, you don't have to sit there."

She glanced at Melissa. "I want to."

"Yeah, but your firm might have a problem—"

"I don't care. I want to."

I nodded and sat down. I took a deep breath and glanced around.

"All rise, Third District Court is now in session. The Honorable Davis Pearl presiding."

Davis Pearl. Hot damn.

A tall man with shaggy blond hair walked in. The descendant of a pretty famous criminal lawyer who'd defended the early Mormons from the US government, Pearl was one of my favorite judges. When Governor Boggs of Missouri issued an honest-to-goodness extermination order against Mormons, stating that citizens had the right to kill Mormon men, women, and children on sight without penalty of law, it was Judge Pearl's great-grandfather who defended some of the Mormons who'd protected themselves with deadly force against the angry mobs that had come to kill them.

Davis had inherited that sense of duty and become a prominent disability lawyer. He was one of the writers of the Americans with Disabilities Act when he was a legislative intern in Washington.

He looked at us with his baby-blue eyes and chiseled good looks—I always thought he looked like Robert Redford—and I glanced over to Garvin and saw the striations in his jaws as he clenched and then relaxed them.

"Good morning, gentlemen," he said softly. He looked to me. "Mr. Game, good to see you again."

"You as well, Judge. Been a while."

"It has." He looked to the defense table. "Mr. Garvin, I don't believe I've had the pleasure."

Garvin hesitated a second and then rose. "No, Your Honor, we haven't met before. It's a pleasure, as I've heard of your reputation for fairness."

Pearl grinned politely. "I'm sure you have." He looked down at some papers in front of him. "I've read the briefs in this case and looked over the discovery schedule. I see no reason to alter that unless either counsel has any objections."

"None," Garvin said.

"It's fine, Judge."

"Good. Then on the 12(b)(6) motion to dismiss for failure to state a claim upon which relief may be granted, I am ruling for the plaintiff."

Garvin laughed. Pearl's face went stiff and he said, "Something funny, Mr. Garvin?"

Garvin cleared his throat and stood up. "No, Judge, it's just I thought you said that you were ruling against us without having a hearing on the matter."

Pearl leaned forward. "It's odd. I listened to the recording from yesterday, Mr. Garvin, and when Judge Roberts ruled in favor of the defense without the benefit of the evidentiary hearing, I heard no objections from you. I assume, based on your objection today, that the microphone must not have picked it up. Am I correct in assuming that?"

Garvin and Pearl stared at each other in silence, and then Garvin smiled his million-dollar smile and said, "Must be."

Pearl nodded. "Regardless, Judge Roberts closed the hearing before recusing himself and was about to make a ruling, so I think it's only fair to both parties that I simply pick up where he left off. Though no evidence has been submitted, it is within the trial court's purview to rule based on the submitted briefs if there's so little evidence for the plaintiff's or the defense's stance on the case that it would not be in the interests of justice to continue with an evidentiary hearing. I am finding that the defense's interpretation of the PLCAA, though accurate, is not clear on the novel argument the plaintiff is making.

"Mr. Garvin, you are stating the PLCAA bars any type of suit against a firearm manufacturer, retailer, or any other person in the chain of sale, for any harm caused by that firearm. And, that the exceptions Congress has carved out of the PLCAA do not apply to this case, most notably the negligent entrustment exception. However, the plaintiff is arguing that the negligent entrustment is not the result of a gunman using one of their guns, but that this *specific* weapon—originally intended to be used by the military—is available to the public at all. The plaintiff is in fact arguing that by making this weapon available to the public, Tanguich Rifles has negligently provided the weapon to unstable individuals and that the weapon should be confined to the military as, again presumably, initially intended. I find this argument persuasive and novel enough to survive a motion to dismiss and go to a jury, and am therefore denying the defense's motion. Now, is there anything else?"

Garvin, his eyes appearing like slits, slowly said, "Nothing, Your Honor."

"Nothing, Judge. Thank you."

"Stick to the discovery schedule, gentlemen, and please keep it civil."

"Oh," I said, "one more thing. Judge Roberts had issued a gag order against my client, myself, and any third parties as to anything pertaining to this lawsuit. He claimed it harmed Tanguich Rifles to have us talk about it. I was hoping the court would be willing to remove the protective order so that my client can give interviews about her son."

Pearl looked to Garvin and said, "Protective orders are issued to protect victims from further harm or harassment. What harm, exactly, would Tanguich Rifles suffer should Ms. Bell give an interview about her son's death?"

Garvin stood up to his full forty feet or however tall he was and said, "My client asserts that they have already suffered a massive pecuniary loss due to lost sales, and the loss is ongoing while this litigation drags forward. To have the plaintiff go out in public and repeatedly point the finger at my client as the cause of this tragedy would harm my client's reputation and, in turn, their finances."

"By how much?"

Garvin grinned. "That would be difficult to calculate, Your Honor."

"Well, you have one week to get that to me. I have an economist I trust who can run the numbers once you get the data to him as to the exact amount of money your client will be losing by having Ms. Bell give an interview. However, should I rule against you, any documents you have submitted become part of the court record and, as such, public record. I'm not sure how your client would react to all their financial documents being made public."

Garvin sat down and huddled with his team. The other four seemed to move in unison, almost like pigeons, their heads bobbing up and down. It was, somehow, mesmerizing. I couldn't really look away.

Finally, some sort of consensus was reached and Garvin stood up and said, "We withdraw the request for the protective order."

Melissa leaned over to me. "Does that mean I can talk about Danny?"

"It does."

Judge Pearl said, "If there's nothing else, Counselors, I'll thank you for your time and adjourn."

When everyone cleared out, Melissa, Craig, Kelly, and I lingered. I said, "A lot of places probably want to interview you. Some press is good, but you don't want to overdo it. You have to assume that any interview you give will be seen by one of the jurors on your case. So keep it short and to the point. In fact, why don't you come by the office tomorrow so we can develop some talking points?"

She shook her head. "I just want to talk about my son, Peter. For any other parents who have lost their children. Maybe my talking about it can help them, if nothing else, to at least feel like they're not alone."

I glanced at Kelly. "Sure. But let's meet to go over some questions you'll probably be asked. Would you be okay with that?"

"I guess so."

She hugged me, and then said goodbye to Kelly and goodbye to Craig, who mumbled something incoherent in response and stared at the floor, and then she left.

"Wow. Lucky break you got Pearl, huh?" Craig said.

Kelly said, "Yes and no. He's not biased, not really. He's fair. That means he'll rule on whichever side he thinks is correct about the law. Tanguich Rifles has the law on their side. Unless we find some other evidence or case law that can help us, all this did was drag that woman's pain out."

I exhaled loudly and said, "I need a drink."

Craig had classes. Kelly checked her watch. "I've got a couple hours. I'll join you."

46

There was a pizza joint by the University of Utah called The Pie that all the students ate at. We ordered a large pepperoni pizza and a pitcher of beer and sat in the corner booth. Bob Dylan was playing. The walls were covered in posters and the permanent marker scrawlings of people who had written their names or messages to future generations on the exposed brick. Also, a lot of penis drawings.

"I haven't thought of this place in ten years," she said.

"We went on our first date here."

She took a sip of beer as she shook her head. "No, it wasn't here. We went to the capitol building and got ice cream."

"That was our second date. Our first date was here. Technically, I was with your friend Marcy and you were with Kyle with the flipped-up collar."

"Oh, you're right. Yeah. I forgot about Kyle with the flipped-up collar. You hated him."

I gulped down some beer. "He was everything I hated at the time. Rich, condescending, felt the world owed him, treated people worse off than him like garbage . . . who knew I'd end up working with a field full of Kyle-with-the-flipped-up-collars?"

The pizza was greasy and I had to wipe my lips right after every bite to make sure the grease didn't dribble onto my shirt or tie.

"It's really great what you're doing for her, Peter."

I shrugged as I took another bite. "She's just a client."

"She's not just a client. I've seen how you interact with just clients and it's not like this."

"I just can't imagine it, you know? If I had to go down to the morgue and identify Michael. I mean that poor woman has been through hell. The strength it's gotta take just to get outta bed in the morning . . ."

"It's this suit that gets her out of bed. She told me it's her purpose in life now to try to prevent these shootings in any way she can. You've given her that."

Her cell phone rang and she answered it. She rose from the table and went outside so she could hear, and I watched her. She was laughing and I knew it was Joey who had called her. She came back in and said, "Peter, I'm really sorry, but—"

"You gotta go. No need to be sorry. Really."

"I'll make it up to you."

"No need. Really. I'm fine."

"Okay. I'll probably see you tomorrow then."

"Sure."

I wiped my lips as she left to be with her boyfriend. She glanced back once and waved and I waved back.

When she was gone, I sighed and took a large drink of beer. The Doors' "People Are Strange" started playing.

Ain't that the truth.

47

The next morning, I grabbed some Coke for breakfast and then drove into the office. I had items on my calendar today for two other cases: a car accident and a dog bite case where a neighbor's dog dug underneath the fence and bit my client's six-year-old son. Both cases were settling soon and I just had to hammer out the details with the adjusters. Normally, a nice payday would lift my mood and I'd celebrate with a massage or a trip up to Park City to buy a nice steak or something, but I didn't have that urge now. I didn't feel like eating, or pretty much anything else.

I trudged up to the office and went inside. Craig was already there. I'd set up a desk for him in the room next door and given him a key, and he came and went as he pleased, but I'd never arrived in the office earlier than he did, and he was usually still working when I left.

"I gotta show you something," he said.

"Later. Right now I need you to get the adjusters for the Mendoza and Brown cases on the line. We're gonna settle those babies today."

"Okay, but I really should show you—"

"Later, my chocolate-loving friend. Money comes first."

He shrugged. "If you say so."

The first adjuster on the line was Harvey from Wasatch Mutual Homeowners. Dog bites were covered under the homeowner's policy but they had low policy limits. This one was only for ten thousand, but that was still a nice third in my pocket. Better than a sharp stick in the eye.

Harvey answered on the second ring and Craig said, "Please hold for Mr. Peter Game, Esquire," and then handed the phone to me.

I got on and lifted the receiver a bit from my mouth and said off in the distance, "Yeah, yeah, and tell that bastard that if he doesn't play ball, I'll have him tied up in court for so long his grandkids will be the ones finishing this lawsuit." I waited a beat, and then said into the phone, "This is Peter Game. Who is this again?"

"Um, Harvey Gibby. I'm an adjuster over at Wasatch—"

"Wasatch Mutual. Right. The Brown case. Helluva a case, ain't it, Harvey? I mean, the determination that dog must've had to dig its way under a massive fence like that. I mean, he must've really wanted to hurt that kid."

"Well, my clients don't see it that way. They say that the McNetts knew about the digging, and that the dog could get onto their property but they did nothing to stop it."

"What're they supposed to do, plant landmines?" I hesitated a second, as though I were thinking, and then said, "Listen, we're getting off on the wrong foot. I'm gonna be honest with you, I'm up to my eyeballs with trials and discovery schedules right now, and I sure as hell don't want to throw a silly dog bite on the pile just because you and I weren't adult enough to reach an agreement. The policy limit is ten thousand. How about we settle for . . . eight? Just under policy for something that is clearly your client's fault. And enough to cover medicals and a little extra for the college fund for my client's son, and maybe they can still be cordial as neighbors. What'dya say?"

He sighed. "Alright, but it's gotta be seventy-five hundred. Twenty-five percent under limits is enough that no one here will take a second look at the case."

I quickly calculated how much a third of seventy-five hundred was. "Yeah, alright, I can sell that to them. Pleasure doing business with you, Harvey. Great name by the way."

"Thanks. I'll get a check drafted and sent over with the release this week."

I hung up and cracked my knuckles like I'd just taken the winning shot from the three-point line and scored. There were few things I enjoyed more than settling a case I hadn't worked that much on. The old juices started flowing again.

"Craig, get me the next one," I shouted.

The car accident case took about two hours to settle. I had to do a back-and-forth between the adjuster and my client and then two three-way calls. We settled for about 10 percent less than my client wanted, but they still saw it as a win, and the insurance company resolved a case where liability couldn't have been clearer against their insured.

Craig came in and sat down once I'd gotten off the phone. He lifted his glasses and said, "We done?"

"Craig my man, we're going out to lunch. On me. And guess what? There's a French place near here, Gourmandise, that has about the best chocolate eclairs you're ever gonna have. You'll love it."

"Cool. Oh, can we talk about what I was going to show you this morning?"

"Yeah, sure," I said, searching my drawers for my car keys.

Craig rose and then came back a second later holding a large box. He put the box on my desk with a thud.

"What's that?"

"Résumés."

"For the new interns? No way. That's great."

"No, Peter. It's résumés from Tanguich Rifles. These are the résumés for the experts they're calling to trial."

I stared at him a second and then flipped through the contents of the box. They were indeed résumés. Before a trial, each side was obligated to share the CVs of every expert that side intended to call. I quickly counted the CVs. Eighty-six. Everyone from statisticians and gun experts to child psychologists and Second Amendment scholars.

"I mean, crazy, right?" Craig said. "Why would they call all these people?"

I slumped back into my chair. "They're not. Call Kelly and ask if she can come down here. Tell her it's an emergency."

48

Jake sat munching on a weed cookie, Craig stood in the corner playing on his phone, and Kelly and I were reading through the CVs as quickly as we could. When we got to the end, she shook her head and said, "Serious assholes."

"We're screwed, right?" I said.

Kelly folded her arms and stared off into space. After half a minute she just said, "Assholes," again.

"I don't get it," Craig said. "It's just résumés."

Jake said, "Not just résumés, kid. These are experts they're saying they're gonna call to trial. That means we have to depose each and every one of them before the trial."

"Wow. That's a lot of depositions."

"No shit," Jake said, taking another bite of cookie.

"But I mean, we can get through it, right? We just tell the judge it's going to take longer."

I rubbed my head. "If they were in Utah, sure. But we got experts in Hong Kong, in Australia, in China . . . and to depose them, we have to pay the costs. That's the cost of the flights, the court reporters, any videographers we want . . . We're talking . . . what, Kelly?"

"Easily half a million for the depositions alone."

Jake whistled.

Craig said, "Couldn't we just depose them over the phone?"

I shook my head. "They have to agree to that, and I'm guessing not a single one of these experts or Garvin is going to. And we can't only depose a few of them; we can't go to trial with an expert we haven't deposed and have no idea what they're going to say."

Kelly said, "And I'm guessing that's what Garvin's hoping for. The second that trial starts he'll overwhelm us with experts we haven't deposed and then make a motion for ineffective assistance during the trial, stating he has to try to protect the plaintiff from their own counsel. Pearl isn't the type of judge to be alright with us being unprepared. He would probably declare a mistrial and report us to the Bar himself. I mean, we're talking at the very least a suspension, maybe even disbarment given Garvin's connections over there. And then I'm sure another suit from Tanguich for damages and attorney's fees would be in the pipeline. Not to mention the fact that your malpractice insurance carrier will have dropped you and—"

"Yeah, yeah, I get it." I rubbed my temples. A headache was coming and I thought a couple beers and some ibuprofen might do the trick.

"Assholes," Craig said.

49

We brainstormed through lunch and my headache just kept getting worse. Every feasible idea was pitched, from calling a cheap airline and trying to get bulk discounts, to hiring temporary counsel in every city to do the depositions for us. The cheapest we could depose these experts for was just over three hundred thousand dollars. And that was barring any unforeseen difficulties.

"How much do you have?" Jake said.

"In my bank account right now? Enough for two or three depositions, maybe four or five if we fly on cheap airlines."

Kelly said, "We could go to the judge. Maybe see if we can have a hearing to whittle this list down to only the experts they really need."

"Yeah, and how often have you ever seen that work? They're entitled to who they need. No judge is going to bar that. It's an easy appeal." I shook my head. "It's over. We all knew something like this was coming. I just didn't think it would happen so soon."

Jake rose and stretched his back. "I got a serious case of the munchies. I'll see ya, pal. Sorry about the case."

Craig had to leave for class, and Kelly stayed back and sat across from me.

"Helluva way to end it, right?" I said. "Before it even really begins."

"You tried. What else could you do?" She looked out the window. "Sorry about yesterday. I shouldn't have just run out on you like that."

"You don't ever have to apologize to me." I inhaled and leaned back in the seat. "Damn. I guess I better go tell Melissa."

"She's stronger than you think. She'll handle it well. She's started volunteering for that gun safety group like you told her to. I can't think of the name."

"Really?"

She nodded. "Yeah. She did it because you suggested it. She thinks you're a saint right now."

"If she only knew the truth, huh?"

She grinned in a sad little way. "You're a good person. And I know you've always had the best of intentions." She rose. "Sorry about this. I mean that."

I watched her walk out. I felt like a claw was around my throat squeezing the air out of me. I needed to get out of here. Go someplace else. Out of the city, maybe the state. I gathered my stuff and headed out to tell Michael to take the next few days off from school and come with me. Because I sure as hell wasn't going to be here to see Roger's and Garvin's smug faces on television talking about justice being done after we withdrew the suit. Justice had taken a vacation on this one.

50

Michael's school was on lunch break and I drove around to the doughnut shop near the back. Most of the kids ate there, and I wondered who the lucky prick was who got rich because he happened to open a doughnut shop in a place they eventually built a school next to.

Michael and a group of other kids sat on a bench, snacking on doughnuts and soda. He saw me and put his food down. He came over to the window.

"I already ate, Dad."

"I'm not here about that. I was thinking maybe we could take off for a few days."

"Take off where?"

"I don't know. Doesn't really matter. Anywhere you want. Pick a place."

He leaned against the car. "You never wanna just take off. What happened?"

"Nothing happened and I resent that accusation. I'm plenty spontaneous." We looked at each other a second. "My gun case is going to be withdrawn. So I just need to get outta here, pal. Just for a little bit.

You're moving out soon and I thought maybe we could go on one more trip together before you do."

He wiped powdered sugar off his hands. "Yeah, okay."

"Yeah?"

"Yeah."

"Great. I'll see ya at home and we'll decide where to go then."

"Sounds good."

The smile that came to my face immediately vanished when I realized my next stop was Melissa's. Then I thought that maybe I should give it a day. Just to really think about what I wanted to say. An "I'm sorry your son is dead but the case you have every right to bring is being dismissed because I don't have enough money to pursue it" wouldn't do. I had to spin it in a way where she felt she wasn't getting screwed by the system. Still, this couldn't wait. It had to be done now.

I stood in front of Melissa's house, knocking and ringing the doorbell, but no one answered. I sent a text and then sat down on the steps to wait for a reply.

It really was a beautiful day. Warm with a blue sky and a slight breeze. The type of day I remembered from summers as a kid when I got out of school and didn't have a responsibility to my name. I closed my eyes and leaned my head back, feeling the breeze on my throat. The neighbors had a peach tree in their yard, and I could pick up the sweet smell of the peaches rotting at the base of the tree.

"She's not home," a female voice said.

I opened my eyes to see the neighbor from a few weeks ago walking up to me from the sidewalk. Martha was wiping her hands on a rag and stood in front of me a second before she tossed the rag over her shoulder and sat down on the steps next to me with a groan.

"Gorgeous day," she said.

"It is."

"Pleased to see you again," she said, holding out her hand.

I shook it. "Peter."

"Oh I remember who you are. Melissa talks about you all the time—how happy she is she found you to represent her."

"Well, she may not be after today."

She looked at me. "Bad news I take it?"

I nodded, staring down at a crack in the steps. "And it's my fault. I shouldn't have ever taken her case to begin with. I gave her hope. Someone told me hope is a terrible thing and I think I'm starting to believe them."

She smiled and looked out over the quiet neighborhood. "Whoever said that is a man who lives with misery as their best friend. And that sort of man you can't trust."

51

When Melissa didn't reply to my text, I headed home and packed a gym bag full of clothes. Had no idea where we were going yet, so I packed for the cold and for the heat. I thought maybe the beach in Los Angeles. Michael had always loved the beach as a kid. But he also loved skiing. Something his mother would take him to do because I hated being cold and wet. Maybe he would finally get to go skiing with his Pops like he was always asking to do when he was a kid.

I was drinking a beer with my feet up on the coffee table when Michael got home. He saw me and grinned. "You look a lot different than this morning."

"Oh yeah? How?"

"You seem happier."

"Just glad to be taking off for a little while."

"Lemme pack first. And I need a shower."

"Look at you all grown up needing a shower."

He smiled again as he went into the kitchen. "So how was school?" I called.

Maybe he didn't hear me because he asked, "So where we going?"

"I was thinking either Los Angeles for the beach or Aspen for the skiing."

"You hate skiing."

"Never too late to try new things, right?"

We decided on Aspen but it was almost evening, so we finally got on the road the next morning. I stopped at a sporting goods store and bought some ski pants, gloves, wool socks, a cap, and goggles. Michael said we could rent everything else there.

We played music, some weird Norwegian techno that sounded like malfunctioning instruments, but that Michael seemed to thoroughly enjoy, and snacked on hamburgers and fries from a drive-through.

Michael seemed light and open. He was talkative, which he rarely ever was. He told me about school and his grades, about the colleges he was thinking about applying to, and what he wanted to do with his life.

"So what about you?" he said as Google Maps informed us we were on the fastest route to Aspen.

"What about me?"

"You don't want to be handling dog bites forever, do you? What's your plan?"

I glanced at him. "My plan was to get a huge case, a retirement case, and then retire. I thought I had one, but it didn't work out."

"The gun one?"

I nodded. "See, the gun manufacturers and lobby groups are rich, and my client and I are not. It takes money to litigate things, and they just overwhelmed us with money. I mean, don't get me wrong, I knew from the start it would happen at some point, but you know, you hold out hope that it'll work out."

He thought for a second. "How much do you need?"

"Three hundred grand, just to do the depositions for their experts. Then we have to hire our own experts. Probably half a million dollars."

"You could try a GoFundMe."

"What's that?"

"It's a site where you can raise money from people for different causes." He took a sip of his soda. "Maybe enough people care about this that they'll donate."

I glanced at him and then back out to the road. "GoFundMe, huh?"

He shrugged. "Worth a shot. It'll take you five minutes to write something and upload a video, so why not?"

52

So apparently, we learned when we got there, you can't ski when it's almost summer. Even in someplace as remote and cold as Aspen. Didn't matter, though, because everything was so green that we were struck by how beautiful it was the second we drove into the city.

We stopped at a pub and ordered steaks with mashed potatoes and wine for me, and soda for Michael. We ate and laughed and the steaks were good. Afterward we went up to one of the resorts and got a room and then changed into hiking clothes. The front desk told us a trail around the back led to the top of a mountain that had views of the entire valley.

As we climbed, we didn't speak. No one was out so the only things we could hear were the birds and the wind through the trees. Occasionally a squirrel or something would scramble around and cause loose pebbles to be flicked toward us downhill.

The summit took about forty-five minutes to reach, but when we did we sat down and neither of us wanted to move. We had a view of the valley in every direction. A tree sat at the top and covered us in shade.

"Sorry about your case, Dad. Your retirement case. I'm sorry it didn't work out."

"Well, that's just how it is sometimes. There'll be others and we only gotta hit the lottery once, right? I mean someone always has a winning ticket, so it might as well be us."

"I didn't mean sorry about the money. I mean sorry you couldn't help that lady."

"Oh. That. Yeah, well . . . that doesn't work out all the time either." I looked around once more. "Let's head back. I'm dying for a drink."

When we got back, we stayed up in the lounge area with some of the other guests. Michael made friends and they mostly hung out together and talked and played pool while me and two other dads sat like idiots on the sofas around a fire and occasionally grinned to one another. I nursed a Long Island Iced Tea and eventually told Michael I was heading up to the room.

"Don't stay up too late."

I loved that ability of the young to make friends wherever they went. Something no adult seemed to be able to do. Where the hell did that talent disappear to in middle age?

I got to the room, which didn't have a view, so I kicked off my shoes and turned on the television. Flipping through the channels twice, I saw nothing interesting so I googled "GoFundMe" on my phone and read about it. Sounded silly, but worth a shot. I didn't have anything to lose.

After getting my shoes on, I went down to the business center and sat at one of the computers. Actually, a pretty nice one considering most hotels had computers that were thirty years out of date. I pulled up GoFundMe and clicked around. It seemed to be mostly for charities or people with medical conditions. But the sign-up process was easy, so I took a chance. I aimed the little computer camera sitting next to the monitor at myself and began recording.

"Hello, this is Peter Game, attorney-at-law."

I stopped the recording, cleared my throat, and tried again.

"Hi, Peter Game here, with an important announcement regarding—"

Damn it.

I decided I needed something to talk about, more than just saying a shooting happened and people died. I went onto some forums on Facebook to see what people were saying about the case. It was a mistake.

One lady, whose username was "Freedom Ain't Free," had posted a link to a study conducted by two Harvard professors that said more guns did not mean more violence. One of the researchers was a former lobbyist for the gun lobby and the other was a lawyer who defended gun companies.

Another woman compared guns to bottles of water and said it's all in how they're used. They can be used for good or for evil, depending on the person who used them . . . Didn't understand exactly how someone would use a water bottle for evil, but okay, A for effort.

I read the forums for a good hour before turning on the camera again.

"Hi, this is Peter Game. I'm the attorney for a mother who, probably like many of you watching this, lost someone she loved to gun violence."

53

I cleared my throat and continued. "I am out of money. It takes money for lawsuits, and it's just me and my client Melissa Bell. She lost Danny, her seven-year-old son, in the shooting that took place at Holladay-Greenville Elementary in Utah. We're suing the manufacturer of the assault rifle that killed Danny and so many other kids that day, as well as taking the life of a teacher. We're suing them not just on Danny's behalf, but on behalf of all the families of all the children that are going to die because of guns in this country. On behalf of everyone who's had to go to a funeral because our government refuses to lift a finger to help us against the gun companies and the gun lobbies.

"People are dead. Children. And I'm sitting here on a forum reading the comments of people and I can't believe the stuff I'm seeing. This lady with the handle 'Fat Frida' says guns are like water bottles. That she was hit once with a water bottle that was full, and it hurt, but she didn't blame the water bottle. She blamed the person yielding the bottle. Okay, Frida, I'm gonna send you a freaking water bottle, and I wanna see how many people at a mall you can take out with it.

"Another person with the handle 'MissyQueen' says that we're just a culture of violence, and until we fix the culture that pushes violent movies and video games and books, we'll always have shootings like this. About a thousand people liked that comment and said things like 'amen.'

"You think so, do ya, Missy? Well I've got some bad news—people are the same everywhere. Britain, Australia, and Canada have the exact same games we do, they have the same movies, the same books. How many mass shootings in Canada did you hear about last year? How many in Britain? Because we average one a day in this country. It's a bullshit argument the gun advocates keep pushing: it's not the guns, it's *you. You're* the violent ones using guns the wrong way. Are we using them the wrong way? Look at this."

I held up on my phone a side-by-side photo of a Tanguich BL-24 assault rifle and a competitor's AR-15.

"Look at these guns. Just look at them. We're selling these to whoever wants them. It's insane. 'JollyGreenGiantofGuns42' says we need these guns for hunting and home protection and the first step toward tyranny is for the government to take away our guns. Well, Jolly Green, let's take a look at that.

"The AR-15 fires ninety rounds a minute, depending on how fast you can pull the trigger. The BL-24, a hundred and twenty rounds a minute. If you pumped ninety rounds into a buck, you'd have nothing left but fur-and-antler pie. Don't give me this hunting nonsense. And home protection? That's a joke. Have you ever been the victim of a home invasion? It takes like twenty seconds. They rush into your house before you have time to slip on your shorts. Unless you're sleeping with an AR-15 or BL-24 under your pillow with the safety off, you're gonna get jumped and it's going to happen faster than it takes you to realize what's going on. You know what protects you from home invasion? An alarm. And it has the added benefit that you won't accidently shoot Aunt Bertha in the middle of the night while she's up to pee."

I stopped for a minute and stared into the camera. "I don't know. You're probably thinking I'm the lawyer and I'm just in this lawsuit for the money, and you're probably right, but that doesn't mean what's happening to Melissa Bell is right. She doesn't get her day in court because the people in charge are in the pockets of the people with money, and about half this country doesn't seem to care that her son has died because they don't want to even talk about any sort of restriction on what types of guns we can buy." I held up my phone again with the photos of the assault weapons. "These are *not* for hunting. These are *not* for home protection. These are made for killing as many human beings as fast as possible. These are weapons of war. And there's a war on our streets right now against us, and our leaders have abandoned us to the gun lobbies and manufacturers."

I inhaled and put my phone down and ran my hands through my hair. I felt fatigue crawling through my muscles and had the sudden urge to just sneak into bed and not come out.

"Anyway, if you want to help, donate some money. We need about three hundred grand to continue with this lawsuit. I know that's impossible, but at least I can say I tried everything . . . thanks."

I turned off the camera, uploaded the video, hit the business center lights, and went upstairs to bed.

54

It was the smell of coffee that woke me up. I opened my eyes to sunlight streaming through the windows and a branch that was slowly bobbing with a breeze. I could hear birds out there, and for a second, I thought I was dreaming. It wasn't until I heard the toilet flush and the shower start that I knew I was awake.

I checked my phone and saw that Kelly had texted last night.

Stopped by your apartment to talk. You weren't there

I sat up in the bed and responded right away.

No. I'm in Aspen. Little vacation for me and Michael

My phone dinged a moment later. *Why Aspen?*

Why not? Hey, I recorded a GoFundMe video last night. Michael's idea. Would you look at the video and make sure I don't sound crazy? We won't raise anything, but I don't want to appear crazy either

Sure, I'll check it out. Text me when you're back in town

A smile came to my face though I didn't intend it to. *She* had texted *me*.

I went into the bathroom to urinate, and Michael shouted from the shower, "Dad!"

"Oh please. I changed your diapers for three years. It's nothing I haven't seen."

"Dad!"

"Fine." I stepped out of the bathroom and had to wait a good five minutes until the shower stopped and he came out. I grumbled as I went to pee and then took my own shower. I dressed in shorts and a T-shirt that said, "Bad Decisions Lead to Good Stories" and threw on some flip-flops.

"You look like a tourist," Michael said.

"I am a tourist. Let's head down. I'm starving."

Downstairs the lodge was serving free breakfast, and I filled a plate to the brim and sat by the window. The women at the table next to us looked over and smiled, and I smiled back.

"That one on the left has been eyeing you since we got here."

I glanced back at her. "She's clearly got good taste."

"You should talk to her."

"Nah."

Michael chuckled. "You're a successful, handsome lawyer, Dad. You gotta have more confidence than that."

"It's not a matter of confidence," I said, digging into some scrambled eggs with salsa. "She's not my type."

"You haven't even talked to her."

I chewed for a second. "She has all her makeup on, and her hair is done up. She's dressed in workout clothes, but look at those shoes. They're brand-new. Basically unused. Her whole outfit is basically new. She's trying to signal an 'I don't care' look that actually takes an hour to perfect. Someone who cares that much about the impression they make with other people isn't for me. I'm not saying she's a bad person; we all have our hang-ups, I'm just saying she's not my type."

"Who is your type then?"

I stared at him a second. "You know who. And of course like a jerk off I left her before our wedding."

"Kelly? Not mom?"

I looked away, to a family seated across the restaurant. "She was, at some point. Or I thought she was."

He hesitated. "Listen, Dad, I have something to tell you. I was gonna wait till we got back, but it's something you need to know so I thought it'd just be fair if I told you now."

"What?"

"I'm . . . moving out."

"I know. Next year when you graduate. I told you I'd help out with the rent at first."

"No, like soon. Like next month."

"What're you talking about?"

"Mom and I talked and we thought it best that I move down there to Tahoe with her. Just to . . . I don't know. Get away. She said you'd be cool with letting her have custody until I turn eighteen."

"Get away from what?"

"You know what, Dad. It's so weird at school I can't handle it. I'll go down the hall and hear whispers, or I'll be standing by my locker and someone will yell out 'fag' and by the time I turn around they're already gone. Two months ago, a kid at our school wanted to start a club for LGBT kids to have someplace to go and talk after school. He got the shit beat out of him, and the school said they would cancel all the clubs rather than let that one go forward, since they can't constitutionally ban one club. My friends are drifting away. The teachers look at me weird . . ."

"Mikey, I got news for you, the kids you know from high school are going to disappear in a flash after graduation. You are going to be absolutely shocked at how little contact you're gonna have with them. I know the school system has beat it into your head how important high school is, and that if you fail in high school or don't have enough friends, then you'll fail at life or not have enough friends in life, but it's not true. It doesn't matter one bit. And moving won't help. You can never run away from your problems."

"You're one to talk."

"Hey, I'm your father. You don't get to speak to me that way."

He folded his arms and looked away. "Whatever. I knew coming here was a mistake. Can we just go home?"

"No. I spent good money on this lodge and we're going to enjoy it, damn it." I angrily took a bite of eggs and then tossed down my fork on the plate.

55

Driving home wasn't exactly a walk in the park. For the first two hours we said nothing to each other. The next hour our conversation was, "You hungry?" "No," and that was it.

When we got home, he stormed into his room and shut the door. I stood there a few seconds and then went over. My hand came up to knock, but it stopped short a few inches. I lowered it and stared at the wood. I remembered a time when I didn't have to knock. When he was young enough that Dad could walk into his room without an objection or a feeling of invasion of privacy. I sighed and went to lie down on the couch.

It was only when my phone buzzed that I realized I had fallen asleep. It was Kelly.

Um, have you looked at your GoFundMe?

No. Why?

Take a look at it

I got up and went to the Mac at the kitchen table. I put in my password and looked at the account. For a second, I didn't understand what I was seeing. Some sort of numbers on the screen that I thought could've been an account number. Then it hit me that it was money, so

I thought that it must be an error. That I'd logged into someone else's account, or maybe it was a glitch. Slowly, like warm water dribbling over my head that I couldn't feel until the moment I was completely wet, it hit me: It was our money. Money raised for us.

It read: $976,435.

56

I texted Kelly, *This can't be right*

It's right. You should see how many people donated. Your video struck a chord. And it's not stopping. People are donating as we speak

I kept watching as the number slowly ticked up. My hand came up seemingly on its own and touched the screen, as though to make sure it was really there.

We have our war chest, Kelly texted. *Send a screenshot to Garvin*

At nine in the morning, Craig, Kelly, and I sat in my office. I kept insisting Kelly not bother with this and go to work, but she wouldn't hear it. The case had dug itself deep inside her, and I was worried Corey would fire her. He'd fired people for far less.

The phone rang and I answered it.

"Hello?"

Garvin's slick voice said, "Very inventive, Mr. Game. I'm impressed. I applaud you."

"Yeah, well, you can applaud me by opening up that checkbook for my client."

He chuckled, but it didn't sound like the kind of chuckle people make when they find something funny. It was more like he was laughing at me in the most mocking way possible.

"Brennen, I got enough to fight this out now. We can be in court for the next six years if we need to. Save us that time. Talk to your client and settle this thing and apologize. I know any apology seems like an admission that maybe, somehow, in some weird way, guns had anything to do with this tragedy, but just have the CEO suck it up and apologize."

He inhaled deeply with a little scoff at the end and said, "You could've raised twenty times what you did and it still wouldn't touch how much money I could spend on this case in a month if I wanted to. Do you really think we care about how long this takes to fight? This is about precedent. You have none, and we will do anything, *anything*, to ensure precedent doesn't get set. My clients aren't thinking about this lawsuit or a lawsuit next year or even ten years down the line. They're thinking about twenty and thirty and fifty years down the line. We pay out one lawsuit claiming negligent entrustment, and fifty more get filed. One of them would eventually get precedent set. It's not a risk we're willing to take."

I leaned back in the seat and put my feet up on the desk. "I get it, they want to make sure that there's no incentive for others to file a lawsuit because you settled with us. I really do understand. But this is different: this is children. You don't want this in the press every day. Just talk to your CEO and see what he thinks about an apology."

"Goodbye, Counsel. I'll see you in court."

I hung up and Craig said, "No dice, huh?"

"No. He wants to fight it out."

Kelly shrugged. "You've got the donations now. One point two million last time I checked. You could fight this case out for ten years if you wanted to."

"Yeah, that's what I want, to be in court for ten years on a single case."

"Hey, beats what I do. You got a real client and a real cause."

"A real cause, huh?"

"Yeah, a real cause," she said, looking me in the eye.

I took my feet off the table and rose to walk around a bit. I'd been sitting too much lately and had noticed aches in my back that weren't there before. "We've got to get this taken care of as soon as possible. Otherwise, they'll just drain us. They'll fight until we're out of money, and then we'll have to go through this thing again."

"So what's your plan?"

"We gotta get through all these depositions as quickly as possible and get into a trial. We need this in front of a jury while it's still in the headlines. Craig, start lining all these depositions up. We have to hit all of them. If any experts are willing to do it by phone, great, if not, just book a flight for me to head out there."

"And me," Kelly said. "I'll take half of them."

"You can't leave work like that."

"I'll take a little hiatus."

"Kelly, no, you can't lose your job over this."

"This is important to me, Peter. This is the type of thing I went to law school for." She hesitated. "Isn't it what you went for?"

Craig sighed and rose. "I'll be making calls in my office for the next forty years if anyone needs me."

57

I stayed and helped Craig out until a little past midnight, since some of the experts were on the other side of the world.

We called expert after expert, and lo and behold, none of them would stipulate to holding the deposition over the phone. One guy got angry with me and called me un-American for trying to take away people's right to defend their homes and their families.

"From what? Packs of wolves? What does someone living in the middle of Chicago need with an assault rifle?" I said.

"They're not called assault rifles damn it! They're assault weapons. And it's a slippery slope. You take away one gun, you can take away all of them."

"We should let babies drive. You deny one person a driver's license, you can deny all of them."

He seemed to grumble something and then hung up on me.

In all, between the two of us, we'd set up over thirty depositions. It would take the next four months to get through them all, and then another six months to get through the remaining fifty or so, we figured. I scheduled Kelly for only a handful. She could say what she wanted about it, but I wasn't about to let her lose her job because of my case.

"Hey, Peter," Craig said, poking his head into my office.

"Yeah?"

"Can you give me a ride back to the dorms? I took the train up here and they don't run this late."

"Yeah, sure, pal."

We drove on the freeway and he pulled out a candy bar, a Snickers, and chewed on it softly. He looked out the window and said, "The city's prettier at night. I like the lights more than the sunshine."

I glanced at him. "I've been meaning to ask you something. This Satanism stuff . . . you really believe in it? I mean, a guy with horns and a pitchfork sitting in a basement trying to tempt us to do evil things? You seem too smart for that. How'd you even get mixed up with it?"

He chewed for a few moments. "My dad was . . . well, he wasn't someone you'd want to get to know." He paused. "He would take me to the bathroom and make me hold the shower rod while he pulled down my pants and beat me with his belt. He was miserable and he didn't think anyone else should be happy either. Anyway, he was a preacher."

"No way."

He nodded. "Fourth Episcopal District Church in Lehi. The thing he was most frightened of, that he would always warn us against, was Satan. That Satan was around every corner and hiding under our beds and ready to make us do anything he wanted us to do. So when I was old enough, and they knew I wasn't going to join their church, they said I had to choose a religion even if it wasn't theirs. I found the nearest Satanic church, which by the way, is freaking hard in Utah, and I joined." He smiled. "His face, when he saw me walk into the house that first time with a pentagram necklace around my neck . . . I've never forgotten it."

"So what'd he do?"

Craig took a bite of Snickers. "He kicked me out, but I knew he would, so I had it planned out to sleep at my buddy's house. I couch surfed for a while until my scholarship came through and then moved into the dorms." He stared out the window for a minute. "Are you religious?"

"No."

"So, like, you think those kids that died are just gone? Doesn't that make you sad? That they were here for just a little bit and then taken away?"

"Life is sad, Craig."

He shook his head. "I wouldn't want to live that way. Thinking that. There's gotta be something to all this."

"There is: Look out for you and yours and make as much money as possible. Hopefully you'll have a little happiness here and there and that's it. That's what we can hope for."

"Always put yourself before others. I like it. You'd fit right in at the Satanic church. But if you believed that, you would've dropped this case the second you knew it was going to cost you something. I don't think you believe that."

I looked at him a second and then said, "You got any more Snickers? I'm starving."

I dropped Craig off in front of the dorms, and he said he would be in early tomorrow to help me schedule more depositions. No reason to, but I waited until he went into the building before driving away. I liked the kid and I tried not to like anybody.

A twenty-four-hour shooting range was on the way home in a town called Taylorsville. I'd gone at all hours before to alleviate stress. Though I'd seen it bare, I'd never seen it this empty. When I pulled in, the only car there was the owner's. I walked in and he nodded to me.

"Peter, how are ya?" he said while cleaning a Glock on the glass gun case.

"Feelin' like a baby crapped on me all day. How are you?"

He chuckled. "Had a good day today. Didn't talk to the ex-wife all day, sold me some nice rifles I'd bought wholesale at a show, had a good burrito for lunch . . . what else a man need?"

"Nothin'."

I stood over the glass case and looked at the guns. "I'll take the nine millimeter tonight."

"Sounds good."

He took a couple packages of ammo, a few targets, and the gun, and laid them on the counter. I paid with a credit card and headed back to the range, picking up my safety glasses and earplugs. The place, for once, didn't smell like burned gunpowder, and no casings littered the cement floors. I wondered why he stayed open if not that many people came through at night. Maybe he had insomnia and liked having something to do to distract himself from it.

I loaded the gun and sent the target out. When it was in position against the wall, I got into the Weaver stance and lifted the weapon. Looking down the barrel, I aimed, and felt the smoothness of the trigger. The gun was heavy in my hand. Not a particularly well-made firearm, but the kickback was minimal and I'd found I could hit the target well.

I tried to pull the trigger and nothing happened.

I thought maybe the gun had malfunctioned, but then I realized my finger hadn't moved. I took a breath and tried again, but it was like my finger had a mind of its own: it wouldn't pull the trigger. A sickening feeling went down my throat and into my guts like I'd swallowed rancid milk or something.

The only image in my head was Danny Bell, struggling to get on his bike and pedal. But instead of Danny Bell, it was Michael scrambling on the bike, and then toppling over. Screaming.

I put the gun down and leaned against the wall, slipping off my glasses and taking out the earplugs. I stared at the gun lying in front of me, and still felt its weight in my hand.

"Damn it."

I packed up the ammo and went upstairs to give it back to the owner and see if he'd refund me the money.

58

It was well past one in the morning when I drove back to my apartment and I was listening to the local AM radio station. I liked the late-night call-in shows because clearly anybody willing to call in to a radio show at one in the morning had some seriously batshit crazy stuff to get off their chest.

The host's claim to fame was that he had once cussed out the left-wing mayor of Salt Lake City for five minutes on air because the mayor had the tenacity to say 9/11 wasn't an inside job but actually committed by the terrorists. It had earned Morgan Van Loren his tinfoil hat with the conspiracy community and he was a local hero now.

He was entertaining me with his rant about climate change being a Chinese conspiracy, and then he said, "Speaking of hoaxes, let's talk for a minute about this elementary school shooting."

Oh shit.

"I'm sure you've all heard of it by now if you follow this program, but there was an alleged shooting at Holladay-Greenville Elementary, which the media wants you to believe killed numerous children and a teacher. Now of course the mainstream media and the anti-gun groups and unions will use this as an excuse to bring up gun control again because that's what they do. They use tragedy to their advantage. But don't be fooled by it, ladies and gentlemen, because we've done the research for you, and can tell you definitively, here tonight, the shooting is a hoax. It is a false flag. We will delve into it tonight, but there is proof that paid actors were there, who you can see on the videos weeping and screaming, and we'll hear from an expert, Dr. Philip Stroke, on staging tragedies that will explore the psychology of the sick people that did this. That used children to forward their anti-gun, pro-globalist agenda."

Deep breaths, Peter, deep breaths . . .

"And *now*, now, apparently, a lawsuit has been filed by one of the so-called victims, a Melissa Bell, alleging that her son was killed in this fake incident. It is the height of hypocrisy and evil. That's right, I said it, *evil*, to use the death of your son as an excuse to go after legitimate, traditional businesses like the American firearm industry. Now I don't know if her son actually died at some point from something else or if it's all a fabrication, but we'll talk to Dr. Stroke about it here tonight. Whatever the truth, this woman is sick and needs help." A long pause. "She is a sick, sick woman and has bought into this globalist agenda to tear down what it means for us to be American, and she's using this *so-called* tragedy—"

"Son of a bitch!"

I flipped my car around and floored the accelerator.

59

It was nearly two in the morning when I hit the brakes and slid to a stop in front of KHZB. I got out and ran to my trunk and took a photograph from a file I had back there. The doors to the station were open, and there was no security guard and no receptionist either.

My breathing was hard and my heart pounded like it wanted to break out of my chest. I stopped in the lobby and listened until I heard Van Loren's voice coming from a door down the hall. I opened the door. His producer was in a booth. It was dark except for a red light above the producer's workstation that said **ON AIR**.

"Um, excuse me, you can't be in here."

I stepped past her and opened the studio door. Van Loren sat behind a huge workstation with a big microphone in front of him and earphones covering his ears. He glanced at me like he wasn't interested in who I was, but when I rushed toward him, his eyes went wide and he tried to stand.

I leapt at him and latched onto his chest, but he was much bigger than me and we just kind of leaned to the side. I slipped off him, but before I hit the ground, I wrapped my arms around his neck and we hit the floor together. I rolled on top of him.

"What the hell are you doing, man!" he shouted.

I pulled the photo up near his face as he put his hand around my throat and started choking me.

"This is Danny Bell," I said.

"What?"

"Danny Bell, you piece of shit!" I said, trying to breathe. "He was shot in the back three times. Three times! While he was getting on his bike to get away from his murderer. I saw the blood. I saw the bullet holes in the walls. It's not a damn hoax, you psychopath."

With the strength of a bull he flipped me off him and I rolled into the wall. He stood and launched a kick into my ribs that nearly made me vomit.

"What the hell are you doing on my show? This is my show!"

He kicked me again and this time some vomit rose into my throat. He went to kick again and I wrapped myself around his leg, biting his thigh. He screamed and I bit harder as we both toppled over his workstation.

Security came rushing in while my teeth were securely embedded in his thigh. They grabbed me and pulled me off. I shoved the photo in his face. "Danny Bell, you crazy bastard! His name was Danny Bell!"

They dragged me out into the hall and put cuffs on me. The police had been called. I was sat down against the wall, and I just stared at the floor. Van Loren was still ranting in there like nothing had happened. I guessed this was not the first time someone had attacked him.

Only one cop showed up: Martin Blackburn. I knew him well from my days at the public defender's office. He was on the DUI squad, which brought in like half the cases public defenders had. I had also helped his wife with a car accident claim where the insurance company was refusing to cough up the money she deserved, even though she had zero liability in causing the accident.

He interviewed the security guards, Van Loren, and the producer, and then came out and sat next to me.

"You look fatter than when I saw you last," he said.

I glanced at him. "There's a burrito cart next to my office. Two a day sometimes."

"Yeah, I've gained about thirty pounds this last year. The wife is just such a damn good cook." He grinned. "I think she likes me fat. Maybe thinks other women won't be interested in me."

"How is Suzie?"

"Fine, just humming along." He looked to the booth and then back to me. "Peter, what the hell did you get yourself into?"

I shook my head. "It was stupid. So stupid. Damn it. I really messed up, Martin. This could hurt that lady's case. The mother of the kid who died."

He nodded. "They want me to charge you with attempted murder." He chuckled. "Van Loren thinks you're a stooge sent by globalists, whoever the hell they are, to attack him. I always thought it was an act but I think this guy's really nuts."

I exhaled and leaned back against the wall, the cuffs pulling tightly on my wrists. "So what're you gonna do?"

"I told them the best they got is misdemeanor assault. But I'm not gonna cite you for that. I'm gonna cite you for disorderly conduct as an infraction. The prosecutor might change that, but he usually goes with whatever I cite."

"Why would you do that for me?"

"You were always decent to me. You treated me like a human being, which not all defense attorneys do. Besides, it's not just for you." He glanced back at the booth, I assume to make sure no one was listening. "We pulled this kid over once, couldn't have been older than nineteen. Just a traffic stop for running a stop sign. I get up to his door and the kid's sweating. He's staring straight forward, his hands on the wheel, and he keeps glancing into his rearview. I thought maybe he hadn't been pulled over before, or maybe he had a little bit of weed on him and was shitting his pants. I take out my flashlight and shine it in the car, and this cocksucker in the back seat sits up from under a blanket with an AK-47. He fires three rounds. None of them hit me, I dove to the ground, but he kept firing, right through the door."

"What'd you do?"

"The kid punched the gas and took off. We blew out his tires a few miles up the road and got him. Little shit said they had some meth in the car and didn't want to go to jail. Anyway, that AK, that wasn't illegal, man. They bought that thing online for a few hundred bucks." He shook his head. "Almost made my kids fatherless." He exhaled. "So no, I'm not getting you for the assault. But you gotta calm down, man. Most cops, despite some of us being gun fanatics, want these assault weapons off the streets. We're watching your case pretty closely. It's our lives, Peter."

I nodded. "I know."

"I'm gonna tell them to uncuff you, but stay away from Van Loren."

"Believe me, I have no intention of doing something like this again."

He smiled. "Just try to keep the anger in check, will ya?"

"I'll try."

He nodded and slapped my back before standing to get the security guard.

60

I slept until noon and kept my phone off. When I rose, I showered and had a Pop-Tart and then lay on the couch and watched television for a bit. It was gray outside, a little drizzly, and the rain reflected my mood. I didn't want to go into the office today. I checked my calendar. I had a call with an insurance adjuster on a slip and fall case in the afternoon and nothing else. I'd hang out here, watch *The Princess Bride*, and eat chocolate and pizza all day.

When I turned on my phone, I saw several messages from Kelly asking me to call her. I called and she answered right away.

"They've dropped their experts," she said instead of a greeting.

"What'dya mean?"

"Craig just got notice. They dropped all the experts except three. Garvin's asking for an expedited trial date and wants to know if you'll stipulate. With the GoFundMe still rising, they must've finally seen we can fight them out on this. Since they can't overwhelm us financially they want to get this into a trial as fast as possible. You were right. They want this out of the press ASAP."

"Three experts? That's it? You're sure?"

"That's what the motion says."

"Huh."

"So, I don't think we should stip. Let's let them sweat it out a bit."

"No, they could easily add two hundred other experts if they wanted to. The eighty-six was a test to see how we'd respond. I think they wanted a quick trial the whole time but wanted to see if there was a chance they could take us out before then. I'm gonna stip."

She exhaled. "I think we need to prep for our own depositions. At least a dozen teachers and administrators will be testifying and then some of the kids."

"No kids."

"We need them to testify, Peter. They can paint an emotional picture for the jury. Think of the impact a kid will have up there."

"They've been through enough. I won't do it. Besides, we have video. It's enough."

"If you say so. But Garvin will use every advantage he can get. He wouldn't hesitate for a second to use kids. Frankly, I thought you wouldn't either."

"Yeah, well, I'm full of surprises lately. I'll give you a call after I talk to Garvin. And, hey, thanks again."

"Just make sure you're doing this for the right reasons before that jury gets impaneled."

"I don't know what that means, but sure, I'll be a good boy."

I hung up and stared at the phone a second, a tingling of excitement going from my feet to the top of my head. Big corporations could drag out litigation for years, arguing about the dumbest, most irrelevant crap possible. Mostly because their attorneys billed by the hour and wanted to inflate their invoices. I hated that nonsense. Spending a court hearing arguing about whether a witness had been properly served according to Rule 4 or whether they were improperly served and had to be served again made me want to tear my hair out. I wanted to be in front of a jury. I wanted Garvin to look them in the eyes and tell them Danny Bell's death was okay. That it was just a natural byproduct of the Second Amendment and needed to be tolerated.

"Hot damn," I whispered.

61

We decided that Kelly should do our depositions. Depositions weren't about influencing anybody; they were about gathering as much minute detail as you could, and the last phrase I would use to describe myself was "detail oriented." Plus, she was logical in a way I just wasn't and could phrase everything so that the witnesses might not get too emotional during the depositions. We wanted to save that emotion for the jury.

We sat at an outdoor café and ate sandwiches. She wore a black dress that I'd seen her wear before. The rain had cleared today and the sun was out. You could still smell the wetness on the pavement and the odor of dry dirt that had turned to mud. It was pleasant. Something like driving through the country. I sat quietly a minute and just inhaled it.

"You sure Corey's okay with you taking a couple weeks off to do this?" I said, staring out at a glimmering puddle in the road.

She shrugged. "He seemed okay about it."

"Did he seem bugged?"

"Not at all. I told him I don't expect him to pay me for the time I take off to work this case and he seemed fine with that."

I grinned. "Yeah, that would make him happy."

She chewed on her mahi-mahi sandwich a second and said, "What about you?"

"What about me?"

"You still think the big retirement verdict is going to make you happy?"

"Yes, actually, Kelly, I do. Like Ella Fitzgerald said, 'I been rich and I been poor and believe me rich is better.'"

"That's clever, but I have to remind you again that this might be a paycheck for you but it's Melissa's life."

"What do you want me to say? It feels like you're trying to get me to say something so just come out with it already."

"Just that you need to be in the right frame of mind. The jury is going to pick up on how you feel in a second. Juries aren't stupid."

"I beg to differ."

"Peter—"

"I know, I know. Look, the case is fine. You worry too much."

A car rolled up in front of the veranda. Joey sat in a convertible Mercedes. He waved to her and then saw me and smiled and waved to me. I half-heartedly waved back.

I watched as she walked to the car and pecked him on the cheek.

I stared at her in the passenger seat for as long as I could as they drove away. She shouldn't be in that guy's car; she should be in mine. With a house to match, and children to fill the house with. That should've been my life.

I inhaled deeply, paid, and then decided I had a helluva lot of work to do so I had better get started.

62

I watched the videos of the depositions every night, skimming through the routine to get to the good questions. And I went through Kelly's notes, and had her highlight places on the video I needed to look at. It was a work of art. She got out of them exactly what she wanted—both our witnesses and the defense's.

Garvin, for his part, was equally masterful. He slowly, almost imperceptibly if I wasn't specifically looking for it, got each witness to admit this tragedy was unavoidable. I didn't think the witnesses even knew what they were saying. He led them like the Pied Piper leading mice. One witness, a cafeteria worker who was there the day of the shooting, admitted that it seemed like even if Varvara hadn't had guns, he just would've used bombs or something else.

Craig went with Kelly when he could, and, on the video, I'd see him lean over and whisper something to her now and again. The two seemed to work well together and it made me happy for some reason.

The big deposition was Melissa, and to my shock, Garvin waived it.

"You sure?" I said into the phone when he called me.

"Positive. No need to put her through that after all she's endured."

"Yeah . . . well, we appreciate that. I'll let her know how gracious you've been."

Kelly sat across from me at my desk, and as usual Craig was in the other room on the phone trying to calm down one of my other clients who I'd been ignoring since I got this case.

"Like hell he'd do something gracious," she said. "He's going to try to exclude her as a witness somehow."

"No. You know it's almost impossible to exclude the plaintiff, and then it'd be in the press that they fought to not have the mother of a dead child testify." I ran my finger over my upper lip as I thought. "No, he's got something on her. I don't know what it is, but he's got something."

"Then you need to meet with her and find out what."

I went home to change before going to Melissa's and found Michael there. He was packing his room up bit by bit. We had argued for days about him moving. There were plenty of horrible things said, lots of doors slammed, and even a remote that he threw across the room and broke. But it was ultimately something Kelly said—that he was almost a man, and I couldn't make his choices for him—that made me give in. Swallowing the most bitter pill I'd ever swallowed, I agreed to let him live with his mother.

As soon as school let out for the summer, his mother would be coming to pick him up to move him to Lake Tahoe. Granted, Tahoe was certainly better than Salt Lake City, and I was glad he'd be somewhere surrounded by nature, but it was the wrong move. I knew his mother better than he did.

"Hey," I said as he took down posters from his wall.

"Hey."

I glanced around the room. My favorite poster of his was still up. A quote by Hemingway that said, "I love sleep. My life has a tendency to fall apart when I'm awake."

"Do you maybe wanna get dinner tonight?"

"Can't," he said without looking at me. "Paul's throwing a going away party for me."

"Oh. Well, maybe tomorrow then?"

"Maybe."

I wanted to say something. Hell, what I really wanted was to throw my arms around the little bastard and beg him to stay. Tell him that the pain of him leaving dug into my guts and made me feel like I wanted to puke. But that wouldn't be fair to him. We each had our own path to walk, and if he thought this was his path, I shouldn't send him down it filled with guilt about how it would make his old man feel.

"Okay, well, I'll see you tomorrow then."

"Yup, tomorrow."

I left the apartment but stood outside the door, staring back at it, hoping he would open it.

I sighed, and went to my car.

63

I called and texted but Melissa wasn't responding. When I went to the house, no one answered the door but it was unlocked. I opened it and went inside.

The house was a mess. Dishes were stacked up everywhere. The floor was littered with clothes and boxes of things that had been ordered from Amazon. The counters were filled with useless items, like trendy water bottles and kitchen decorations. There must've been fifty or sixty things, brand-new and unused. Most of them still in the packaging.

"Melissa, are you here?"

The fridge door was beeping because it had been left open. I closed it and then eased down the hall. I saw her lying on the bed in the master bedroom. She was underneath the covers, softly moaning, the blanket pulled up to her mouth.

"What's going on? What happened?"

I saw a bottle of pills on the nightstand. The bottle was tipped over, the little white pills strewn everywhere, next to two empty beer bottles. I picked up the bottle of pills. Codeine.

"Melissa, how many of these did you take?"

Her eyes rolled up and she saw me and a slow smile crept to her lips. "Peter . . . you're so sweet to come here and check on me," she said, her voice slurring in pitch as though she were so drunk her tongue didn't work anymore.

I sat on the bed next to her. "Melissa," I said softly, "how many of these did you take?"

"I don't know," she said, closing her eyes and rolling to her side.

"Melissa. Melissa!"

"Don't yell," she said, her eyes still closed.

"How many did you take?"

"I don't know. Three or four. My normal dose."

"With beer?"

"You're not my mother."

With that, she started snoring almost immediately. I sighed and sat on the recliner in the corner, playing on my phone as her snores filled the room.

Melissa didn't wake up for about two hours, and when she did, she didn't appear to know where she was.

"Peter? What are you doing here? What time is it?"

"It's three. You feeling okay?"

She rubbed her head with her hands. "Yeah, yeah. I must've just been exhausted."

I put my phone away. "You wanna go grab some coffee?"

She checked her phone and shook her head. "No, no I promised my sister I'd go help her with . . . something. Shopping for something."

I leaned forward. "Melissa, you can't mix those pills with alcohol. Do you understand? You could die."

"I know. It was just a couple beers and I take the pills for my back."

I nodded. "Will you please do me one favor? No more booze with the pills. Please?"

She smiled and ran her hands through her hair. "Sure, Peter. I won't mix them again. It was just a little bit of alcohol to help me sleep. I'm not sleeping at night anymore."

"Yeah, join the club."

"I'm just . . . I'm more lonely than anything I think. Danny used to fill this house with laughter and television and friends . . . there's nothing now. It's like . . . a grave. I've never felt so alone in my life."

"Hey, I'm here. You need to talk, you want to go get lunch, whatever, I'm here."

She sat up on the edge of the bed. Her makeup had run down her face from recent crying and dripped dark splotches onto her sweatshirt. "Any news?" she said.

"Some good news and some bad news. The good news is the defense has waived your deposition. It's a crap experience and would've taken twelve hours, so it saves you that. The bad news is that I think he's got something he's going to spring on us when we're in trial. Can you think of anything that would be?"

"Like what?"

"Like anything. Affairs, criminal records, weird searches online or porn you're into, dating a terrorist or something . . . anything."

She thought for a few moments and said, "No. Nothing. I've never been in trouble in my life."

"Anything with Danny?"

"Like what?"

"Abuse or—"

"Never! How could you even say that?"

"I'm just exploring options." I glanced to the pills. "What about the pills?"

"What about them?"

"Where do you get them from?"

"My doctor. Peter, I'm not a drug addict. These are for my back. I had back surgery last year."

I breathed in deep and let it out slowly. "Well, there are some other things to look at, like why Danny's school was chosen and things like that. I don't know. I could be wrong that he's got some smoking gun to use against us. He could just feel like there's nothing you could add and wants to hurry and get this to trial."

"That must be it because I'm telling you, I'm the most squeaky-clean person you know. I haven't had a traffic ticket since I was sixteen."

"Well, if you think of anything it could be, text me right away." I rose. "You okay?"

"Fine," she said, forcing a smile. "Thanks for checking on me."

"No problem." I turned to leave. "I'll see you in court tomorrow. And hey . . . seriously, you ever need someone who's a good listener, call me."

"Thanks," she said.

Before leaving, I picked up the dishes around the house and put them in the sink and closed the fridge. I straightened up a few things in the living room. At the front door, I looked back to the bedroom but she hadn't come out. I closed the door behind me and left.

The next morning I woke up and my shirt stuck to me with sweat. I was breathing heavily and it felt like someone was sitting on my chest. I'd seen Michael in a dream, lying facedown on the pavement, three holes in his back as black blood spilled onto the ground.

I peeled the shirt off and got into the shower. We had a pretrial conference today to make sure Garvin and I were on the same page. He had five lawyers with him now. Lawyers were falling out of the sky and landing at the defense table.

"I have to say," Judge Pearl said, "that I've never had a civil case of this magnitude move through litigation this quickly before."

Garvin gave him a smile and said, "We want justice as quickly as possible, Judge. There's no reason to hold things up and clog your docket."

The judge raised his eyebrows and said, "Well, it's your dime. Other than the matters and motions in limine we talked about, anything else before the trial?"

Garvin looked to his team. The five lawyers huddled, broke huddle, and then did a single nod to him. "No, Judge," he said.

"Um, I don't have anything else, Your Honor, no."

"Alright, well, the trial is set to begin tomorrow and I expect everyone here at eight a.m. sharp. I'd like to get the jury impaneled by noon if that's not pushing it too quickly. It's the custom in my court for you to submit voir dire questions to me the night before by eight p.m. and I'll choose the ones I wish to ask. I don't allow counsel-led voir dire in my court. Is that understood?"

"Yes, Judge."

"It is, Your Honor."

"Good. Then if there's nothing else, we're adjourned. See you gentlemen tomorrow."

Melissa said, "I'll be here early," and squeezed my shoulder before she left. Kelly wasn't here and neither was Craig. Garvin and his team cleared out and I found myself standing in the courtroom by myself for the first time in years.

I looked up at the flag. Framed behind it were the Constitution and Declaration of Independence and, prominently above that, the Bill of Rights. I stared at the Second Amendment. "A well regulated Militia, being necessary to the security of a free State, the right of the people to keep and bear Arms, shall not be infringed."

Madison, you brilliant bastard, you couldn't throw in a few more words to tell us what the hell it means?

I picked up my briefcase and left.

64

When I got home that night, Michael wasn't there. I went into his room, nudged aside a suitcase, and sat on the bed a minute. I hadn't even thought about what to do with his room when he was gone. Maybe I'd move out and get someplace smaller? The thought made me uncomfortable and I decided I would keep the room in case he ever wanted to come back or if he just needed a place to crash in Salt Lake sometimes.

After I finished the voir dire questions for the jury panel and emailed them to the judge's clerk, I went for a run, and then watched television and drank a few beers. None of it helped. I knew sleep wasn't coming, but I did all I could anyway.

I swallowed some herbs, drank some milk, and took a hot bath while listening to Yanni. Nada. Sleep just wouldn't come on the night before a jury trial. The anxiety would keep me awake and usually power me through the trial the next day, although one time I did fall asleep during a trial and woke up after my head bonked on the wood of the desk.

I lay in the dark, staring at the ceiling until I couldn't handle it anymore, then I got dressed and headed out. There was a bar not far from my house and I stopped there and got a drink, something fruity, and sipped it slowly. About two dozen other people were there, and as more and more people came in, the music got louder and the place got more annoying.

I drank the rest of the cocktail and asked for my check, and the bartender said, "That's it? You sure? You look like you could use some more."

"That obvious, huh?"

"You do this job long enough you can tell. Woman troubles?"

"That's definitely one of them. But it's because of me, not her."

He chuckled. "I got news for ya, pal. It's always because of us."

I sighed, and left the bar to go lie in bed again and hoped I could maybe catch an hour or two of sleep at least.

65

The morning of a jury trial for me was always the same. I got up, puked, shot coffee down my throat with a cannon, and then puked it all up again.

Michael was at the breakfast table. I got some oatmeal even though food was the last thing I could tolerate, and sat next to him. We ate in silence a minute and I said, "This is freaking ridiculous. You're leaving soon. Are you really going to spend our last days together being mad at me?"

"Yes."

"Do you even remember what you're mad at me for?"

"Yes . . . I . . . I . . ."

"See, you can't remember. Your mother would do the same thing. She'd be mad at me for weeks and I'd ask her why and she couldn't tell me."

"It was something," he said, his brow furrowing.

"Yeah, it's always something." I exhaled and said, "I don't want to spend our last days together like this."

"It's not our last days, Dad. Man, you make it seem like I'm going to the moon."

"You think we're gonna hang out all the time? You know how much I hung out with my dad after I moved out? Once a month at first. Then once every couple of months, then every few months, and eventually we'd just talk on the phone and see each other at Christmas. That was it."

His lips pursed. "I don't want that."

"I don't want that either."

I reached over and put my hand over his. I held it a minute and then he pulled away and said, "I better go."

"Can we have dinner tonight?"

He watched me a second. "Sure."

I got up to get dressed. I'd forgotten about the trial and then as soon as I remembered I ran to the bathroom to puke again.

Courthouses always looked ominous to people who didn't frequent them, but as a lawyer, you got so used to them, they didn't look any different than any other building. Until trial day. Then you forgot what they looked like, and it was as if you were seeing them again for the first time.

The West Jordan courthouse looked like a monolith made by the Galactic Empire. I felt like a lone stormtrooper hoping for the best. When I got screened through security, the bailiff said, "You look pale, Peter."

"Do me a favor, Ted, if I shit myself, run out and get me some new pants, would ya?"

He laughed. "Got some in the locker. You're covered."

I went up to the courtroom. Craig, Kelly, Melissa, and Jake were all sitting in the hallway. They looked at me. An icy feeling shot through my spine and down into my belly. The thought occurred to me to turn around and get back onto the elevator and run to Las Vegas.

"Hey," I said to them, my throat dry.

My stomach made a sound I hadn't heard before, like it was grinding a block of concrete through my intestines. I must've grimaced because Craig said, "You okay?"

"Fine. You guys ready?"

This time, Garvin wasn't late. He sat at the defense table with the COO and no one else. One of the main advantages plaintiff's lawyers had was that we were the underdog. Jurors saw me and my client at a table, and four or five high-priced lawyers at the defense table, and they instantly made the connection that we were the little guy. Garvin, unlike any corporate or insurance defense lawyer I had ever seen, was too smart for that. He sat there looking weak and outmatched. Instead of his normal three-thousand-dollar Armani or Gucci suits, he wore a plaid jacket with slacks that didn't match and a tie with the Utah Jazz basketball team logo on it. His old shoes even had scuffmarks. The COO looked like he couldn't afford a proper suit and had to borrow one from somebody. No pocket square, and he wore a cheap plastic watch. Garvin had no doubt dressed him to look like this case was bankrupting his little company.

Holy shit was this guy good.

Still, he wouldn't want to lose out on an opportunity to bill Tanguich their hourly rate for a team of lawyers, so six other lawyers sat behind him in the first row of the audience. None of them were wearing their usual expensive suits and Rolex watches either. They looked like schlubs just here, watching.

Garvin 1, Peter 0.

66

Judge Pearl came in, the bailiff shouted an announcement that court was in session, and the judge said, "Counselors, do we need to go over anything before we bring the jury panel out?"

Garvin glanced at me and winked. "No, Judge."

"No, Your Honor."

"Bailiff, would you please bring in the panel?"

As the jurors filed in, Pearl said, "All rise for the jury."

We rose. Melissa was next to me and I saw her hands trembling. Kelly sat on her other side, and Craig sat behind us in the first row. He and Garvin's six other lawyers were glaring at each other. Craig flipped them off.

"Ladies and gentlemen," Pearl said when the thirty potential jurors were seated, "thank you for being here today. The case you are about to hear is what's known as a civil case, which means that the plaintiff is seeking compensation for damages allegedly caused by the defendant. We will first be going through a process known as voir dire, in which you are bound by law to speak the truth. Essentially we will be ensuring that all of you selected for the jury will be able to be objective in this matter without bringing any outside prejudice—"

I didn't listen to the judge but instead focused on the jurors themselves. In my experience, there was no magic formula for selecting a juror. I'd read reams of data on jury selection and nobody had found a credible link between choosing the jurors and the outcome of the case. I would try to exclude people giving me or Melissa dirty looks and anyone wearing an NRA hat, which, holy sweet Mary of Mercy, one of the men actually was, and then just select people who looked nice from there.

Garvin, no doubt, would have spent tens of thousands on jury selection. Luckily, in Utah, unlike some other states, we didn't mail out the list of potential jurors months ahead of time. This meant jury selection experts had limited upside in Utah. Still, I noticed one of the men sitting behind Garvin furiously taking notes on the jurors, barely taking his eyes off them. I had no doubt he was their jury selection expert.

The hours grinded on. The judge asked question after question: "Is there any reason you couldn't be fair in this case?" "Do you own firearms?" "Have you ever been in a mass shooting?" "Have you ever shot anybody?" "Do you view the Second Amendment favorably?"

After an hour or so, you could see the jurors getting worn down. By hour three, they had zoned out. By the time we started talking about the actual case, they would have maybe 75 percent of the attention span they did now, and by the end of the day they would have about half. The trial was scheduled to last for one week, and by the end of the week, studies showed that they would have about 10 percent of the attention span they did now. Which meant they would be deciding the case when they were mentally at their weakest and most exhausted point.

"I'm scared," Melissa whispered to me. "I don't want to do this. I don't want to get up there."

"It's just jitters. Everyone gets them. I'll stand right in front of you. Don't look at anyone else except the jury. Pretend they're some friends you haven't seen in a long time and they asked you what happened.

When it gets overwhelming, just turn to me and look at me for as long as you want before looking back at the jury."

We'd practiced her testimony only once: her reactions had to be authentic. But now I wished we'd gone through it a few more times. Especially cross-examining her to prepare her for what Garvin was going to do. Problem was, I didn't know what he was going to do.

I kept a close eye on the panel, but really there was no need. Anything I read from them would just be projection.

After five and a half hours, and four meetings in the judge's chambers, we had excluded twenty people. Leaving the eight actual jurors and the two alternates. I always felt bad for the alternates. They would sit for the trial as though they were on the jury, and then before deliberation be told they're no longer needed. It would be like having sex and then being told right before climax that it was time to go.

We had an even split of men and women. Most wore jeans; a couple wore suits. The guy with the NRA hat had been excluded, even though Garvin fought like hell to keep him on, and one guy, who wore an "I'm With Her" T-shirt, had been excluded by Garvin, even though I argued that his political affiliation didn't necessarily imply he was anti-gun.

The jury was sworn in, and my guts felt like they were going to fall out of me in a hot mess and I would have to grab them and try to shove them back inside.

"Mr. Game," the judge said, "are you ready for opening statements?"

67

Opening statements, we're taught in law school, were a roadmap to the case. A chance to lay out the direction of the facts and what important tidbits the jury should keep an eye out for. Sure. Right. Really, you wanted to convince the jury that the other side was the scum of the earth and couldn't be more wrong. And you had to do it with a smile because juries had been shown to like nice guys and gals.

The plaintiff went first in a civil case. The bailiff had brought out the DVD player and television I asked for. I rose and stood in front of it. My knees felt weak and I kept wiping at the sweat I thought was dribbling down my neck, but when I'd touch it, nothing was there.

I looked each juror in the eye, and then without a word, I turned on the video.

No!

A scream from the video shattered the silence of the courtroom. I had purposely turned the volume almost all the way up.

No! No! Run. Tyler, get over here! Get over here!

The video had been filmed by one of the teachers on her cell phone. In the background, the crackle of gunfire was audible. Children screamed, adults screamed, and every few seconds the video would spin and shake as the teacher sprinted. She had wanted to make sure she captured the shooter's face in case he decided to take off, so she would stop every once in a while and get a good shot of him, her breathing frantic through her sobs.

In one frame, Varvara stood, pointing his rifle at a crowd of young kids running the opposite way. The rifle boomed, and smoke came out of the barrel and drifted into the air, vanishing shortly after.

Some of the jurors couldn't watch. I turned the volume up as far as it would go.

No, Lord, please no!

The teacher's scream was bloodcurdling. The type of scream someone makes when their entire existence comes down to one action: one final chance to express themselves. It made my blood run cold the first time I heard it in my office, and it had the same effect on some of the jury. One woman made the sign of the cross and then wouldn't look up from the floor.

Lord, the teacher cried, *Oh Lord help us. Help us please!*

More children shrieking as the rifle kept firing.

The teacher screamed one more time, and then the phone dropped, and the video ended.

I let that scream be the last thing they heard for a minute. It seemed like it was bouncing off the walls. I stepped in front of the television and looked at each juror.

"That video was shot by Mary Thomlin, a teacher at Holladay-Greenville Elementary School, on the date of April tenth, at ten twelve in the morning, during the children's recess. A man named Nathan Varvara walked in with a BL-24 rifle and several other firearms in a bag and began firing into the crowd of children who were playing outside. He followed them as they ran for cover anywhere they could. He got up close to the doorway of the school and shot them in the back as they ran down the hall to get away. He shot teachers, he shot administrators, he shot anyone who moved, and he did it with a smile on his face.

"He brought over five hundred rounds of ammunition with him. The BL-24 fires over a hundred rounds per minute and he fired for a solid three minutes. As he stopped to reload, the school police officer kept him busy until other police officers arrived, and Varvara got into a shootout with them. The police, though, were outgunned. They didn't have anything like the BL-24."

I walked over to Craig and he reached down and came up with the BL-24 I had bought from a pawnshop a week ago. The rifle was heavy and long. The jury gasped. The judge said, "Mr. Game, I did not approve that rifle in my courtroom!"

"It's obviously not loaded, Judge."

"Put it down," the bailiff said, his hand on his gun.

"Easy, easy." I set the rifle on the plaintiff's table and the bailiff came over to get it. He lifted it and checked the chamber and then held it like it was hot lava before disappearing into the back. I apologized to the judge and to Garvin before continuing.

Though I apologized, that had gone exactly how I wanted it to. The jury saw how big and ominous the rifle was, felt the fear upon seeing it out of nowhere, and saw how upset and frightened the judge and bailiff had been. For just a moment, maybe, they felt what those children felt when they saw that rifle come out of Varvara's bag.

I took out a photograph from a folder on the table and showed it to them. "This is Danny Bell. He's facedown with a bicycle tangled between his legs, and that woman covering his body is the woman who took the video, Mary Thomlin. When the shooting started, he got on his bike and tried to pedal away. His hands were probably wet with sweat, his heart like a drum, the fear turning his blood to ice . . . and then he felt three hot rounds enter his back. He lived for about a minute, lying on the cold pavement, the bike between his legs, and the last thing he heard before he died were the screams of his friends."

I glanced at Melissa. "One of the witnesses said that the last thing he did . . . was cry out for his mother."

Melissa slumped down and covered her mouth with her hand. Her sobs quietly echoed in the courtroom as she tried to fight them back.

I held up another photo, a woman on some grass with her daughter in her lap, both smiling. "This is Mary Thomlin. She was a teacher at Holladay-Greenville. Mother of two. Sunday school teacher at church. She volunteered at the local disability center two evenings a week to teach children with disabilities how to read. She had a chance to get away from Varvara and make her escape, but she didn't. She threw her body on top of Danny Bell to protect him from the gunfire, and she was shot six times. She died on top of Danny, still clutching him to prevent more bullets from getting to him."

I walked over to Melissa and stood next to her. "I would like you to imagine what it would be like to be Danny and see your friends dying. To hear the screams, to smell the gunpowder, to see the blood . . . and then to feel those rounds tear into your flesh. To not fully understand what is happening, but to have the rudimentary instinct that children have and know that you're going to die. I'd like you to imagine that, and then I'd like you to imagine what it would be like to be his mother. And to know that's what he saw, and what he went through before he died."

I pushed the television closer to them. "I'm going to show you another video, from the crime scene investigation unit. I'm so sorry to have to show you this. I struggled for days about whether I could do this to you or not. I really didn't want to. But in the end, I knew I had to. You deserve the truth."

I turned the video on. It opened to a clear picture near the entrance of the school and two men speaking softly. It was quiet now. This was about an hour after the shooting.

"In the media, in movies, in video games, even in the news, we see shootings. We see people die, and it doesn't seem like anything. People grab their chests and fall over, or they don't die, they just fall down and are able to talk while other people stop the bleeding and take them to a hospital, or worse, they just keep going. As if bullets don't really hurt us.

You ever ask yourself where that idea comes from? When someone gets slashed with a knife or a sword in a movie, they bleed. It cuts muscle and tendons just like it does in real life, but we don't show what bullets really do. Why? Because of the gun lobby and the gun manufacturers that own our government and our media. The millions and millions they spend everywhere are to make sure that we, the citizens, never see what guns really do. What bullet wounds are really like. They say that if slaughterhouses were made of glass, we'd all be vegetarians. Well I'm about to show you the glass slaughterhouse."

The men in the video turned the corner, and there it was.

68

The two crime scene investigators stopped in their tracks. One of them whispered, "Sweet Heaven have mercy."

Lying near the entrance were the bodies of four children.

"This is Laia White, Thomas Smith, Meghan Melendez, and Crystal Stoddard. This is what a real shooting looks like. Blood, and guts, and bone, and pain, and screams. It's not people clutching their chests and falling over like the gun lobbyists want you to believe. It's nightmares come to life. This is what our first responders have to see whenever they go into a mass shooting scene like this one."

You could hear something on the video. Something quiet, but definitely audible. One of the crime scene techs was sobbing.

"That's Marcus Tyrell. He's been with the Salt Lake County crime scene investigation unit for over twenty years. He's seen over a hundred murder scenes in his time, horrific traffic accidents . . . and he's crying. Because even he has not seen what guns really are. What they really do.

"People call nuclear, chemical, and biological weapons 'weapons of mass destruction.' You know how many people have died from nuclear weapons? About one hundred seventy thousand if you include the radiation poisoning that took their lives years later. Chemical weapons in every country since the First World War? About one hundred thousand people. Biological weapons? About fifty thousand people." I stepped closer to them. "The Civil War in this country killed about five hundred thousand people. World War Two took the lives of about four hundred thousand Americans. Vietnam, about fifty-eight thousand . . . From 1968 to 2015, over one and a half million people died in the United States by gun violence on our streets. More than all the wars in American history combined. If we include the entire planet, guns have killed over a billion people; that's *billion* with a *B*. There has never been and never will be a more potent weapon of mass destruction than the gun. It is the greatest killer in the history of our planet. In the United States, it is the ultimate murderer."

I pointed to Garvin. "The gun lobby and manufacturers buy politicians to ensure that you don't see these things. That all you see is the heroic cowboy riding into town and taking out the villains. That the gallant soldier takes out the bad guy and saves the day. And those things do happen. We have the finest soldiers in the world, soldiers who lay down their lives to protect us. But their causes make up a sliver, a *sliver*, of what guns are used for. The primary use of the gun in this country is to murder innocent people.

"Nathan Varvara was a disturbed young man. So what? There are a lot of disturbed young men in every city on earth. What separated him from the guy who just sits in his basement and does nothing was Varvara's ability to purchase military-grade weapons. And that's what the BL-24 is: a military weapon. A weapon Tanguich negligently sold to the public. The weapon was made for soldiers in a field of war, and they decided to unleash it on the public, who has no training in its use or its ability. And then they act like they had no idea that's what the rifle would be used for." I shook my head. "If that's not negligence, I don't know what is."

I paused a second and glanced back to Garvin again. "So what do we do? What has every other nation done for this problem? Australia had the worst mass shooting in history, up until that point, in 1996. They banned guns. No mass shootings since. Scotland had a school shooting in March of 1996 where sixteen children were killed. They banned guns. No mass shootings since. New Zealand had the worst mass shooting in its history in 1990. They imposed strict gun laws that consisted of interviews with police, mental health checks, background checks, and a national gun registry. They haven't had a mass shooting since. Taiwan had a mass shooting in 1959. They imposed a national gun registry and restricted the sale of firearms, included interviews, random police checks, and inspections every two years. They haven't had a mass shooting since.

"India, Japan, South Korea—restrictions on gun sales and no mass shootings. Thailand, Malaysia, Iceland, Norway, Switzerland . . . the list goes on and on. You would have to be blind"—I looked at Garvin—"or purposely trying to fool people to not see that gun control works to reduce murders."

I stepped forward and leaned on the banister in front of the jury. "Guns are not tools, they're not toys, they're not even for self-defense since a home alarm has been proven in study after study to be more effective at home defense than guns . . . They are weapons meant to murder. And that's all. Tanguich Rifles will argue today that Varvara didn't use the assault rifle how it was intended. Don't buy it for a second. He used that gun exactly how it was intended." I glanced at all of them. "To kill us." I held up Danny's photo again. "To kill him."

I sat down and unbuttoned my suit coat. Melissa was staring off into space. I reached over and gave her arm a squeeze and it seemed to snap her back to the here and now. She blinked a few times and cleared away whatever thoughts she was having. Kelly gave me a slight nod, a sad little grin on her face.

Garvin stood up to his full height. He towered over everybody else there. But his demeanor was different. It wasn't that of the confident giant he had always held himself out to be: he seemed a little slouched, a little humbled. He stood in front of the jury with a shy smile on his face as though he was embarrassed to be there. I looked over the jurors' faces and realized, to my horror, they liked him.

"Randy Miller is a hardworking construction worker in Mesa, Arizona. He has two children, Mark and Vincent, and a wife, Blanche. He and Blanche met in high school and were married shortly after graduation. They have the white picket fence, they vote, they pay their taxes and support the local high school football team, the Mesa Warriors.

"On March fourth of this year, Randy was asleep when Blanche woke him up. She'd heard a noise downstairs. The children's bedrooms were down there. Randy had grown up around guns. He had a gun safe in his closet, like all responsible gun owners do. When he heard the noise himself, he recognized it: someone was walking up the stairs.

"Randy jumped out of bed in the dark, got to his closet, unlocked the gun safe, and he took out his Smith & Wesson pistol. Carefully and quietly he left the bedroom and told his wife to stay in bed. His greatest fear, every responsible gun owner's greatest fear, is that they might accidently shoot a family member, thinking it's a burglar. Doesn't happen often, but it does happen—to those who are untrained and haven't taken the necessary steps to ensure they know when to pull that trigger and when not to.

"Randy slowly makes his way over to the stairs and looks down, and sees two men coming up the stairs. One of them is holding a shotgun. In a moment that must've been pure terror, the men all see each other, and freeze. Time slows down.

"The man lifts the shotgun to fire and Randy fires first. The other man reaches for the nine millimeter he has tucked in his waistband, but Randy, thankfully, is able to fire first.

"Immediately, Randy calls nine one one. The paramedics and police arrive. One of the men passes away but the other lives. The police run their names. A few days later they meet with Randy and inform him that the two men are wanted for murder and multiple home invasions. The last home they entered was that of a young couple, newlyweds. Just twenty-four and twenty-six years old. They pushed their way into the apartment and raped the young wife and made the husband watch, before they shot them both, and stole what little valuables they had. The man who lived confessed to the police that their plan had been to do the same to the Millers . . . including killing their two young sons.

"Ask yourselves, why haven't you heard this story? Arizona is right next door to Utah, and I can't imagine this wouldn't be news here, so why haven't you heard this story? Because our mainstream media has a bias built into it: a bias against our God-given right to own firearms. Mr. Game is right that they don't want you to know the truth, but it's not the truth that Mr. Game thinks it is. They don't want you to know that responsible gun owners save lives—theirs, their families', and other people's."

He took a long pause and walked across the courtroom to right near where the jury was sitting. "My mother was an alcoholic. She did everything she could to stop drinking but it just never happened. The alcohol was too powerful. She drank herself to death . . . and I was the one who found her on the bathroom floor. At first, because I was a child, I blamed alcohol itself. Then, when I became an adult, I realized that it was not the alcohol, but her. Something within her caused that demon to kill her. The alcohol really had nothing to do with it. If it wasn't vodka, it would've been heroin or something else.

"Nathan Varvara was a disturbed young man. But guns, like my mother's alcohol, are not to blame. The demons inside him are what caused this tragedy. To blame guns is to do what I did as a child, and displace my anger." He looked to Melissa. "I'm so sorry for your son, more sorry than you'll ever know." He looked back to the jury and said,

"But guns didn't kill him. Nathan Varvara did. And if he didn't have those guns, it would've been something else. Bombs, or knives, or crossbows. The sick and disturbed can find ways to hurt others without guns.

"This case is not about guns. It's about a lawyer who is using a mother's pain to line his own pockets. You've probably seen Mr. Game's billboards around town. 'The Best Game in Town,' they declare. Best game at what? At getting money from companies that have done nothing wrong. Tanguich Rifles is a family company built on the Second Amendment and our God-given right as American citizens to be armed."

He stepped close to the jury and put his hands softly on the banister. "Don't let the fancy plaintiff's lawyers fool you: this case has *nothing* to do with guns, but with greed. It's about Mr. Game gaining as much from his client's tragedy as he can. Don't let him get away with it. Don't be fooled by the tragedy and heartbreak. He doesn't care one bit about those children. If he did, he would be giving any money he got for this case away, but dollars to doughnuts I'll bet you he's not. Because this case is about one thing and one thing only: money."

He sat back down and the judge said, "Mr. Game, first witness."

69

I asked for a quick break after opening statements. Garvin had done such a good job, I didn't want my first witness to get up there with that opening still in the jury's minds. Kelly and Craig went to the bathroom and I sat on the bench outside the courtroom with Melissa. She said, "That was really good. Everything he said. He almost had me convinced."

I nodded. "It's a basic straw-man argument. You ascribe to the other side arguments they're not really making. The examples he gave were a guy defending his family with a handgun. No one's arguing that handguns should be taken away. Our argument is that if Tanguich Rifles is going to sell military assault weapons, they should bear some responsibility for what lunatics do with them. Garvin doesn't want the jury to frame this case that way. He wants them to frame it as 'They're trying to take away your guns.' It's what every gun manufacturer and lobbyist argues in every case. Don't worry about it, we'll refute all that through the witnesses and in closing statements. Opening is really just to make the other side look bad so the jury has a bias as they hear the evidence."

I glanced over to the bathrooms and saw Kelly come out with the phone glued to her ear. She seemed upset and her voice was raised, though I couldn't quite make out what she was saying.

I sighed and said, "We better get back in there."

My first witness was one of the teachers who initially heard the gunshots. He went up to the bailiff and put his hand on the Bible and the bailiff said, "Do you affirm that the testimony you are about to give is a fair and accurate description of events to the best of your recollection?"

"I do."

He sat in the witness chair. He was a thin guy with bad skin and a mustache that could've been pulled from any '70s movie. I stood at the lectern and said, "Name please."

"Tobias Robert Smith."

"Mr. Smith, where were you on April tenth of this year?"

"I was at work. I work as a sixth-grade teacher at Holladay-Greenville Elementary in Holladay."

"What happened that day?"

He swallowed and glanced at the jury and then back at me. "Well . . . we were out for recess, our first recess break of the day. I was near the playground watching the kids. The teachers alternate who goes out to monitor the children each day. It was my day so I was outside."

"What happened while you were outside?"

"I, um . . . there was nothing until the very end of recess. Then I noticed this guy dressed in black walking onto the school grounds. He got through this hole we have in the fence and walked about halfway across the soccer field. I really didn't think much of it. I mean, he looked so young I thought he was a kid from the high school cutting through. But he had something on his back which, I didn't even . . . I thought it was a musical instrument or something like that. Then he bends down and takes the thing off his back."

"What'd he do after that?"

"He opened it up. It was like a beige sack, a long sack. And he unzips it and pulls out a rifle. Big long thing. I mean huge. I was in the army and I know what the large magazine autos and semiautos look like. I knew it had to be an AR-15 or a BL-24."

"So what were you thinking at this point?"

"Once I knew what it was, I knew what he was going to do. I mean, you can't turn on the news without another school shooting on there. We're really cognizant of that in the school community. After Sandy Hook we paid some of our budget to the county in exchange for a full-time police officer." He inhaled deeply and fidgeted in his seat. "I knew what it was right away."

"What'd you do?"

"I yelled for the kids to run. I grabbed as many as I could and shoved them into the building." He looked down to the floor. "I was running onto the soccer field to get more of the kids when I heard the first gunshot. Just a loud snap that echoed across the school yard." He paused for a long time. "Then the shots really started. He fired at two teachers and hit one. Then I saw when he hit a young girl named Suzanne. She was ten years old. She died at the hospital later that day."

He looked at Garvin, and anger filled his eyes, but he was able to keep it in check and didn't say anything.

"You see Suzanne dying, what do you do then?"

He exhaled loudly and looked up at me. "I don't know. It was really quick. I think I ran out more into the field and pointed as many kids toward the school as I could. The ones playing soccer were farther out. They started running around to the back of the school to get away and he started firing at them." He glanced at Garvin again. "As he walked by the playground, he fired a bunch of shots there. Probably twenty shots. The younger kids were at the playground. The kindergarten class."

"What'd you do when you saw all this?"

He shook his head. Tears came to his eyes. "I . . . I froze."

"What do you mean?"

He shook his head again and was now sobbing. "I saw Suzanne lying there. Her chest was going up and down so quick. That's what got me. Her chest. Her little body was trying so hard to stay alive. She was fighting so hard. I saw her lying there and I heard the gunshots and I froze. It was like I had tunnel vision and couldn't move." Tears streamed down his face and he had to take a few seconds to compose himself. He inhaled deeply and then let it out through his nose.

"What'd you do then, Toby?"

"Umm . . . I ran to Suzanne and I picked her up."

From Craig, I grabbed a large poster board with a photo on it. I placed it on the easel I had set in front of the jury. It was a photo of Toby holding a young girl in his arms. Blood covered his shirt and hands. The girl looked unconscious, her head dangling over Toby's arm.

"This you?"

He nodded. "Yeah," he said, taking a quick glance and looking away. "After I picked her up I ran inside the school. The guy, Varvara, went around the corner and I didn't know if he'd turn around so I needed to get Suzy inside. I ran her in and gave her to the first teacher I saw, Mary."

"Who's Mary?"

"Mary Thomlin. She died during the shooting. But I gave her Suzy and I ran back out. Our school officer, Officer Mitchell, was there directing the children, but he was . . . I don't know. He was scared, terrified. You could see it in his eyes. I don't blame him. When you're in that situation it just . . . you feel like you're in a movie. It doesn't feel real. But after a minute I think we all knew what we had to do. It wasn't something we spoke about, but the officer and I decided we'd rather die than hide and let him keep firing into those kids. So I went around one side of the building and Officer Mitchell went around the other and I heard gunfire. Two sides. They were shooting at each other. Officer Mitchell wouldn't fire much. Just a round here and there, and then you'd hear Varvara's BL-24 and it sounded like the machine gun on a fighter plane. I thought Officer Mitchell was dead. I didn't think he would survive that."

I glanced quickly at the jury. They couldn't take their eyes off Toby, not one of them.

"So what'd you do?"

"I came around and saw Officer Mitchell pinned behind a dumpster. The rounds just kept bouncing off the metal. Varvara was trying to go around the dumpsters to get a better shot. I knew Officer Mitchell wouldn't make it if that happened so I distracted Varvara."

"How?"

"I grabbed a chair that was outside. We had a dance event with some of the younger kids that morning on the lawn. A practice. And not all the chairs had been taken back inside. They were stacked against the wall. I picked up two and tossed them at Varvara. I mean they were just these plastic chairs, they weren't going to do anything to hurt him, but it was enough to piss him off." He looked sheepishly to the jury. "Sorry. Enough to upset him. He left Officer Mitchell and walked toward me."

"What'd you do?"

"I sprinted around the building. I was going to run through the parking lot and away from the school to try to draw his fire away from the kids. I got about halfway to the parking lot when we heard the sirens, and the police arrived." He closed his eyes. "I can't tell you what that felt like. To hear those sirens. To hear that help had come. It was . . . I don't know. I don't know. No other feeling will ever be like the sound of those sirens."

I stepped around the lectern and leaned against it. "Was he still shooting at you?"

"No, he had to reload. But the BL-24 is made for easy reload. It takes like five seconds. It didn't look like he had any firearms training so it took him quite a bit longer, but still only twenty or thirty seconds. Once he was reloaded he knew the police were there. He turned around and fired at the kids that were still outside." Toby's face turned red and his jaw muscles flexed and loosened. "The bastard knew he was done and he just wanted to take as many children with him as he could."

I pretended to shuffle some papers around so that could sit with the jury for a bit.

"He killed seven children and one teacher, and injured another twenty-three children and teachers. Would he have been able to do that in such a short time without the BL-24, using different rifles or handguns?"

"Objection, speculation," Garvin said.

"I'm asking for his opinion as someone with experience in firearms, Judge."

Garvin said, "He hasn't been qualified as an expert in firearms."

"Sustained. Move on, Mr. Game."

I said, "Toby, how quickly did he kill all those people?"

"Couldn't have been more than a few minutes."

"How fast was the gun firing?"

"Nonstop. The only time it stopped was, like I said, when he reloaded. But that was maybe twenty seconds each time. The rifle just kept firing and kept firing. Civilian rifles can't be automatics, they're very difficult to get as a civilian, but they want to sell semiautos that approximate automatics as closely as possible for the people who want automatics without the extensive background checks. So these rifles have really fast firing rates. They're made to take out as many targets as possible within the shortest amount of time."

Garvin stood up, and with that shy smile on his face said, "I'm sorry, Your Honor, but again, the witness is speculating. I'd like to just hear about what happened on that day."

"Sustained."

"No further questions," I said.

I sat down.

Garvin stood at the lectern and loomed over it. He stayed there only a second and then casually came around it and stepped halfway to the witness box. Though he appeared shy and unassuming, he was so tall that stepping closer was clearly a move to intimidate the witness into saying what he wanted him to say. Looking at the jury, I wasn't sure they saw it.

"I'm so sorry," he said. "Mr. Smith, I can't even imagine what you went through. To see that . . . no one should have to see what you saw. Please know that my prayers are with you and your family."

Toby's jaw muscles flexed again but all he said was, "Thank you."

"Mr. Smith, how did Varvara look to you that day?"

"What do you mean?"

"I mean how did he look? Did he look like someone who was unsure of himself? Scared maybe?"

He shook his head. "No. He didn't look scared."

"From the video footage I've seen, he looked confident. Maybe even arrogant, wouldn't you say?"

"Yes, I think that'd be accurate."

"He was determined. No matter what, he was going to kill as many children and teachers as he possibly could, right?"

"I think so, yes."

"In fact you even said when he knew the police were there and it was over for him, instead of running, instead of firing on the police, he immediately turned around and fired at the children that were still outside, correct?"

"Yes, that's correct."

"Someone *that* determined to kill, to the point that they just want to take a few more lives before they die, I mean that person is going to be hard to stop from hurting people, isn't he?"

"I guess."

"Are you aware that after the police searched Varvara's home, they found pipe bombs?"

"I was aware of that, yes."

"Have you ever seen a pipe bomb explode?"

"Yes."

"Describe it."

He shrugged. "I don't know. It was in high school. One of the kids made it and stuck it in a mailbox. It blew it to shreds."

"How far would you say the blast radius was on the one you saw?"

"I don't know. Maybe six feet."

"Would it have hurt or killed anyone in that blast radius?"

"Certainly. It was pretty powerful."

"So a bomb made by a high school kid to blow up a mailbox would've killed people. I think we can imagine that someone like Varvara, who planned this for weeks and wanted to kill as many as he could, I think it'd be fair to say his pipe bombs would've had a blast radius of much larger than six feet, right?"

"I would think so."

"In fact the police bomb technician stated that he would guess they were meant for a blast radius of—"

"Objection, Judge. As Mr. Garvin has pointed out, Mr. Smith is not a firearms expert and certainly not a bomb expert. Also, it's hearsay. The bomb technician is on the witness list and Mr. Garvin is free to call him should he wish."

"Sustained. Move on, Mr. Garvin."

"Do you know how many bombs were found in his house, Mr. Smith?"

"I think nine or ten."

"Ten. Ten bombs," he said, looking at the jury. He turned back to Toby and took a step toward him. "If Varvara had been unable to purchase those firearms, and he had used those bombs instead, he probably would've killed more people, wouldn't he have?"

"Objection."

"Sustained."

"Is it fair to say that if Varvara hadn't been able to purchase firearms, he still would've killed a lot of people?"

Toby swallowed and nodded. "Yes. I think he still would have."

70

The next testimony came from another teacher, and then the vice principal of the school, and then a recess monitor. All of it was the same. Horror, blood, and chaos. But I wanted the jury to feel it. I wanted them to imagine being in the middle of something like that.

I would go through the event with each witness, what they saw, how quickly the deaths occurred because of how quickly the assault weapons were designed to fire, and then Garvin would bring up how Varvara could've killed even without the guns. He was laying the foundation for his closing argument, for his theme of the case, that it wasn't guns that killed people and that psychopaths would find a way to kill no matter what. And that by ruling for Melissa and creating precedent to sue gun manufacturers, all the jury would be doing is punishing legitimate, law-abiding gun owners because psychopaths like Varvara would just buy guns and bombs on the black market.

Our gun expert, a detective with the Salt Lake City Police, a former marine named Alan Kia, laid down our case that the BL-24 and other assault weapons like it were not made for civilian use. They were designed for use by German soldiers in WWII, solely for offense on the battlefield by the frontline infantry. "They're meant to be used for war. Period, end of story."

"Thank you, Detective Kia."

Garvin got up and approached the detective. He stood by the witness box, his giant hand resting on the wood paneling only a couple feet from the detective.

"You ever go out and shoot bottles in the desert or the woods, Detective?"

He nodded. "Sure."

"It's fun, isn't it? At least to most of us."

"Sure, yeah, it's fun."

"You ever shoot them with a rifle?"

"Sure."

"Pistols?"

"Of course."

"Shotgun?"

"Occasionally. Not my favorite weapon, but occasionally."

"Semiautomatics? Or what you called assault weapons?"

He hesitated. Shit.

"Yes," Kia said.

"How many times have you taken out semiautos to shoot?"

"I couldn't say exactly."

"Say approximately, then."

He thought a second. "Maybe . . . fifty."

"Fifty times," Garvin said, glancing at the jury. "You've taken out semiautomatic rifles to shoot, for fun, fifty times."

"Somewhere around there, yes."

"Was what you did dangerous?"

"I mean . . . firearms are always dangerous. It's never a hundred percent safe, but I take the necessary precautions to ensure that I minimize the chance of an injury."

"In other words, you're a responsible gun owner, isn't that right?"

"That is correct."

Garvin took a step back. The guy was masterful. He stayed up close, imposing himself over Kia until he got Kia where he wanted him, and then started easing back so it wouldn't seem to the jury like he was trying to bully him.

"Have you been there when an accident occurred?"

"Yes."

"Tell us about it."

He shrugged and glanced at me and then at the jury before looking back at Garvin. "Nothing really to tell. I was with some friends and one of them wasn't paying attention like he should've been. Was trying to talk on his cell phone while holding a rifle. The rifle slipped from his hands and hit the ground and fired a round. Luckily it was just a twenty-two so it only cut through his foot without serious damage. Just some nerve damage, but nothing serious."

"Well thank goodness he wasn't hurt." Garvin took a few steps toward him again. "What did your friend do right after he was shot?"

"Nothing really. Just said he was shot. Then we wrapped the wound and took him down to the hospital."

"That's all he said, 'I was shot'?"

"Yeah, pretty much."

"He didn't blame the gun for shooting him?"

"No."

"Why not?"

"It wasn't the gun's fault. It was his."

Holy shit.

Garvin looked to the jury. "It wasn't the gun's fault . . . It was his. Thank you, Detective."

The judge looked at me. "Redirect, Mr. Game?"

"Yes, Judge. Thank you."

I stood at the lectern again. "The BL-24. Are you familiar with that model specifically, Detective?"

"Sure am. I own several."

"Tell us its history."

"It was developed at Tanguich Rifles as a competitor to the AR-15. They wanted a rifle that was as powerful but with a higher round capacity along with more ease of use for modification. Fully automatic weapons aren't illegal in the US, most people don't know that, but they are hard to get, so Tanguich wanted a weapon that could be turned into a fully automatic weapon easily."

"Objection," Garvin said. "Speculation. He has no idea what the intention of the creators of that rifle were."

"How do you know this, Detective?" I said.

"I heard it from one of the designers directly."

"Then it's hearsay," Garvin said.

"Mr. Game, response?"

It was completely hearsay, but the jury had already heard it so it didn't really matter to me. "I'll move on, Judge. I just have one more question anyway. So, Detective, in your expert opinion, is the BL-24 safe for public purchase?"

"Absolutely, positively not. It is a military weapon meant for military personnel. I enjoy mine. I love guns, and I love hunting and shooting, but if giving up my assault weapons meant the life of even one child would be saved, I would do it in a heartbeat."

"Thank you, nothing further."

71

We finished the day with the third teacher to testify. A young teacher, just twenty-two, who had since quit the profession. She testified that she had entered therapy, and she and her therapist decided it was best she take time for herself. She had been shot through the wrist and had lost the use of her hand due to tendon and nerve damage.

Court during a trial was not nine to five. The judges packed in as much as they could. By the time the last witness was done, darkness had fallen and I checked my phone. It was ten at night. The judge admonished the jury not to discuss the case with anyone, even their spouses—yeah, right—and not to read about it online—again, ha ha.

Melissa rose and stretched her neck when the jury had left. Garvin sat quietly a moment and then conferred with his team.

"I'm going home," Melissa said, rising. "I'm exhausted."

"Okay," I said. "Just be here at eight tomorrow. It's going to be another long one."

When she'd left, Kelly sat on the edge of the desk and stared at Garvin, who spoke quietly to the jury consultant on his six-man team.

"He's good," Kelly whispered. "Really good. Subtle. He got all those witnesses to say exactly what he wanted them to say."

"I know. They don't teach you how to defeat a guy like that in law school."

"You got in some great testimony. Emotionally, the jury is with you. I'm not sure that's going to be enough, though."

I rubbed my face with my hands. Exhaustion had crept its way up my spine and into my head. A throbbing migraine pounded in my skull. I closed my eyes tightly a second and then opened them again before rolling my head around to stretch my neck. "Too late to do anything about it now."

She nodded and said, "Let's have a late dinner and talk."

"Actually," Garvin said, coming up to us, "why don't we have a late dinner and talk, Peter?"

Despite having dressed down for court today, Garvin, of course, wanted the fanciest restaurant he could think of. A place in Deer Valley, near his home, that served a hundred-and-fifty-dollar steak and forty-dollar mashed potatoes, which came separately. I told him if he wanted to talk, he had to come to my turf.

Guadalupe's was about as much of a Mexican dive as you could find without actually going to Tijuana. But the burritos were out of this world. The type of burritos that melted in your mouth and dripped down your chin in gooey, cheesy goodness. The type of place that Garvin wouldn't be caught dead in.

When we walked in, and those flies were buzzing, and that smell of dirty mop water hit, his face contorted in a mixture of disgust and disbelief. It was the first time I'd seen him not completely in control of his emotions.

"I'll order for us," I said.

The cashier, a little Hispanic lady with a tattoo on her forearm, shouted, "Peter! *Hola!*"

"Hola!"

I gave her a kiss on the cheek and said, "This is my friend Brennen. He's never been here so let's make something extra special for him. What do you think, Maria?"

"Hextra especial, sí."

I left a ten on the counter for the burritos and a ten in the tip jar and led Garvin to a booth. The restaurant was surrounded by thick, bulletproof glass, but you could still see little chips from where a stray bullet, sometime in the past twenty years, had missed its mark and struck. Garvin was staring at the cook, who wasn't wearing gloves, and then looked back at me with an expression that said, *I wish I could punch you in the face right now.*

"I'll get us some salsa," he said.

"I wouldn't hit that salsa bar, man. They don't really replace anything or clean out the bowls. You'll get the Tennessee Two-Step for sure. And it'd be a shame for one of your dozen henchmen to take over the trial."

He exhaled, and with the exhalation, all the tension and disgust seemed to pour out of him, and he was back in control.

"You did well. The jury felt the emotions you were trying to convey. Nonetheless it won't be enough."

I shrugged and looked out the window at the passing traffic. "Maybe, maybe not. We're too far in it now to second-guess, aren't we?"

He folded his gigantic paws in front of him on the table and I noticed how shiny his nails were. Perfectly cut and trimmed, not a speck of dirt or an uneven cuticle anywhere.

"That was a nice touch about the death of your alcoholic mother," I said. "Where is she really? She practice with you?"

He grinned. "Maybe I'm telling the truth. Juries can sense deception much of the time. It's good to open with something genuine."

"You can't bullshit a bullshitter."

He chuckled. "She's an insurance defense lawyer in St. Louis."

"Mine passed away. Bad heart. She was sixty-four, and her father died of the same thing at sixty-four, and his father, my great-grandfather, died at sixty-four of the same thing. I got a couple decades left by my math. And you know how I'd like to spend those years, Brennen? Fighting lost causes. Those are the coolest kind of causes. Anyone can settle or win an easy case, but a case everyone tells you is impossible to win? That no one has ever won before? Well that's just a feather in my fedora, am I right?"

The burritos came. Thick as steel pipes. I picked mine up, steaming hot, and bit into it. As the cheese dripped out, the salsa inside spattered over Garvin and onto his tie.

"Sorry," I said with a mouthful of carne asada.

"It's fine." He took out a handkerchief and dabbed at his tie. "Listen, I came here with a purpose. I'd like to make you an offer."

I shook my head. "Without an apology—"

"Three million dollars."

I choked on the burrito. I went for the water but before I could, Garvin slapped me on the back. It was like getting hit by a bear. The bite of burrito shot out and onto the floor in a globby mess.

"Thanks," I croaked. I took a long drink of water. "Will you say that again, please?"

"Three million dollars. No apology, no more public interviews or discussions. We both walk away."

I drank some more water. "Why would you do that? By my calculation we were neck and neck today with that jury."

He shrugged and said, "Call it an act of charity."

"Yeah . . ."

He rose and buttoned the top button of his suit coat. "You have until before court starts tomorrow to let me know. As soon as the judge steps through those doors, the offer expires, and you will not get another."

He was leaving and I said, "Hey, Brennen?"

"Yes?"

"Can I have your burrito?"

He looked annoyed and turned and left without a word.

72

Kelly met me at Melissa's. I paced back and forth in her living room while they sat calmly and talked. I kept running through the numbers: one-third of three million . . . and then I realized that my representation agreement said that once we went to trial, I got 40 percent of any settlement or verdict. One point two million . . . no. No, I wouldn't take 40 percent from Melissa. A third was good. Enough to pay off everything and retire.

I went out to the porch. I sat down and looked up at the stars. The night air smelled like pines and it was warm and pleasant. The type of night you settle multimillion-dollar cases on. I kept crunching the numbers, not that my brain gave me any choice, and figured, after paying off all my debts, I would have a little more than seven hundred grand left. If I was frugal and worked part-time still, whether in the law or something else, that should last me the rest of my life. If I continued to work full-time but only took the cases I wanted to take, I would live like a king and never have to worry about money again.

As I walked back into the house, a smile permanently affixed to my face, the first thing I heard made my heart stop.

"I don't want it," Melissa said.

"What?" I blurted out.

"I don't want it. Not without a public apology and a public donation to the AnyPerson organization. This is about them taking responsibility."

I stepped closer to her. "Melissa, this is about doing what's best for you. Even after my fee, you would have almost two million dollars. Enough to donate to your anti-gun charity something serious and make sure you never have to work again. And I don't know how GoFundMe works but I bet they wouldn't mind if we donated that money, too."

She folded her arms and shook her head. "I don't care about money. They took my son, Peter."

I bent down so that we were looking in each other's eyes. The hardest part of my job was bringing reality to situations that reality didn't seem to apply to. We'd gotten further than I'd ever imagined with this case, but Garvin was right: we'd lose. This case would make no difference in preventing more of these guns from being sold, no matter how much we wanted it to. To pass up three million dollars and all the good it could do for both of us was crazy.

I said softly, "Nathan Varvara took your son. How much Tanguich had to do with it is debatable, but Melissa, Nathan was the one who pulled that trigger."

Her mouth dropped open. "You don't believe in this."

"Melissa—"

"No, no. All that sympathy you showed me, all that talk about doing the right thing . . . I mean, I knew you were doing this for the money, but I thought you actually believed in it. You don't even believe in this. You think they're not responsible."

"What I think is irrelevant."

"The hell it is. You're my lawyer. *My lawyer*, Peter. You're supposed to be fighting for me."

"I am fighting for you."

"You're fighting for money for a cause you don't believe in." She shook her head. "You're as bad as them."

"How can you say that?"

"Please leave."

"Melissa, don't—"

"Please leave, Peter. I need to be alone and think."

I stared at her a second, and then left the house. Kelly wasn't far behind me. We stood out near my car and I rubbed my temples as she leaned against the car next to me. I could smell her perfume.

"Did you expect her to take it?" she said.

"I did."

"I think it could've been ten million and she'd still turn it down."

"Yeah, well, when an offer like this comes around, you gotta take it. Everybody's just getting by in life and money like this can make sure you're set. You become one of the few lucky ones in one signature of a check." I put my hands on my hips and stared at the house. "I'll give her until morning and then I'm going to tell her she has to take it."

"Why? It won't change her mind. This isn't about money to her."

"It's always about money," I said louder than I would've liked. "It's always about money. And this is enough. It's a good offer, more than we deserve."

She shook her head. "It doesn't make sense. The case went fine for them today. Not a slam dunk but not a guaranteed loss either. There's no reason for them to make an offer like this."

"Their jury consultant probably recommended they settle. Consultants are full of shit, but if they tell Garvin to settle and he doesn't and loses big, I'm guessing his partners aren't going to be very pleased."

"Yeah, maybe."

I glanced up at the stars. The light pollution in Salt Lake City was getting bad enough that most nights you couldn't see very many.

I remembered as a kid that the sky was always clear and bright, but it didn't look that way anymore.

"You really serious about that guy?"

"Joey? Why?"

"He seems . . . not your type. Too safe."

"Oh, no, Peter, you don't get to criticize anybody, and you certainly don't have the right to discuss my love life. I'm on this case for Melissa, not for you, so let's just stick to talking about that."

"Bullshit."

"What?"

"You heard me. You feel it, too. We're not finished."

She took a step toward me and said, "We were finished the second you broke my heart."

She went to her car. I watched as the headlights disappeared into the darkness.

"Shit!" I shouted. "Shit, shit, shiiiiiitttttttt!"

73

On the drive home I got a call from Craig.

"Yeah," I said.

"Hey, it's Craig."

"Yeah, Craig, I have your number in my phone for crap's sake. What's up?"

"Where are you?"

"Driving."

There was a pause. "Um . . . I got some bad news."

"It couldn't possibly be worse than mine: Melissa doesn't want to take the deal."

"Three million?"

"Yeah, three million."

"Um, well, this kind of pertains to that. I have a friend that clerks for the Tenth Circuit. We've been chatting about this case the past couple weeks. He sent me a text that a decision is coming down in two days that's relevant to this. He emailed me an advanced copy. You need to read it."

"I'll read it tomorrow after court. My head's not exactly in the game right now."

"Peter, you better read it."

"I'll read it when I get home then."

"No, I think you should pull over and read it now. I'll email it to you."

"Ugh, fine. It better be worth it."

I pulled the car over and waited for the email. The Tenth Circuit Court of Appeals was the federal appellate court that handled many of the Western states, like Colorado, Utah, and New Mexico. It was one step down from the United States Supreme Court, and when the Tenth Circuit spoke, every lawyer in the Mountain West listened. It was binding authority on the judges here and what they said was set in stone until the United States Supreme Court had their say. The fact that Craig got an advanced copy of a decision was unethical, but clerks proofed the opinions and the decisions had a way of slipping out a few days beforehand to parties that might have an interest in the cases. Mostly it was about money. If someone had a huge investment in a tract of land and the court was going to come out with a decision that wasn't favorable, miraculously, the land would be sold a few days before the decision was published. Of course, it was always the super-rich that just happened to be so lucky. Never guys like me. Except apparently now.

The email came. The case was *Cortez v. Sagan Chemical.* Sagan was a successful entrepreneur who owned a chemical production company making formulas for toothpaste and other similar items for bigger companies. They had made a type of nitroglycerin, advertised as a quick solution for getting rid of large rocks and trees in people's yards. The nitro was extremely potent, much more potent than anything anyone could buy before its release, and designed for serious landscaping and stone work.

A man named Guillermo Cortez had used the nitro to blow up his wife's car with his wife in it. She survived, because Cortez had put it in the trunk and she was in the driver's seat, but had third-degree burns over a quarter of her body. She filed suit against Sagan Chemical, saying that they had been negligent in advertising the sale of a product that it was foreseeable could've been used by someone to cause harm. Negligent entrustment. The same argument we were using.

Uh-oh.

I quickly skipped to the end of the case, the holding, the portion in which the judges made their ruling. My stomach was doing backflips and I held my breath.

> *We find neither proximate nor real cause in the sale of Sagan's product, nor in its advertising. No matter how dangerous a product, the manufacturer cannot be held liable for every foreseeable or unforeseeable event in the chain of use. After all, even a fork could cause enormous harm if used the wrong way. And advertising a product is a normal business practice that should not lead to punishment of the advertiser simply because a deranged individual takes it upon himself to use the product for harm.*

Oh man. This was bad. I called Craig.

"What the hell? When did you get this?"

"Just now. I called you right when I read it."

"This is a disaster. When does it get published?"

"Two days. But I mean, we're already in trial, right? Because the case came out after the trial started, they can't use it, right?"

"They can use it. If Garvin reads this he can say there's been a substantial change in the pertinent law. He can file an interlocutory appeal directly to the Utah Supreme Court and then the Tenth Circuit if he doesn't get what he wants there. When you file an interlock, it freezes the trial. I mean, when it resumes, we'll have the same jury and pick up where it left off, but he'll win on this. These are almost the exact same facts as ours, and it's even worse because guns are so prevalent."

"So . . . what does this mean?"

"It means if we don't settle or win this trial by the day after tomorrow, we're sunk."

74

Two days . . . two days.

I kept running that through my head as I drove home. *Two days . . . two days . . .*

Maybe not even two days. I had no idea what time the case would be released on the day of publication. If it was in the morning, maybe one of Garvin's goons would pick up on it and file the interlock that day. If it came out in the evening after court, they would certainly find it and file the interlock that night. I might have only a day. I absolutely *had* to get Melissa to take the three million. If I had to beg on my knees I would. In fact, I should call Garvin right now and tell him we would take it to lock it into place and then talk to Melissa about it afterward. After I explained the Sagan case, there's no way she wouldn't see my side of it.

I glanced in my rearview and saw the cop that had been following me for a while. I quickly ran through the checklist that everyone runs through when a cop is following them: Registration valid? Check. Correct address on license? Check. No booze in the car? Check. No booze in my system? Check.

I decided it was just a coincidence about a second before his lights turned on.

Well a ticket would be the icing on the cake to this day.

The officer took a minute in his car and then came up to me with the flashlight glaring.

"How are you, sir?"

"Good, Officer. How are you?"

"License, proof of insurance, and registration, please."

I handed him the docs. He returned to his car and then came back a minute later and handed them back to me.

"Any drugs or weapons in the car, Mr. James?"

"No."

"You certain about that? I'm smelling an odor of marijuana."

"What? No, I don't smoke pot."

"Step out of the car please, sir."

"Hey, hey, listen, I'm an attorney, and I'm giving you my word that I don't smoke pot. There is no pot in this vehicle."

"Then you won't mind if I give it a quick search?"

"If it gets me outta here quicker, then no, knock yourself out."

I went over to the curb and sat down while he searched my car. A few minutes into it another officer came and helped him. They stopped near the back seat for a while and then the original officer strutted over to me with a small baggie of a green leafy substance.

"What the hell is that?" I said.

"You tell me."

"I have no idea."

"Really? It was under the driver's seat of your car."

"What?" I said with a laugh. "There's no way—"

Holeee shit.

I started laughing. I was laughing so hard it hurt.

"Holy shit, Officer. Holy shit he's brilliant."

"Who?"

"Three million," I mumbled through my laughter. "Three million my ass! He had no intention of giving us anything. He knew I'd be desperate to take it and rush over here. They just wanted to make sure they knew where I was so they could toss that into my car." I was laughing so hard now I was crying.

"You alright, Mr. James? Do you need medical attention?"

I waved my hand, indicating I just needed a minute.

When the laughing subsided, I said, more to myself than anyone else, "He is one dazzling son of a bitch. This was genius. I'm not even mad. I'm more impressed." I wiped away some tears and said, "I'm really tired, Officer, and this day has been one of the shittiest I've ever had. Can I just get my citation and go, please?"

"I'm afraid we're going to have to take you in, Mr. James."

"What? For a little bit of pot?"

"We see that you have another pending case. It's our policy when someone has a pending case if they get another misdemeanor to take them in. We can't just issue you a citation."

"What pending case?"

"A disorderly conduct out of the Salt Lake County Justice Court."

"Oh . . . right. That. It's just an infraction, though."

"Sorry, policy is policy. Please stand up and put your hands behind your back."

75

I'd been booked into jail once before for mooning a cop while I was drunk in college. Granted, I didn't remember much about it other than that the place smelled like urine. The scent hadn't changed in all those years.

Processing—taking my photo and fingerprints—ate up only about twenty minutes. Then they gave me the orange jumpsuit and slippers with no laces. I was led back to a cell to await assignment to another cell, and there was a tall white guy with a gray beard that ran down to his belly sitting on a bench. I could smell the alcohol coming from him from across the cell.

"Them bastards get ya when ya least expect it, don't they?"

I nodded. "They sure do, old timer."

I was in the cell maybe an hour before the guard came and got me. I was given a towel, a toothbrush, and a small bar of soap, and led out into the general population of the Salt Lake County Metro Jail.

One guy whistled. I was flattered.

The new cell was small and dingy and the bars were rusted and chipping. The cement floor had a drain and the toilet looked like it hadn't been cleaned in about a year. I sat on the cot and put my head into my hands and stared at the rusted drain in the floor.

I was there awhile before a guard came and said my attorneys were here. The officer had been nice enough to let me make a phone call before arresting me. The guard led me out to the visiting room, which was steel benches on both sides of a thick glass partition. Melissa and Craig sat on the other side.

"What happened?" Melissa asked.

"Brennen Garvin happened. They planted pot in my car and called the police on me."

"What? They can't do that. We'll go to the judge."

"It's my word against theirs. That's not why I asked you here, Melissa. The offer, the three million, isn't real. They just wanted me somewhere they knew they could find me, and they knew I'd rush over to your house with the offer and then they could call the cops when I left. I don't know if I'm going to miss the trial tomorrow and Kelly will have to take over, but I wanted you to hear it from me. I've decided I need to withdraw from your case. This is . . . way over my head. These guys don't play like anyone I've ever seen. So, as soon as I can get ahold of her, I'm going to tell Kelly to withdraw us and ask the judge to give you time to find other attorneys."

She was silent a long time. "If you think that's best."

"I do. You should know there's a case coming out of a higher court in two days that destroys us. Your next attorney is going to have to deal with that. They'll have to try to show that the new case is substantially different from this one. I just don't have the juice to keep going and do that. I'm so sorry. I'm sorry . . . for everything."

She nodded. "It doesn't feel right."

"Life usually doesn't."

She swallowed and her eyes glistened with tears. "Goodbye, Peter."

When she left, Craig and I watched until the steel door slammed shut. Craig turned to me and said, "I hate to do this right now, Peter, but I just want to get it over with. You know I like you and I've liked my time working for you. I've learned a lot . . . but I think I need to get another job. The case is over so there's really no reason for me to stick around."

"What're you talking about?"

"You don't have enough work to justify a clerk. I was here just for this case and it's done."

I thought for a second. "I was hoping you'd stick around for other cases."

He shook his head, and I got the impression he didn't think there would be other cases given where he was talking to me right now. "You don't need me anymore."

He rose and left without another word, leaving me staring at my reflection in the glass.

76

When I was taken back to my cell, someone else was there. A little Hispanic guy sipping on a Sprite and lying down on a cot.

"How's it goin'?" he said.

"Shitty. How about you?"

He chuckled. "Stupid question, I guess, huh?"

I sat down on the cot across from his. "If we were smart, we wouldn't be in here, right?"

He laughed and set his drink down. "You look like I seen you before. You famous?"

"No."

"But I seen you, right?"

"I'm on some billboards and on the back of the phone book. Probably there."

He grinned. "That's right. You got a billboard near them trailer parks in Taylorsville. I like them billboards, they funny."

I sighed and lay down, staring at the ceiling. "What are you here for?"

"DUI. You?"

"Pot. Is it laughable if I tell you I was set up and didn't do it?"

"Yeah, man, I was set up, too. So was everybody in here. Ain't no one guilty of anything."

"Yeah . . ."

He swung his legs around and said, "You know how you got that cot, right?"

"How?"

"My cellie that was in here, Chuck. He died."

"No shit?"

He nodded. "Had a heart attack right where you lyin'. Barely got his body outta here before they stuck you in. Ain't that shit? You die and they just pull you out and stick someone else in your place."

The cell door slid open. I looked up. Standing at the entryway . . . was Dane Howick. The ass grabber that I'd gotten demoted to the jail staff.

"Of course," I said. "I forgot about you, Howick. You're very forgettable, you know."

He stepped inside the cell, a grin on his face, as he said, "Umberto, go grab a drink."

"I already got one."

"Go grab another one."

Umberto looked between the two of us and then left. Howick stepped closer to me and said, "I told you to watch your ass. Now you're in my house."

"I'm not in the mood, Howick. You wanna hit me, go ahead and just get it over with. I just wanna go to sleep." I stood up and faced him. "Go ahead, take your best shot."

"No, I think you're gonna take your best shot."

"I'm not hitting you, man. Just hurry this up so I can get some sleep."

"You're gonna have to hit me, Counselor."

"I'm not hitting you."

Howick glanced out of the cell, and then popped me in the nuts with his retractable baton. It stung like getting them caught in barbed wire. He struck again, and even though my hands were guarding the goods, it still felt like my testicles had popped. I felt ill and it knocked the breath out of me. He struck again and puke came up into my throat.

"Only way this is stoppin' is if you hit me. Go ahead, Counselor. I won't even put up a fight. Let's see if you got the balls." As he said "balls" he struck me again and I toppled over onto the cot. He lifted the baton to strike me again and as he did I slammed my fist into his groin. Shouldn't have done it, knew I'd pay for it, but it was still worth it.

It sent him sprawling onto the other cot, his face turning bright red, fury in his eyes. He clicked the little radio strapped to his shoulder and said, "We got a three nineteen in D four."

He hit the ground, holding his balls, just as two other guards ran in. They saw him, looked at me, and I could see exactly what they were thinking.

"Fellas, it's not what you—"

They pulled out their batons and jumped on me like leopards on a fat warthog.

77

Administrative segregation was where they kept inmates considered too dangerous to keep anywhere else. The psychopaths, the murderers, the people who didn't know the difference between reality and imaginary worlds. Among them was me, Peter Game, attorney-at-law. The Best Game in Town.

Ad Seg didn't have windows or even bars to look through. It was a brick room with a bucket in the corner and a dirty sink and faucet attached to the wall. The guards tossed me in, after a few more good shots in the stomach and groin. Places that wouldn't leave much evidence they'd roughed me up. My balls and stomach were on fire, and I just crawled over to the wall and leaned my head back against the brick and closed my eyes.

I don't know how long I slept until one of the guards woke me up with a kick. I looked up at him and he said, "You got a visitor. Your attorney."

I rose to my feet without asking any questions and let him lead me out of the cell. He took me down a labyrinth of hallways before we ended up somewhere with a table and two chairs, the attorney-client contact room. Kelly sat across from me, wearing a hoodie. She had no makeup on, and I could see the tattoo of my name on her wrist. It wasn't covered. I sat down.

"You okay?"

I shrugged. "I been better."

"Craig called me. Said he was worried about you."

"Little shit quit on me. I didn't think he would care."

"Well he does. We all do."

"Even you?"

She looked down to the table, twirling a bracelet in her fingers. "Melissa gave me your message. I'm not withdrawing from the case."

"You're gonna do it by yourself?"

"No, you're going to do it."

"Yeah, right," I scoffed. "Kelly, look at me. I'm in freaking jail. My entire life I've been chasing a case like this, and never once did I consider what the price would be. I didn't realize I wouldn't have what it takes to win. And so this is my lot: just barely getting by, just like my dad, working himself to death. That's my portion in life. To bust my ass, never quite make ends meet, and then die from it." I shook my head. "I'm no one to waste your time on. Go be with Joey and tell Craig good luck. Forget about me."

She stared at me a second. "Do you remember when you were a law clerk at Corey's, when I worked there the first time? I remember you getting a case, a divorce. The woman was afraid her husband was going to hurt her when he found out about the divorce. You were supposed to turn those cases over to your supervising attorney, me, but you didn't. You paid the deposit and first month's rent on an apartment for her and then drafted the divorce petition. You remember that?"

"Yeah. So?"

"So you blew your money for the month on that. I remember you couldn't even eat and I had to bring sandwiches to work so you would actually have some food." She twirled the bracelet. "You didn't have a dime, and I'd never seen you so happy. Do you remember?"

I sat quietly a second. "What's your point?"

"My point is that it doesn't matter if you're rich or if you're just getting by. You're so scared of just getting by because you think you saw your father die from it, but guess what, Peter? Most people are just getting by, and they're happy. It doesn't matter if you're just getting by because this life is all we got, and it's a gift. Every day is a gift. And I think, when you spent every penny you had on that woman who didn't have anyone else to turn to, I think you knew that. You forgot it along the way, but I think you knew it then."

I felt a lump in my throat and had to swallow to keep it down. I held out my hands in front of her and said, "I can't . . . I can't even help myself, Kelly. How the hell am I supposed to help anyone else?"

"You found a way to help that woman, and you'll find a way to help Melissa, too. Because that's who you really are. Not that guy on the billboard." She hesitated. "Not the guy who rips out the heart of the person they care most about without even having the courage to look them in the eye while they do it. That's not who you are, not really."

I couldn't look at her so I looked down at the table. Tears came to my eyes. An overwhelming sense of something went through me, and it felt heavy and uncomfortable. Like putting on a thick, itchy wool sweater. It was shame.

"I was scared."

"Peter, you don't owe me anything."

"The hell I don't. I was scared. I loved you so much . . . so damn much, that the thought of you being with me didn't even make sense. I thought that I didn't deserve it and that it would be taken away from me. So I figured it was better to not even be in that spot. I'd had it happen once, out of the blue, with Jollie. And I didn't love her a tenth as much as I did you. I knew if you took off one day, too, and never came back, it would break me. I thought it was better I just end it quickly." I looked in her eyes. "I thought it was a good idea then, and now, when it's too late, I realize it was the worst mistake of my life."

We sat quietly awhile and she said, "What're you going to do? You going to stay in here or are you going to try to find a way to be in that trial tomorrow?"

I swallowed and looked at the guard, who wasn't even paying attention to us but was playing a game on his phone. "Call Jake. He knows the screening prosecutor at the DA's office. Tell him to call in a favor and get my bail set tonight. Like right now, as soon as he can, and then put up the money. Tell him I'll pay him back tomorrow. And then call my investigator and tell him I need the address for Jamal Williams."

78

I was out of jail within three hours. Jake was waiting for me outside, his hair a mess, still wearing his silk pajamas. He was on his phone, and when he saw me he said, "You look like shit."

"I need you to drive me somewhere."

"It's like five in the morning."

"Trial starts at eight. I gotta go now. Please, please, please, please, please—"

"Okay, okay. Man, you're worse than a toddler. I gotta hit Starbucks first then."

We grabbed two coffees and headed to Magna to the address my investigator had texted me when I got out of jail. Magna was little more than factories and fields, but at five in the morning, with hardly anyone out, it was peaceful and quiet. The sun was breaking over the mountains.

"I really appreciate this, Jake. How much did you have to pay in bail?"

"Just a few hundred bucks. Don't worry about it. So you really got set up, huh?"

I nodded. "I got played like a fiddle."

"Dude's that good?"

"Better. Never seen anything like it."

"Well, shit. Glad it's not my case then."

After a few turns, we were there. The home was white and two stories with a yellowed lawn and a run-down Lincoln in the driveway. I got out and told Jake to wait there. I knocked and it took a while, but finally a woman in a blue robe answered.

"Hi, um, I need to speak to Jamal Williams please."

"And who is you?"

"I'm an attorney-at-law, ma'am. It's very important I speak to him. He's been involved in something very serious and this couldn't wait. I'm sorry for waking you, but we have a deadline to keep and I need to speak to him immediately."

She stared at me a second and then said, "Wait here."

I turned and looked at Jake, who was sucking on a latte, and a voice said, "I'm Jamal. Who are you?"

I turned around. He was just a kid. No older than seventeen or eighteen.

"You're Jamal Williams?"

"Yeah."

His mother stood behind him a few feet and I said, "Let's talk out here in private. You're not going to want your mom to hear this."

He glanced back at her and then stepped out onto the porch with me. When he shut the door, he said, "Yeah, so, who are you?"

"I'm an attorney suing Tanguich Rifles for that mass shooting at Holladay-Greenville. You know the one, right? You sold the shooter his guns."

His eyes went wide and he took a step back, and I thought he might make a run for it.

"I'm not here for you. I don't give a shit that you sold him the guns. But I know you're the scarecrow. You're the guy who buys the guns legally and then sells them to people like Nathan Varvara. Well, I'm going to level with you, Jamal: I'm getting my butt kicked. I'm up against people who will do anything to screw the little guy, guys like you and me and him." I held up a photo of Danny that Melissa had given me from their home. "He died on his bike with his teacher covering his body. They both died."

He looked away from the photo. "Yeah, I heard about it."

"Well I need your help. I got nothing else, Jamal. If you can't help me I'm done, and these guys are gonna get away with it. Over and over again." I held up the photo once more. "He was seven, Jamal. Seven."

He looked at me and folded his arms. "What you need?"

"Run down for me how it works. How do you get the guns and get them to people like Varvara?"

He took a deep breath and glanced at Jake, then said, "I'll get the fliers when they havin' a sale. Then I just go down and pick up what I can. I got a clean record so don't take long. Then I post on Craigslist and we get 'em out. Sometimes the cops try to bust us but we just set up drops and they sell out so quick we ain't never been busted. That dude, Varvara, paid the money into my PayPal and I left the guns for him behind a dumpster near the Denny's. That was it. He coulda got the guns himself at a gun show but he said he wanted them quick, didn't want to wait. So, I mean, it weren't really illegal what I did since he could buy them himself."

"Wait, what fliers? What are you talking about?"

"The fliers. They put out these fliers at the Y when there's a sale."

"Who does?"

He shrugged. "I don't know. Just whenever they got a sale on guns they put out them fliers. They got 'em all over. At the Y, they down by the liquor store, sometimes they down at the strip club, places like that."

"You got one of these fliers here?"

He shook his head. "No, but they probably got 'em down at the Y."

79

Jake, despite being a little stoned, drove me down to the local YMCA in Taylorsville. We went inside and I asked the young girl behind the front counter where the bulletin board was to post ads.

"Right over there when you're going into the locker rooms."

Where she pointed, there was a massive corkboard with fliers and advertisements all over it. Jake and I scanned the thing from top to bottom. Near the right lower corner was a red flier with a big, bold, all-caps **FIREARMS SALE!** written across the top. I plucked it off.

It held a list of the firearms for sale: 9 millimeter, shotgun, TEC-9 . . . BL-24. The ad didn't say who it was by, but they were all Tanguich-made weapons.

"Jake," I said, barely able to get the words out, "look."

He looked at it. "It's an ad for the guns. I don't get what your point is."

"Why would they put out an ad like this? Fliers for guns at the YMCA? How many hard-core hunters you think they have here? What they do have in this area is a lot of poverty. The type of poverty that creates a lot of drug dealers and scarecrows. If you were trying to reach people like that, a flier right here would be perfect for it. And look at the retailer, Tom's Firearms. I know that place, they specialize in Tanguich firearms. Especially the rifles."

"So you think that's an ad from Tanguich?"

"Jamal said they advertise at the Y, the liquor store, strip clubs . . . They're placing them intentionally in poorer areas to find scarecrows to buy guns, so they can get around the laws preventing felons from getting them. The bastards found a way to get around the law."

Jake looked down at the flier. "I am way too stoned for this shit."

I sat in Craig's dorm room. He read the flier and I explained to him what Jamal said. He shook his head and said, "That's just some evil right there."

"I need your help, Craig. That ruling comes down tomorrow, and I have no idea when. Garvin's the best I've ever seen. No way he doesn't have a team of people who will get notice the second that case is published, and we'll be done. I can't do this without you."

He thought for a second and looked down to the carpet. There was a stain by his feet and he rubbed it with his toe. "Remember when you asked me if I believe in it? The Satanism?"

"Yeah."

"I don't. Not for a second. You just fall into this thing where you've believed something for so long that it's like, comfortable, you know?"

"I know. I was there, too, until someone reminded me that you don't have to be stuck there. Is that why you quit?"

He nodded. "You get told you're a loser enough times and you start to believe it. I just wanted to make sure that I would get a job and . . . just be a good lawyer. Just get that job and—" He stopped a second. "And that my dad would see it. He'd see I made it."

"That's not making it, man. If you're miserable, you haven't made it. You've fallen right into their trap. You got close to fifty years of work left. You really wanna be doing something you hate? That's just condemning yourself to fifty years of misery. Do you really want to sit in the back of a law firm and write memos and briefs while everybody else gets the credit, or do you want to be the one making the moves and helping people? The reason, I'm willing to bet, you actually went to law school and not into science is because you get to help people directly. Am I wrong?"

He shook his head. "No." He exhaled loudly and took out a candy bar from his pocket. "What do you need me to do?"

80

It was nearly seven in the morning when I showed up at Melissa's door. I handed her the flier and told her about Jamal. She had to sit down.

I said, "We think they did this on purpose. It's the only thing that makes sense. If it was on purpose, the sale of the guns to Varvara wasn't reckless or negligent on their part. They sold to scarecrows so they could get around the laws barring certain people from owning guns. That's knowingly and intentionally violating the law. We're talking criminal charges, not just money anymore. This is it. We got 'em, Melissa."

She looked up at me. "And that boy's going to testify?"

"Yeah. He seemed as shaken up as anybody about the shooting, so maybe this is his way of doing penance. Garvin can object because he's not on our witness list, but judges don't like excluding people because of notice. I think I can get him on that stand. But we only got today and maybe some of tomorrow. There's that case I told you about coming down from a higher court that is going to destroy our arguments. This helps, but it's not guaranteed. Garvin can get the trial delayed while he files an appeal saying there's new pertinent law that the court needs to consider, so this trial has to wrap up today or tomorrow, and I think Jamal can do it. After they hear his testimony, and yours, I think they're going to make another offer. A real offer, with an apology and maybe we'll ask for a fund set up in Danny's honor helping victims of gun violence. Everything you wanted."

"I don't want to testify."

"Melissa, we talked about this."

She shook her head. "I'm sorry, Peter. I can't do it. I can't get up there and talk about it. I thought I could but I can't."

"Well, I mean, Jamal is probably going to be enough. Once they know that we know about the fliers, they should make the offer. And even if they don't, if we get his testimony down, the appellate court is going to read the transcript. It'll help us a lot, but I think, with this bombshell, they've got to settle this and make sure it doesn't get out to the news."

"That's crazy, right? They're so powerful they don't need to do any of it."

I pointed to the flier. "If this is real, can you imagine what the headlines would say?" I shook my head. "No way. We get Jamal up there and we introduce this flier, they're gonna settle. Even if it's not true and they had nothing to do with this flier, the appearance of it looks so bad they'll have to make an offer. But like I said, it's gotta be quick. I got Craig on a flight to Denver to visit a buddy of his at the Tenth Circuit and beg him to delay the publication of the case another day or two, but who knows if it's going to work. It's now or never." I bent down to eye level with her. "Do you trust me?"

She nodded.

"Then trust me now. We can still win this thing."

81

I didn't have time to go home and change, and the jail had wrinkled my clothes, so I stopped at a Target by the court and bought a suit off the rack that kind of fit. I met Kelly and Melissa there. When I walked into the courtroom, Garvin smirked. As I sat down he said, "Rough night?"

"You could say that."

The judge came out, the bailiff announced him, and we all stood. Once the computer was booted up, he said, "Any issues that need to be addressed, gentlemen?"

"None, Judge."

"No, Your Honor."

"Alright, then let's bring out the jury."

The jury filed in and we remained standing. I looked at each of their faces, trying to glean something from them, but I never could. They hid themselves well. Once they were seated, Judge Pearl said, "Next witness, Mr. Game."

"The plaintiff would call Jamal Williams to the stand."

Jamal, who'd been seated in the back, headed to the front of the courtroom. Garvin's team immediately began another huddle and one of them whispered something in Garvin's ear. He shook his head and dismissed them with a wave. Then he leaned back in his seat, putting his prodigious hands across his stomach as he calmly watched Jamal get sworn in and take the stand. No objection. I mean, there'd be a recess while we argued it, and the judge might allow him time to interview Jamal, so why not make the objection? I could only assume he felt the trial was going so well he didn't want to break to interview a witness he thought wasn't going to impact the outcome.

"Name?"

"Jamal Williams."

"Jamal, you know why we're here, right?"

He nodded. "Yeah, it's about that shooting at the elementary school."

"That's right. The shooting carried out by Nathan Varvara on April tenth, correct?"

"Yeah."

"And what's your relation to that shooting?"

He hesitated, looking once to the judge and to the jury and then said, "I sold that dude the guns."

A couple whispers went up in the courtroom behind me, though I couldn't tell from who. I glanced back at Melissa and Kelly at the plaintiff's table and then looked at Jamal.

"When you say 'that dude,' you mean Nathan Varvara, right?"

"Yes."

"How'd you get the guns?"

"They advertise them to us. They put up these fliers at the YMCA by my house when they got a sale, and I just go down and buy the guns. They look at my license and I get 'em right away. Nathan wanted the guns fast so he didn't want to wait for a gun show, and he told me he didn't want to buy them from a store 'cause of how expensive they is. He was gonna buy them online but a friend of mine told him 'bout me. I buy 'em on sale from them fliers and then sell 'em cheap."

"May I approach the witness, Your Honor?"

"You may."

I showed the flier to Garvin before I headed up. No reaction from him, but the five people directly behind him looked like they were about to crap their pants.

"What is this?" I said, showing the flier to Jamal.

"That's one of the fliers."

"Your Honor, we'd move to introduce plaintiff's exhibit, I believe twenty-six, into evidence."

"Any objection, Mr. Garvin?"

"None."

I held the flier up to the jury. "And what does this flier say, Jamal?"

"It says there's a sale on them guns. So I go out and bought 'em and I met that dude, Nathan, through my friend, and I sold him the guns. He told me he was a hunter and was going hunting for deer. I didn't think nothin' of it. If I would've known I would've thrown them guns in the garbage."

"What's a scarecrow, Jamal?"

"It's someone that buys guns and sells them."

"Are you a scarecrow?"

He hesitated. "I guess you could say that, yeah. But I just done it a few times."

"Who does a scarecrow sell guns to?"

"I mean . . . anybody, but that's not really our customers."

"Who are your customers?"

He was quiet. I looked at him. This was it. This was the question. If he said he sold the guns to people who couldn't normally buy them, like felons, Tanguich would be sunk. If he said that his customers were just normal gun buyers, I wouldn't be able to show that Tanguich was getting around the laws. I had told Jamal that if he were charged with a felony, I would defend him for free. Reluctantly, he'd agreed to testify. I couldn't imagine he was sleeping well after seeing the carnage his sale had led to.

"Our customers are people that can't buy guns. People that have felonies. That's why they advertise with these fliers. So those people can get guns."

"Objection," Garvin said, rising to his feet.

Before the judge could rule on the objection, I said, "You're telling me Tanguich Rifles advertises at places like the YMCA on purpose to get scarecrows to buy guns, so they can get them into the hands of people the law has said can't own them?"

"Mr. Game," the judge said, "I haven't made my ruling on the objection."

I glanced back at the jury. I was worried they wouldn't quite get the link, wouldn't quite connect the dots. I hoped to hell they had.

"No need, Your Honor. I withdraw the questions." I paced a second. "Where did you go to buy the guns?"

"This place called Tom's."

"Tom's Firearms in Taylorsville, right?"

"Right."

"What type of guns do they sell there?"

"They only sell them guns I sold to that dude, Tanguich guns. They um, a distributor or somethin'."

"So these fliers go up at the YMCA to come down to Tom's Firearms, and Tom's Firearms only sells Tanguich guns."

He nodded. "Yup. They the only type of gun they sell there."

I debated for a second and then took the shot. "I know Tom's, they only got Tom and his wife that work there, right?"

"Yeah, I think so."

"Tom ever say he posted these fliers?"

"Objection, hearsay."

"Goes to state of mind, Judge. We need to understand Jamal's thinking when he purchased these guns, and the person selling them to him—what they said, what they did, what their intent was—massively influenced that."

"I'll allow it."

I turned back to Jamal. "Did Tom ever say he posted these fliers?"

He shook his head. "Nah. I don't think it was him doin' it. One time I had a flier with me and his wife looked all surprised and shi— and stuff. She didn't know nothin' about it. She said the gunmakers sometimes advertise without telling them when they got too much inventory."

I could've kissed Jamal right there.

I glanced to the jury again and said, "I tender the witness, Judge."

I left the flier near the jury, and sat down as Garvin buttoned his suit coat and approached Jamal.

82

Garvin approached slowly. He stood in front of Jamal at his full height. He stared at the boy a few seconds and then smiled. My phone kept buzzing: it was Craig trying to reach me. I turned it off.

"Who really made those fliers?" Garvin said.

"The company, man. The gun company. Y'all make those fliers so people like me buy the guns."

"Are you sure?"

"Yeah."

Garvin strolled to the defense's table and opened his briefcase. He came out with several fliers. He showed them to me; they were all identical to the flier I had.

Garvin then asked to approach the witness. He went back to Jamal and laid them in front of him. Jamal looked up at Garvin and then back down to the fliers.

"How'd you get this?" Jamal said.

"You recognize them then? Please tell the court what they are."

He was quiet a long time. "I don't know."

"You know it's a felony to lie to a court, don't you? Felony perjury. It's a second-degree felony. So I'm going to ask you again what these are, and if you lie, I'm going to prove you lied, right here, on the record. And I'm going to ask the judge to take you into custody. Do you understand, Jamal?"

He closed his eyes. "They're fliers."

"Whose fliers?"

He swallowed. "Mine."

"What do you mean?"

"I made them."

"You made them," he said, looking to the jury. "And you also made that one that Mr. Game just introduced, didn't you?"

He looked to me, as though to say he was sorry. "Yes."

Mumbles went up in the courtroom again, and Kelly leaned toward me and said, "What the hell is going on?"

"I have no idea," I whispered. My heart had begun ramping up, my throat dry, my hands starting to shake. I felt like I was on a roller coaster.

"You need to object," Kelly said.

I stood up. There was technically nothing to object to. So I just said, "Objection . . . speculation."

"About what?" Garvin said.

"About the fact of the fliers coming from him."

Those sounded like words coming out of my mouth. Good enough.

The judge gave me a quizzical look and said, "Overruled."

"You made these fliers yourself, to distribute around these places and raise interest for these guns."

Jamal couldn't look him in the eyes. "Yes."

"And the reason it doesn't say Tanguich Rifles on any of these fliers is because they didn't make or distribute the fliers."

"Yeah."

"You did."

"Yes."

"And you did this because you wanted people to buy these guns from you, after you'd purchased them legally from Tom's Firearms. Correct? So this was your advertising, not Tanguich Rifle's."

He nodded. "Yes."

Garvin stepped really close to him and said in a serious tone, "And you were the one who sold Nathan Varvara the guns that he used to murder those children, weren't you?"

Jamal hesitated, and then said, "Yes."

"No further questions."

83

Immediately after Jamal's testimony I asked for a recess. Jamal left the courtroom without looking at me, his mother holding him. I tried to talk to him and his mother told me that if I ever spoke to her son again she would call the police.

He looked back once from the elevators. A sorrow I couldn't even imagine filled his eyes, and I knew right then he hadn't made those fliers.

Kelly, Melissa, and I went to a side room and sat down.

"What happened?" Melissa said.

"They must've gotten to him. They played us. Again."

"How?"

I shook my head. "They probably paid him off knowing I'd go to him. These guys have been one step ahead of us the entire time."

Kelly said, "But he just admitted to a felony up there, selling guns to felons. The DA will file charges."

"With what evidence other than what he just said? He said just enough to tank our case but probably not enough to get a conviction against him. Even if he did, it'll be knocked down to a misdemeanor and he'll get probation in court. What if someone offered you a hundred grand to do that? If you saw your mom struggling to get by on thirty grand a year, would you take a misdemeanor for a hundred Gs? I have no doubt they paid him off. The real question is when? Did they know I'd go to him and they got to him first, or have they been following me this whole time and went to his house right after I did?"

Melissa said, "Well let's prove it. Let's talk to that boy and find out."

"I tried. No way the mother lets me, and I sure as hell don't feel like getting arrested again the day I got out of jail."

She shook her head. "I can't believe this."

My phone buzzed. It was Craig again. I answered. "Tell me some good news."

"I've been trying to reach you for like half an hour."

"I'm in trial. Did you get the publication delayed?"

"No, the opposite. It's gonna be published today."

"What? How the hell did that happen?"

"My buddy said the chief justice wants it out today. So it's either a really big coincidence or—"

"Or Garvin has connections up there, too." I rubbed my forehead. Another migraine was coming on and it was starting to pound away like a jackhammer. "Shit."

"Sorry, man."

"You did your best. Thanks, Craig."

I hung up and set my phone on the table.

"What is it?" Kelly said.

"That ruling from the Tenth Circuit is coming out today. We would never find proof of this, I'm sure, but I bet Garvin's got a connection up there, or his firm does, or UGAA does."

Kelly leaned against the wall. "I'm so sorry, Melissa."

"That's it?" she said, looking back and forth between the two of us. "I mean, they're just going to get away with it?"

Kelly said, "Sometimes the law isn't about what's right. It's about how the real world works. And this one we lost."

"No," I said.

"Peter, it's over. Your star witness just tanked our case and Garvin's going to file an interlock by the end of the day. I bet it's already drafted and in his briefcase."

"Jamal wasn't my star witness. You are, Melissa."

She looked from one of us to the other. "I already told you I can't get up there."

"You have to."

"I can't."

"Listen to me, I know how hard this is for you. Talking about what happened to Danny in front of a courtroom full of people. But sometimes you gotta not think about yourself and you just gotta do what's right." I glanced at Kelly. "If you run away from something, it never works. There's no running away from your problems. You either face them head-on and conquer them, or you run and they conquer you. The appeals court is going to read the transcript of the trial, maybe even watch the video, and they gotta hear what you have to say. You're the victim here. We have to put a face to that, otherwise it's all abstract. You gotta do this. For Danny and for you."

She thought a second and closed her eyes before she said, "Okay . . . I'll do it."

84

Melissa looked like she might faint. When she was sworn in, her hand trembled on top of the Bible. If we could get her testimony, and then get it out to the press and start interviews while this was up on an interlocutory appeal, there was a chance Tanguich would give us what we wanted if the public pressure was strong enough. It was a long shot, but a shot.

She took the stand and I let her get comfortable. I went and got a drink of water so the jury would focus on me instead of her. When a minute had gone by, I turned to her and smiled, giving her a quick nod to let her know she could do this.

"Name, please."

"Melissa Bell. I'm Danny's mother."

"And you've heard everything in this trial, haven't you, Ms. Bell?"

"Yes, I have."

"Tell us about what happened on April tenth."

She looked at the jury. "I was at work when they called me. The school called and said there'd been a shooting and Danny was . . . Danny was hurt. So I ran down there as fast as I could. The police had blocked everything off but I could see the school." She paused. "They had these black tarps over the bodies that were on the playground and the soccer field. The tarps were made for adults so they were really large." She inhaled deeply and I could see the tears welling up in her eyes. "A lot of people were crying; some of the parents were screaming. Even the police there were crying. The chief of police came up to me and held me. I still believed that Danny was alright. You don't think that your child will be . . . You always think it's someone else's kid, not my kid." She wiped some tears away. "But they had me identify the body. I don't remember anything after that. I think I screamed and fainted, I don't know. But I woke up in a hospital bed."

"What happened then?"

"They told me how everything happened. That teacher, Mary Thomlin, she tried to protect my Danny. She was running to him to cover his body with hers when she was shot. My Danny was . . . he was trying to get on his bike to get away." She broke down and started sobbing. "He was trying to get away and he was shot in the back. When they found him the bicycle was between his legs and he was dead . . . My Danny was dead." She wiped a few tears away and I brought her some tissues. She looked to the jury and said, "He was all I had. His father left us and it was just me and Danny. And they took him from me. And the next day . . . the next day the Gun Advocates Association held a rally. Can you believe that? They held a rally about guns to make sure that everybody knew how important they are and that no one would be forgetting them. I mean, yes, they have the right to hold a rally, but you're going to hold a gun rally before the bodies of those little ones are even cold? They're monsters," she said, staring right at Garvin. "They're not human."

I sifted some papers to leave that with the jury a second. "What did you feel like when you saw this rally?"

She shook her head, still sobbing. "I felt like 'how could they?' It was a slap in the face. It was like they were telling me it was okay that Danny was killed because that's just the price we pay to have these assault rifles." She looked to Garvin. "Well, you didn't pay the price, I did. And all the other parents of those kids did. You guys never pay the price."

Garvin, smartly, said nothing. Any type of objection to a grieving mother would instantly paint him as the villain, and that was something he certainly wouldn't let the jury see.

"These guns," she said, "they're used to kill our children and we can't even have a discussion about it. Just having a discussion about it is a threat to them. I tried to talk about gun control after this shooting and everybody told me it's not the time, that I'm exploiting a tragedy. Well, when is the time? When we're all dead? We're prisoners in our own country because they've paid off all the politicians, and they think there's nothing we can do about it." She looked at Garvin again. "Well I did something about it. I'm here, and I'm not going away, and I'm going to devote the rest of my life to making sure you pay, Mr. Garvin. You and all the rest of you who sit back and line your pockets on the blood of people like me."

"Melissa, if you could say anything to this jury, just one thing you want them to know for when they go back and deliberate this case, what would it be?"

She reached into her pocket and pulled out her phone and brought up a photo. It looked like a school photo of Danny. "He was my entire world, and I lost him to guns. I know it was a mentally disturbed man who had those guns, but if he didn't have those guns, my Danny might still be alive. They tell us guns are tools like anything else, but they're not tools. They're weapons. The most dangerous weapons ever, like Mr. Game said. They talk about their Second Amendment right to guns, and that it's guaranteed and that it can't be infringed upon. What about my rights? What about Danny's rights? Do we not count because we don't have the money to fight them? Do *you* not count? What I would tell you is that Danny was killed this time, but next time it might be your child. And there will be a next time. As long as they keep getting away with it, as long as our politicians take their money and refuse to do anything about it, as long as we won't even have a discussion about it, there will be more Dannys . . . and next time it could be your child. It could be yours . . ."

She turned the screen toward herself and stared at the photograph.

"No further questions," I said.

85

Garvin waited a beat before he stood up. There was no winning this for him. Melissa had lost her child. No matter how lightly he took it on cross-examination, the jury would be hypersensitive and protective of her. And, anything he said that could seem like an attack would be in the press the next day, courtesy of me. The last thing the gun manufacturers and the gun lobbies wanted was the public to see them not as the great defenders of the Second Amendment, but as greedy leeches putting the dollar above the lives of their fellow men, women, and children.

Garvin stood up, opened his briefcase, and took out two documents. He laid one on the plaintiff's table, and gave the other one to the bailiff to deliver to the judge.

"Your Honor, a new decision was just published by the Tenth Circuit. It is on point in this matter and the controlling law. I'd like to take a recess in chambers to discuss it, please."

We sat in Judge Pearl's chambers while the judge read the *Sagan* case. Garvin and I were quiet. Not cross-examining Melissa was the right move. I was hoping his aggression would overcome him and he'd want to strike back at her, but he'd controlled himself and made the correct strategic decision.

"I assume you have a motion, Mr. Garvin?" Pearl said.

"We will be filing an interlocutory appeal to dismiss this matter when we're back on the record, Judge."

He nodded, laying the papers down on the desk. "They usually release these on Thursdays. Rather odd that it would be released on a Wednesday."

Garvin shrugged. "The Tenth Circuit does what the Tenth Circuit does. We're all just pawns to the higher courts, aren't we?"

Pearl tapped his pen against the desk. "Certainly looks like it." He exhaled through his nose. "Mr. Game, what say you?"

"There's nothing to say, Judge."

"Okay, well, we'll go ahead and excuse the jury and recall them once the higher courts settle the matter of the motion to dismiss. Thank you both for your hard work."

When we were leaving, and Garvin was already out the door, Judge Pearl said, "Mr. Game?"

"Yeah, Judge?"

"You did a helluva job with what you had. It was great work."

"Great work would've been if I could've gotten that little boy some justice."

He grinned. "Who says you didn't? You can never predict how far the ripples in a pond will go once you've tossed in the pebble."

86

I sat out on the court steps and watched the people coming in and out. The joy and elation, the heartbreak, the anger and sense of injustice, the vindication . . . it was all there. Shakespearean dramas played out every day with people's lives.

Someone sat next to me. It was Melissa. We didn't say anything at first, just watched the traffic, and then I said, "I'm so sorry."

"For what?"

"For losing."

"Kelly said it's going up on appeal."

I shrugged. "Yeah, but . . . I mean, I pretty much know how that's going to end." I shook my head. "I never should've taken this case. I should've let a better lawyer take it over."

"A better lawyer? First off, no other lawyer would touch it. They were too scared. And also, you didn't lose. I told you this wasn't about money for me. You're just thinking about it in terms of money." She put her hand on my arm so I would look at her. "I got to sit up there, and stare at those men, and tell them they helped kill my son and that they're not going to get away with it. That's what I wanted, Peter. And you got me that when no one else could. You encouraged me to follow through. I can't thank you enough, but I want you to know that, no matter how this eventually turns out, I'll be grateful to you the rest of my life."

Now it was me who had tears in his eyes, and I had to look away from her. She put her arm around me.

"If it's any consolation," I finally said, "Garvin didn't get away scot-free."

"What'd you do?"

I motioned down the street with my head. Six men huddled around a car with the hood open, including Garvin, who had a phone glued to his ear. "Car broke down. Almost like someone put sugar in their gas tank. But you'd have to be a real bastard to do something like that when they probably had flights to catch."

She smiled, and laughed, and a smile came over me, and I said, "Let's get outta here and grab some dinner with Kelly. I happen to know she's a big Richard Pryor fan and would love to hear your story."

87

It was later that night when I showed up at Kelly's house after I asked if I could stop by and she texted me where she lived. It was in the same condo complex she had lived in before moving to LA. Joey wasn't there.

"Hey," she said. "Come in."

We sat down on the couch and she stared at me. No makeup over the tattoo on her wrist.

"I feel bad I never got your name tattooed like I said I would."

"You don't have to feel bad."

"Well I do." I paused. "That was fun, us working together."

"It was."

"In fact, I think I'd like to do it again."

"What do you mean?"

I leaned forward. "You don't wanna work for a prick like Corey. He'll make your life miserable just like he did last time. Come with me. Let's start our own firm. Baun and James. We'll be unstoppable. And Craig said he'd like to join us when he passes the Bar. So we've already got our first associate."

"Peter . . ."

"Look, what I did, leaving you before our wedding like that, was horrible, inexcusable, but that doesn't mean this isn't a good decision. I'm sick of fighting this fight alone, and you're sick of working on cases you don't give a shit about. Come with me, and I promise I'll work every day to make sure you're happy." I placed my hand over hers. "Please."

She stared at me awhile. "I don't know . . . I guess you will need help with this appeal. I mean, it could take years to go through the courts."

I glanced around the condo. "And sorry about not getting to know Joey. If you like the guy, I'm sure I'll like the guy."

She inhaled deeply and said, "No, you were right. He wasn't for me. I dumped him this morning."

"You did? Why didn't you tell me?"

She shrugged. "I don't know. I like seeing you jealous."

I looked down to her coffee table. There was a deep scratch and I ran my finger over it. "I meant what I said. Leaving you was the stupidest decision of my life. I want to make it up to you, if you'll let me."

"Maybe. We'll see what happens down the line. For now . . . let's find some new office space. One with fewer cockroaches maybe."

I drove home with butterflies in my stomach. I rolled down my windows and let the air hit me. My phone rang. It was Michael.

"Hey pal."

"Hey, Dad. Um, I was wondering when you're gonna be home?"

"Few minutes. Why? Is something wrong?"

"No, I just wanted to talk . . . I've been thinking a lot about what you said. About how running away from your problems doesn't make them go away. I mean, I've been hiding who I am for so long that . . .

I don't know. It just feels wrong to run away to Tahoe with Mom now just because of some people at school. I wanted to talk to you about it."

My heart swelled. "Um, yeah, we can talk as much as you want, pal. Give me five."

"Okay. Love you, Dad."

As I was driving, I passed the homeless shelter and saw my billboard. I stopped the car at the curb and got out. I walked over to it. There was a ladder leading up to it and I took it, climbing up onto the platform to stare at the billboard. I was hitting an insurance adjuster in the face with a boxing glove on my hand and proclaiming, **PETER GAME: THE BEST GAME IN TOWN.**

I went to the edge and took out a key, and scraped along the vinyl coating until it ripped, then I peeled off the cover and tore the whole thing down. About half of it stayed up, but you couldn't see my face or most of the slogan. I took down as much as I could and tossed it on the ground. Eventually, I crumpled it up and put it in a nearby dumpster. I looked at the billboard again, at the smooth white imprint that had been underneath.

I glanced up at the night sky. It was a clear night and the stars sparkled. I had thought a storm might be coming, but it looked like it had passed by.

I got into my car and drove home to my son.

88

The firm of Baun & James buzzed with activity. In addition to Craig, Jake had come over a few months after the Tanguich trial. We didn't have much money to pay ourselves yet. Still, I don't think any of us regretted the decision, even though, except for Craig, we all made less money than we did before we joined up.

Every night after work, we went out for a drink or dinner and talked about our day. Michael had decided to stay in Salt Lake and finish his final year of high school, and he would meet us sometimes. He had enrolled at the University of Utah half an hour away from our apartment and would be majoring in philosophy starting next fall. He had me proofread his essay to the admissions department, and the theme was that running away from problems never solved them.

I sat at my desk and signed some paperwork while our two paralegals were outside talking about an insurance adjuster they were dealing with. I heard Kelly on the phone in the office next to mine. We had been taking it slow, but gradually, she had stopped wearing makeup over the tattoo on her wrist, and we'd been spending time alone, just me and her. We had a trip planned to Hawaii tomorrow. Every day I would look at my calendar and make sure it was still there, that she hadn't deleted it.

Craig was yelling at a prosecutor about a case. He had decided that criminal law fit his personality the best. He'd tossed his pentagram necklace and replaced it with creepy red-and-black suits. One time, I even caught him eating a low-fat granola bar rather than a candy bar.

I leaned back in my chair for a second and enjoyed the noise. I had grown so accustomed to working alone that I didn't realize how much I craved having people around me. Kelly had been right—this was what I had been missing. I'd been so focused on not being "the guy who just got by" that I forgot why I didn't want to just get by: so that I could have the freedom to do what I wanted and spend my time with the people I wanted to spend it with.

Kelly ran into my office.

"What?" I said.

"You're not gonna believe who's on the phone."

"Who?"

"Brennen Garvin. I'll transfer him."

The phone rang and I picked it up.

"Brennen. How are you?"

"I'm good," he said, his voice smooth and calm as always. "How are you?"

"I'm good. I got my charges tossed the other day. You remember those pot charges, right? Craig got them tossed on a bad search. Apparently there had been an anonymous tip to the cops, but the tipster didn't leave any information. See, you gotta give enough info that the cops have reasonable suspicion to pull someone over, *and* that they know it's from a reliable source. They just didn't have enough info."

"Well good for you. I'm happy to hear that."

"Yeah, I bet. So what can I do for you? Our hearing isn't for a few months."

"I wanted you to know that I filed another request for a protective order today and will be asking for an expedited hearing on the matter. Your client has been a busy bee."

"Yeah . . . that interview Melissa gave on MSNBC where she destroyed that UGAA guy was particularly brutal, wasn't it? She works with AnyPerson now. Did you know that? Crazy, isn't it? She's really been doing some great fund-raising with that group. Do you know they outspent gun lobbies in some states? First time that's ever happened."

A long silence.

"You there, Brennen?"

"Do you stipulate to an expedited hearing?"

"Sure. Why not? You happened to catch me in a good mood. You sound kind of upset, though. The partners didn't take too kindly to all the press this got, huh?"

"Goodbye, Mr. Game. See you in court."

Kelly was still standing at the doorway when I hung up and she said, "Happiest I've seen you after someone just told you they want an expedited hearing."

"They're desperate. If there's even a chance we could win at the Tenth Circuit and set precedent, the gun lobbies and manufacturers will be flooded with lawsuits left and right. I don't mind more hearings; the longer this takes the better. I might even hit him up for another offer. Bigger this time of course."

"If you say so." She looked behind her to make sure no one was listening and said, "I'm looking forward to our trip."

When she left, I opened my calendar and checked the dates for Hawaii again. They were still there. I smiled and put my feet up on the desk. I listened to Kelly get on the phone with another client, Craig still shouting at a prosecutor, and Jake flirting with one of our paralegals, who just called him disgusting.

I turned and looked out the window. The skies were blue and clear and the sun was out. It would be a good day. But tomorrow, there was something I still had to do.

89

Melissa answered when I knocked. She wore makeup and a business suit. It was early morning and I wanted to catch her before she left for work.

"Peter, what are you doing here?"

"I just wanted to give you this in person." I pulled the check for one point two million out of my pocket and put it in her hands. "It's the leftover money from the GoFundMe. I posted a message to the donors and said I wanted to give the money to you. No one objected to it."

She stood with her mouth open a minute, staring at the check. "Well, you're entitled to a third of this."

"I don't need it. It's your money. Do with it whatever you want. If you want to donate it, great. If you want to stop working and move to some tropical island, that's great, too. But it's yours, not mine."

"I can't let you do that. You worked your ass off. I mean, this must be the type of payday you dream about as a lawyer."

I grinned. "Not anymore."

I turned to leave.

"Hey, I don't see your billboards on my drive to work anymore."

"No," I said, turning to look at her again. "I don't need those either. I'll see ya."

"Peter, wait." She threw her arms around me. She held me a long time and I felt her sobbing quietly. "Thank you."

She pulled away and I said, "What are friends for?"

I got into my car, waved to her one more time, and then left. Kelly was waiting for me at the airport, and soon, I would be lying on a beach sipping mai tais and listening to the waves roll in to shore.

As I pulled away from the curb, I remembered I had one last thing to do. I took out my cell and texted a number.

Hey, Brennen, it's Peter. I just wanted to say something from the bottom of my heart

It's been a good fight, the reply came. *No need to ruin it with sentimentality*

No, not that. I ordered thirty pizzas to your house a few minutes ago, asshole. Have a good day

I turned off my phone, tossed it onto the passenger seat, and gunned the car to the airport with a smile on my face that just wouldn't go away.

ABOUT THE AUTHOR

Victor Methos knew he would be a lawyer at the age of thirteen, when his best friend was interrogated by the police for over eight hours and then confessed to a crime he didn't commit. From that time forward, criminal law was in Methos's sights.

After abandoning a doctorate in philosophy to pursue his childhood dream of becoming a defense lawyer, Methos graduated from the University of Utah School of Law. After graduation, wanting to learn the true practice of law rather than what the law schools taught, he worked for a special kind of lawyer, the kind with neon signs up front, who did anything and everything to win for their clients. Afterward, he sharpened his teeth as a prosecutor for Salt Lake City before founding a law firm that would become the most successful criminal defense firm in Utah.

In ten years, Methos conducted more than one hundred trials, with only two losses under his belt in that time. One particular case—a father who shot his daughter's rapists—stuck with him, and he knew he had to write the story. It became the basis for his first major bestseller, *The Neon Lawyer*. Since that time, Methos has focused his work on legal thrillers and mysteries and produced two books per year. He currently splits his time between Salt Lake City and Las Vegas and continues to defend the poor and the weak against the strong and the powerful.